LMT

Thrift store for 5¢

May 2017

Memorial Day

new book - had
never been read

Memorial May 2018. I still have
Day weekend not read this all the way
5/25/18 about cruelty + injustice +
I will know if it is
I just can't take more
horrible words —

Well, I did read it —
You read it and add
your opinion, whoever you are —

True Fires

Also by Susan Carol McCarthy
LAY THAT TRUMPET IN OUR HANDS

May we hold in our hearts the true fires

that warm the human condition:

love, joy, peace, gentleness, goodness,

faith, meekness and temperance . . .

TRUE FIRES

Susan Carol McCarthy

BANTAM BOOKS

TRUE FIRES
A Bantam Book / January 2004

Published by
Bantam Dell
A Division of Random House, Inc.
New York, New York

This is a work of fiction. Names, characters, places, and incidents either are the
product of the author's imagination or are used fictitiously. Any resemblance to
actual persons, living or dead, events, or locales is entirely coincidental.

Grateful acknowledgment is made to Mid-Florida Publications,
for permission to use excerpts from the *Mount Dora Topic*.

Bantam Books is a registered trademark of Random House, Inc., and the
colophon is a trademark of Random House, Inc.

Library of Congress Cataloging in Publication Data is on file with the publisher.

ISBN: 0-553-80170-8

Manufactured in the United States of America
Published simultaneously in Canada
10 9 8 7 6 5 4 3 2 1
BVG

For Mabel Norris Reese,
my hero

TRUE FIRES

The outermost guard sees it first. The careful footfall, the crack of twigs, the crush and crumbling of dry leaves. She turns and, imperceptibly to the intruder, sends the alarm. "One comes!"

The message is passed from guard to guard, from outer rim to inner wall, from watchful eyes to anxious hearts. "One comes!"

Those assigned the colony's defense ready their weapons. The rest stand and wait, prepared to die, if need be, rather than surrender their treasure. Sensing the alarm ("The children, are they safe?"), She Who Decides emerges from her chambers.

The outermost guard presses forward, peering through the woods and sees, "It is He!"

Once again, word flies to and through the colony. Relief spreads. He Who Provides comes. To collect the golden tablets glistening in the sun. They will offer no resistance so long as the children, their treasures, are safe.

1

Outside the wall of windows, the unrelenting flatness sets Daniel's mind to dreaming, sketching mountains, ridges, and rain gullies in the wasted space between the sparse Bermuda grass and the vast staring-down sky. Suddenly, a flare of light—blazing sun careening off polished car chrome—yanks Daniel's eyes out the open doorway. The light glares in the face of the skinny boy on his left and the girl with the yellow hair in front of him. As the two-toned car comes to a stop in front of the school office, the skinny boy points; the girl gawks. And the two of them whisper, not to Daniel, never to him, "The Sheriff, K. A. DeLuth," their tones at once fearful and reverential.

Haw, Daniel scoffs inside his head, *y'all call that a Sheriff in Floridy? Looks like he couldn't tell a still from a smudge pot, and wouldn't bother dirtyin' his boots to try. Up home, Sheriff Jim is Pap's fifth cousin and he's got two stills. One to keep, he says, and one to share, when the revenuers come through, needin' somethin' to bust up. That still's been moved around and busted up more times than anyone can count. Sheriff Jim brags he's got the least still still in Avery County!*

Daniel snickers at ol' Jim's familiar joke but stops as the

skinny boy and the yellow-haired girl turn on him, their flat
eyes hard with disgust.

He's been at this school ten days now, but nonetheless, the
depth of their contempt surprises him. The first two days, his
fellow fifth graders had seemed entertained, charmed even, by
his tales from up home in Pigeon Ridge, North Carolina.

"Pigeon Ridge? You got lots of pigeons up there?" they'd
asked.

"Nary one." He'd grin. "But we got more ravens than you
kin shake a stick at. Know why the raven's so black? Th' Ol'
Cher'kee says he got burned black, stealing fire from heaven
for the folks on Grandfather Mountain."

Oh, they'd liked him fine then. But, the day after that, the
girl with the hair as bright and shiny as a river trout turned on
him, her blue eyes squinty, her nose squinched, and asked, real
loud, "Don't you have anything else to wear?" That question
and his answer turned everything sideways. The grins of the
others were gone. Now, their eyes either glittered with bone-
naked revulsion or skittered off elsewhere as if he weren't even
there.

Daniel the Lone Ranger he'd become, laying low behind a
mask of amused mockery he didn't really feel, feeding the hungry rumble of his homesickness constant helpings of memory
and imagination.

Outside, the Sheriff's door slams shut. *He's got a fancier car
than ol' Jim, I'll give 'im that. And,* Daniel notes as the big man
hitches up his broad belt, *an even fancier gun.*

The sight of the Sheriff's pistol with its pearly white handle sends the boy's mind wandering. In his lap, his palms fold,
one up, one down, several inches apart. In his mind, he grasps
his own little bolt-action .22, its barrel ice cold as he crunches
through the crisp freedom of the October woods; brown nut

grass, stiff with first frost, crumbling beneath his feet. Here, sun slants bright through the half-bare hickory grove. And just there, the tail of a fat fox squirrel flickers. Daniel stops, takes aim, lets the squirrel back his way 'round the trunk into full view, then, *Bam!* Got him! Easy pickin's for a lover of Mam's squirrel burgoo.

Mam. Without warning, her long skinny face rises up in front of him: grinning at a tow sack heavy with a dozen skinned pink squirrels, grimacing at the pain eating up her innards, composed peaceful-like by old Miz Sary on the pine plank she called her cooling board. This last memory of his mother, colorless except for the strange spots of rouge somebody smudged on her cheekbones, tightens the muscles around his sore heart. All at once, Mam's pointy fingers, never still, ever impatient with any sort of dillydallying, poke him sharply in the shoulder.

"Sammy," the harsh whisper says. Mam never called him that. "Sammy! Teacher want you, up to the front," the grubby boy behind him says.

Dazed, Samuel Daniel Dare stands and shuffles his oversize feet between the desks toward the front. He feels, like pinpricks, the other children's eyes on his plaid shirttail. He drops his chin hastily, hoping they can't see, don't notice the backs of his big ears flushing darkly red. Their sharp laughter tells him they can, and do.

Bullying has always Been

2

Sheriff K. A. DeLuth grabs his hat off the other seat then pauses to center his belt buckle between the stiff parallel creases in his shirt and pants legs. "A fine figure of a man," the President of the Ladies' Auxiliary called him, meaning his six-foot, six-inch height which, with his hat on (an authentic Texan ten-gallon, a gift from the Governor) and the heels of his size-thirteen boots, grows to damn near seven feet tall.

SHERIFF K. A. DeLUTH. The gold letters on his car door glint his arrival. To the voters who will, no doubt, reelect him next month for an unprecedented third term, the ballot reads Sheriff Kyle Ambrose (K. A.) DeLuth, Incumbent. But among his powerful friends, the citrus growers and cattlemen who own and run this county, and among those who dare cross them, he's Kick Ass. *The Honorable Sheriff Kick Ass DeLuth.* He nods, relishing the feel of his hat on his head, the velvety smooth rim of the brim. *At your service.*

This place hasn't changed a bit, he thinks, ducking his head to enter the school office. *Same damn chairs, same old prune face behind the counter, must be—what? seventy-something by now.*

"Good afternoon, young lady," he says, turning on the charm, removing his hat in a practiced arc.

"Kyle DeLuth! Last time I saw you in here, you were on the receiving end of a rather large piece of pine!" Miss May White's attempted grin cross-stitches the folds of her ancient face. "You sure have done well for yourself."

"Thank you, Miss May. And you haven't changed a bit. Boss man in?"

"In for you, I'll bet. Ed*ward,*" she calls loudly into the open door six feet away, "you here for Kyle DeLuth?"

"Ol' K.A.? 'S long as he's not here for me, I am." Ed Cantrell calls, waving him in with a smile.

DeLuth passes through the swinging half door next to the counter, drops his big hat in the center of Miss May's desk, and extends his right hand to grip the principal's squat little paw.

"Missed you at Rotary today," the Sheriff says, settling into one of the uncomfortably small wooden chairs in front of the principal's desk, adjusting the crease in his crossed pants leg.

"Damn district reports, due end of the week," Cantrell says and shakes his bald head at the paperwork blanketing his desk. "What can I do you for?" he asks quickly.

The Sheriff notes the hint of anxiousness in Cantrell's voice, views it as the respect that he considers his due.

"Sat next to Clive Cunningham at lunch. You got the last of his kids here in the fifth grade, sweet little thing named Caroline, pick of ol' Clive's litter?"

"Sure do. 'A' student, too." Cantrell says it a little too heartily, clearly curious why a man of Clive Cunningham's status would involve the Sheriff in a school problem.

"Well, Caroline's come home complaining about some boy in her class. New kid, name of Dare? Not that he's bothered her or anything, but seems he's a little on the too-tan side.

Clive's driven by the playground, given him the once-over, thinks he might be some sort of high-toned mule-otto, tryin' to pass for white."

Cantrell's big chair squeaks as he shifts his bulk forward, alert now. "I know the boy you mean. He and his little sister are new—week ago Monday, October sixth. But they got redheaded cousins who've been here a year already."

"Well,"—DeLuth stretches a foot to admire the mirror-sharp sheen on his boot toe—"with all this nonsense coming out of the Supreme Court, and you know better 'n I do the Governor'll close the schools before he'll integrate, we got to keep an eye out for any sort of left-wing foolishness. I told Clive I'd check this kid out myself, that is,"—DeLuth pauses to make sure Cantrell realizes he's being thrown a bone—"if it's all right with you."

"Of course." The principal nods hastily. "He's in Sarah Burch's room. Want me to call him out?" He's already swiveling toward the P.A. system on the table beside his desk.

The Sheriff shakes his head, rising up and out of the too-small chair. "You got your hands full here, Ed. I'll just stroll over there, take a look-see and be on my way. Fifth grade still where it used to be? And the sister's in—what? First grade? Second?"

"Second," Cantrell says, standing awkwardly. "Sure you don't want me to come?"

"Naw, probably nothing anyway," DeLuth says, waving him back into his seat.

"Haven't changed a bit," he winks at Miss May as he swings his hat off the rack behind her desk.

3

Ol' Miss Burch cuts the others off quick.

"I know y'all have *plenty* to do," she says tersely, stabbing a finger at the chalkboard's list of assignments. "Need I add some more?" She glares the giggling children into silence.

As Daniel reaches the front, her pointing finger drops to the chair beside her, then tilts upward in that way that means, *I'll be with you in a minute.*

He sits down hastily, his back to the class, twisting his hands into a ball, and steps one scuffed shoe on top of the other. The movement sends a flock of dust and chalk particles swooping through the shaft of sunlight from the open door. Daniel watches the specks rise and flutter like a covey of tiny quail; then shifts his attention to the teacher who, rummaging through her desk drawers, reminds him of a giant guinea hen fretting through her nest straw.

"Ah!" she declares, lifting the tidy stack of rubber-banded white cards. "Here they are."

She leans forward, suddenly cheerful. "Now, Sammy . . ."

Daniel, name's Daniel, he wants to tell her but can't figure how. On the first day of school, she took his whole name, Samuel Daniel Dare, and squinched it the wrong way into Sammy. He thought he'd try it on for a while. But, it fits worse than the new shoes the boardinghouse lady tried to give him. He'd given the shoes back. But getting rid of the wrong name had him stumped. Up home, he never had to tell anybody his name. Even folks he hardly knew would squint and call, "Ain't you Daniel, Rachel Wells's boy, one of them dark-headed Dares?" *Up home . . .*

"Sammy? You need to listen to me," the teacher says, staring him into attention. "I see you been struggling with your fractions. I got something that'll help. You have flash cards at your old school?"

"No, ma'am," he says, eyeing the stack.

"Well, if you promise to be careful with 'em, I'll lend you mine. Your mamma can drill you at home, okay?"

My mam's dead, he wants to tell her, but his throat won't let him. *Dead and buried on the broom-sedge knoll up home.* Instead, he nods and takes the proffered stack of bright white cards.

"Goooood," she says, her eyes darting past him to the suddenly darkened doorway.

Daniel turns to see what comes. The giant man grins his way across the threshold, his shadow claiming the entire front of the classroom.

"Sheriff DeLuth!" Miss Burch flutters up to greet her impressive visitor. "May I help you?"

"You sure can, pretty lady," he replies, nodding in her direction. "I've just come from the principal's office where we put the names of everybody at this school in my big ol' hat here," he says, sweeping it off to show the gaping children.

Smith and Wesson thirty-eight, Daniel thinks, admiring the Sheriff's pistol. *Fine leather holster, carved ivory handle.*

"Principal Cantrell did the honors, and the lucky winner gets a free ride home in my brand-new squad car, gets to run the siren and everything," DeLuth says smoothly.

"And?" Miss Burch asks, catching the Sheriff's drift.

"And the lucky winner's in this classroom!" the Sheriff crows with great effect.

"Isn't that ex*citing?*" Miss Burch beams to her students, clasping her hands in front of her ample chest.

"Who is it?" "Who won?" "I want to run the siren!" the other children call.

"A boy . . ." the Sheriff says, deliberately scanning the room, ". . . name of Dare."

"Why, Sammy," Miss Burch cries, her still-clasped hands cupping his shoulder. "That's *you!*"

As the Sheriff turns his steel-eyed gaze to the front, something about the big man makes Daniel uneasy. It's not his size. The redheaded McKennas up home are bigger, and as good as they come, on weekdays. It's not even the reaction of the other children—mock-envy masking relief. It's something about the way the Sheriff's smile doesn't rise to his eyes. And the look in those eyes. Like the look Pap and the other men get when the brush of wild wings breaks the silence outside the duck blind.

When the Sheriff says, "This is your lucky day, boy," Daniel feels anything but. "Ever ridden in a squad car before?"

Lottsa times up home, Daniel thinks, but says nothing.

"Miss Burch, it's—what? Twenty till the bell?" Sheriff DeLuth says. "Mind if we leave early so my car doesn't block the buses?"

"Course not, Sheriff," Miss Burch chirps. "Sammy, get your things."

4

Betty Clayton Whitworth, proprietress of the Charmwood Guest House on Elm Street, stands on the front porch massaging her right hip. Her hurricane hip, she always calls it, gingerly rounding the inflamed joint with the heel of her right hand, scanning the horizon for storm clouds.

Betty the Barometer, Clay'd called her that last December, *shoulda enlisted, coulda been Ike's secret weapon,* he'd teased, marching around this very porch, mimicking Eisenhower's Texas drawl: *"Whus that y'say, Monty? June sixth? Lessee what Betty's hip has to say 'bout it."* That Clay, always clownin'.

The growl and sheen of the Sheriff's car startles her. Betty's hands fly out to grasp the white wood railing. For nine years now, the sight of the Sheriff, even the casual mention of his name, conjures up pieces of the worst night of her life: Sheriff DeLuth's banging knock at the door, his eyes downcast while delivering the news, the horror of standing there in cold cream and curlers, boarders cracking their doors to catch a listen, hearing that Clay, her only son, the town's most conspicuous war hero, had spent the evening at the V.F.W. drinking toast after toast to the unexpectedly dead General George S. Patton—*Biggest sonofabitch ever lived!* Her Clay, who'd survived North Africa, Sicily, the Battle of the Bulge, for heaven's sake, and had a shoebox full of medals to prove it, lay dead no more than a mile from home, wrapped around the unloving arms of a Florida jack pine.

"Why, Sheriff—Sheriff DeLuth!—what brings you to—I mean, what could you possibly—well, really?" Betty calls to the big man making his way up her sidewalk.

"Now, Miz Betty, nothing to fret over," the Sheriff says, stopping just short of the bottom step to greet her eye to eye.

Keepin' his distance, Betty thinks. Was he recalling, as she was, the fat smear of cold cream across his chest when she'd collapsed, hysterical, that awful night? She feels her cheeks flush.

"Got a couple schoolkids, name of Dare?" DeLuth jerks a thumb toward his car. "Claim they live here."

"Daniel and Rebecca?" Betty cranes her neck, squinting at the two dark heads in the Sheriff's backseat. "Yes—poor things—they do. Just a few months—I mean, till the Brysons—they're regulars from Michigan—arrive for the winter." *Quit prattlin' on, sound like an ol' loon,* Betty scolds herself. "What's the trouble?"

"Well, if you don't mind,"—the Sheriff removes his hat and slaps it gently against his thigh—"I'd like a word with their mother. Please, ma'am."

"Mother? Didn't they tell you—haven't got one—that's why I said poor things—earlier, I mean. Father works for Lila Hightower—you know, out at the Judge's place? Well, of course, you do!"

"No mother, y'say?" Sheriff DeLuth cocks his head as if he hadn't heard right. "What happened to her?"

"Died 'fore they came here—cancer, I think—the poor little girl, 'Becca, told me, 'My mam's insides et her up.' Doesn't that sound like cancer to you?"

"Yes. Yes, it does. And the father works for Lila, y'say?" The Sheriff retains the look of someone who either doesn't hear well or is having a hard time believing what she'd said.

"Oh, yes! She's the one vouched for 'em. House rules—I mean, I must have references—so many oddballs, really!"

"Well," Sheriff DeLuth fingers the rim of the big white Stetson, "I'll be heading out to Lila's then. Sorry to have bothered you, Miz Betty."

"But, Sheriff," Betty flutters a trembly hand in his direction. "Is there trouble?—I mean, this is a respectable—I can't afford—"

"Might catch a little rain, don't y'think?" The Sheriff eyes the bank of clouds scuttling overhead. "Then again, might not." He shrugs and strides to the curb.

Betty's hand floats back down to her side, the heel of it testing her sore hip joint. *Rain, for sure,* she decides. *And what else?* she wonders as 'Becca's small wave blurs in the back window of the Sheriff's receding car.

5

Sheriff DeLuth turns left on Beech, right on Oak, then hard-pedals out Old Dixie toward the Judge's place, south of town. In his rearview mirror, his eyes rake over the two tight-lipped children in the backseat and he shakes his head at Ed Cantrell, Betty Whitworth, and, now, Lila Hightower, hearing the words of the prophet—*Jeremiah, Ezekiel, who?*—*The Lord give them eyes, but they do not see.*

Look at the kink in that boy's hair, and the girl—that nose has the black curse of Canaan on it, clear as day. What's Cantrell thinking, lettin' them in school? And Lila vouchin' for 'em to stay at the old hen's boardinghouse?

Lila.

As DeLuth turns the wheel sharply at the bend in the blacktop created by the abrupt arrival of Lake Esther—the one locals christened SonofaBitch Curve after it claimed Clay Whitworth—his thoughts veer toward Lila Hightower.

Lila was nobody's fool. The Judge had seen to that. Even in grade school, when he and Louis Hightower first became friends, Lila had the jump on every kid in class. The Judge taught her to read early—tried to do the same with Louis, too, but it didn't take—and suffered no more foolishness in his home than in his courtroom. "Don't go relyin' on your prettiness,

Miss," DeLuth had heard the Judge warn Lila many a time. "In the cases that count, smart beats pretty every time." And hadn't she outsmarted the Judge himself—damn near broke his heart, too—by joining the Women's Army Corps after Louis went and got himself killed in Africa, for Chrissakes? And hadn't she piled insult onto injury by staying away until just before the ol' man died and was all set to disown her?

DeLuth purses leathery lips as he wheels onto the private side road—paved at county expense—beside the green-and-white sign for Hightower Groves. Once, during the anxious weeks before the Judge passed, DeLuth had flirted with the possibility that all this might be his. The Judge as much as said so. "K.A., you been more of a son to me than Louis ever was." The ol' man was spitting up blood in wads as thick and brown as chewing tobac by then. "S'long as Lila can't see fit to find her way home, I've told Paine to fix things so you're next in line." But, of course, Lila had come home, just in time to usher her father from this world into the next. And blood being thicker than branch water, DeLuth wound up with the Judge's gold watch and a small note, in Lila's broad scrawl, that said, *"Sorry, Kiss Ass."*

For DeLuth, driving down the Judge's grove road sets memories flickering like a Movietone newsreel:

Just there, in the big oak beside the main road, he and Louis built their flight deck out of wood pilfered from the county woodpile—The Dixie Bombers, they were—and, from their secret post on high, hurled rotten, powdery gray grapefruit at the passing traffic. "Bombs awaaay, suckers!" Over there, in the break between the navel trees and the Parson Browns, he and Louis manned the kerosene tanks, choking on fumes, changing off the smudge-pot crews during the endless, bone-chilling night that was the freeze of '34. By morning, everyone's face so oily black you could hardly tell the Niggers from the whites. Here, on this very road, flanked by rows planted a perfect ten yards on center, he and Louis practiced the pinpoint-accuracy passing and receiving that took their high-school football team to the '39 National Championships in Miami. Red Grange—three-time All-American, The Galloping Ghost himself—was there to congratulate them. The Judge, arms around him and Louis, introduced them to everyone as "my two boys." Grange had hands like hams, pink, big, and firm; his ferocious grip and flaming face came at you like a boar out of the woods. His wave to the Miami stadium—a sort of jabbing salute—was the secret inspiration for DeLuth's own Fourth of July "parade wave."

Up ahead, the big white house, white-columned like the courthouse downtown, presides over its surrounding acreage like the Judge's bench over the hard-backed chairs of Courtroom Number Two. It was just there in the corner of the porch shaded by the live oak, the Judge and his cronies gathered to anoint him County Citrus Inspector and, later on, their uncontested candidate for High Sheriff.

From then on, he and Judge Howard Hightower—who courtroom wags called Judge How-High, as in "When I advise you to jump, Counselor, the appropriate response is 'How high?' "—remade this county into their image of Law 'n' Order. They'd brooked no foolishness, either, not from returning Nigger war veterans, union organizers, ungenerous real-estate developers, or anyone except Big Nick, the local Bolita ringleader who lined their pockets with enough cash to build the herd of blue-ribbon Brahmas that was the envy of the state's cattlemen.

Lila'd managed to reel in the Judge's house and vast grove lands. But the cash money was in the Judge's handshake shares of the Brahmas and the Bolita that were now all his. *Sorry, Miss.* DeLuth smiles smugly as he passes the house on his way to the big grove buildings in the back. *Like the ol' man always said, smart beats pretty every time.*

6

Floridy, it seems to Daniel squeezing 'Becca's cold little hand in the Sheriff's backseat, watching the green boulders of Miss Lila's grove trees whiz by, *Floridy's like a giant-size bald, badly in need of trees.* Up home, when lightning struck the flat top of a mountain and set fire to everything in sight, when the local wildlife was left to scratch and claw a life out of the burnt black earth under the hungry glare of the hawks and the sun, when worthless ragweed and goldenrod took the place of the berry bushes and the big cedars and the ancient elms for a hundred years or so, you had yourself a bald and 'tweren't pretty.

Floridy has no trees to speak of 'cept for a bunch of scrawny pines and the occasional live oak. No mountains to soften the edges between night and day and back again, settle the arguments 'twixt the hard dark dirt and the fretful, changing sky. No dirt even, fragrant with the loam of fallen leaves. Just a whole lot of sand and lakes and prickly palmetto bushes and prissy orange trees. 'Tweren't natural atall.

And the folks 'tweren't natural neither. *This Sheriff,* Daniel thinks, *is more bear than man.* Got the big, square head, the shiny black hair, the li'l leery eyes, long nose, barrel-shaped body, even the limpy, flat-footed gait of a big black bear up home.

I seed it right off, Daniel thinks. When the Sheriff dropped a heavy paw on the back of the boy's neck just outside the class-room, and did the same with 'Becca—not even botherin' with the ruse of "names in his hat" and "a free ride home." When he grunted at them to "git in the back," lumbered up to poor Miz Whitworth at the boardinghouse, who looked like she'd spotted a ghost, and shook his head with that great, slow sway and sniffed the air in just the way that bears do, Daniel, a boy raised in bear country, knew what to do—and slipped into a still and watchful silence.

A bear, Daniel knew, *usually has one thing on his mind—he cain't handle two—and the trick is to figure out what it is, let him have at it, and he'll soon be on his way to the next one thing. A bear ain't all that dangerous, unless, of course, you or your dog or the deer you just killed is the bear's one thing. If that's it, you best be careful that your single shot hits home.*

The Sheriff whips his car into Miss Lila's wide, dirt grove yard and gets out in a hurry without his hat. Daniel and 'Becca watch him swivel his big head back and forth, left to right. Under the bead of his gaze, the Negroes in the yard, who are returning their empty picking sacks to the supply shed, shut their mouths, drop their chins, and study their shoelaces, backing into the shade like songbirds silenced by the shadow of a hawk.

The Sheriff approaches an older one, the color of molasses, and demands, "You, boy! Where's Leroy?"

"Ain't here no more, suh." The molasses man shakes his head at his shoe.

"What's that?" The Sheriff leans over him. "I *said,* where's Leroy?"

Daniel watches the molasses man dig his chin a little deeper into his chest. "Leroy ain't here no more, *suh.* Miss Lila's got herself a new tree man. He inside the barn."

"Kin I help ye, Sheriff?" Beside Daniel, 'Becca gasps as the big man turns slowly on the hind of his heels to glare at their pap, who's walked out of the barn into the sunlight.

"Well, maybe you *kin* and maybe you *kin't*," the Sheriff tells Pap, mocking his accent. "Where's Leroy Russell?"

"Like Nate there said, Leroy don't work here no more. Name's Franklin Dare." Pap steps toward the Sheriff, offers up his hand. "Yores?"

The Sheriff's eyes, sliding from Pap's hand up to his face, glitter suspicion. The Sheriff's a full head taller but, Daniel thinks, *Pap's five and a half feet of pure Carolina gamecock. He kin outwrestle any man on our mountain, including the oversize McKennas. Outshoot 'em, too. I seed him drop a possum out of a pine a hundred yards yonder. "Left eye or right?" Pap asked ol' John Trotter, who bet him he couldn't do it. "Either one," ol' John said. "How 'bout both?" Pap said as he pulled the trigger. That possum had turned sideways and Pap's bullet went clean in one eye and out t'other.* On account of his skills and his temper—Pap could be as prickly as a polecat—folks up home had a sayin'. "Don't go ranklin' Franklin Dare," they'd warn the local hotheads. *This Sheriff,* Daniel decides, *don't know who he's talking to.*

A woman's voice behind both men calls, "His name's DeLuth." Miss Lila Hightower strides out of the barn to stand beside Pap, a pretty, auburn-haired woman dressed, as usual, like a man in khaki shirt, pants, and grove boots. "K.A.," she tells Pap, "as in Kyle Ambrose. As in Kick Ass. Or Kiss Ass. Depending on who's got the bread and who's holdin' the butter knife. And he has"—her green eyes flash at the Sheriff—"the manners of a pig."

"Now, Lila." DeLuth's face splits suddenly into a grin, a boy's Sorry-I-spilled-the-sugar-bowl grin, I-wasn't-aimin'-at-the-mockingbird grin, Teacher-it-sure-as-heck-wudn't-me sort of grin that doesn't appear to soften Miss Lila one bit. "What's all this about Leroy? He's been the Judge's tree man 'round here for—what? Eight, nine years?"

"Well, he ain't mine anymore!" Her eyes are sparking fire. "Not since I found the truckload of fertilizer I paid for was pure cane sugar for his moonshine operation in the back corner grove!"

"You fired Leroy for makin' a little 'shine?"

"What? I shoulda called The Law?" she blazes, then catches sight of Daniel and 'Becca in the back. "What're you doin' here anyway?"

"Investigatin' a constituent complaint," he tells her, and opens the car door for them to scramble out. Daniel and 'Becca move mutely to stand beside Pap. "Seems to me and Clive Cunningham that your new tree man is tryin' to bleach the tar brush at Lake Esther Elementary."

Pap slides a protective palm onto Daniel's shoulder. "What ye sayin' about my younguns?"

The Sheriff's eyes aren't the least bit friendly. "I'm sayin' that Lake Esther Elementary is an all-white school, for all-white children. Appears to me, your two don't belong." His tone is a low growl.

Against his shoulder, Daniel feels Pap's clutch turn into a claw. He can see, close up, the anger rushing into his father's face. "They're as white as you are and of better stock!"

"Lila," the Sheriff says, soft, "look at that girl's nose. I don't like the shape of it one bit. And, the boy's hair—ain't as nappy as old Nate's over there—but it's kinked, ain't it?"

Pap's claw is biting into Daniel's shoulder now, his breath's turned to a shallow pant, the fight muscles in his jaw have begun to twitch. *Pap's gonna kill him, I know it,* Daniel thinks. Miss Lila shoots a flat hand out in front of Pap's chest, gives him that woman's look that says "just you wait a minute," and turns back toward the Sheriff.

"Kyle, what's this all about? Hidin' behind Clive Cunningham who, everybody knows, swells up like a tick over anyone he hasn't known all his life. Wasn't it just last month he accused a Fuller Brush man of being a Communist spy? Don't you have anything better to do than bother a boy about his curly hair, embarrass a little girl over the shape of her nose?"

"Gee, Lila,"—the Sheriff grins his I-ain't-done-nothing-wrong grin again—"you been gone so long you forgot the difference between colored and white? This ain't no meltin'-pot state. We got laws about such nonsense. And I'm here to enforce 'em."

"You sonofabitch," she says quietly. "This is another one of your preelection stunts, isn't it? Last time, it was the Communist labor organizers, I heard. Sheriff DeLuth had to put his big ol' white hat on and ride their Red asses outta town. And, now, it's desegregation, isn't it? Find some kids with curly hair and call out the Sheriff to save our lily white souls! You're barkin' up the wrong tree, Kyle. This dog won't hunt."

"On the contrary." The Sheriff laughs, then says sweet as chess pie, "I think this dog's done treed himself a couple mule-ottos who best stay the hell outta the white folks' school."

Pap's had enough. To everyone's surprise, except Daniel's, he flies past Miss Lila and pins the Sheriff backward against his car. His fingers, clutching either side of the Sheriff's starched shirt collar, jerk the thick neck, the heavy head, eye to eye. "Name's Dare, ye blamed fool!" His face, which had earlier turned the color of a cock's comb, was now way past red, the bridge of his beak-shaped nose streaked with white.

"Son of Samuel Franklin Dare, tenth generation down from Ananais Dare, brother t' Virginia Dare, first white child born on this cont'nent!"

"Franklin, let him go! Now!" Miss Lila commands. She grabs Pap's arm, glares him into retreat, and steps into the sudden open space between the two men. "Kyle, I'll thank you to get in your car and get out of my grove!"

The Sheriff, eyeing Pap over Miss Lila's shoulder, elbows himself up off the hood of his car and takes his time adjusting his collar, lining up the parallel creases in his shirt and pants legs, centering his belt buckle, his holster on his hip. He shifts his eyes to Miss Lila, then drawls, "Well, he's got more guts than any Nigger I ever saw. I could shoot him right now for assaultin' an officer. But, then who'd pose for the publicity shots when I run 'em out of town, restore Law 'n' Order to the good folks of this county?" The Sheriff rolls baleful bear eyes around the clearing, taking in the Negroes still standing hushed in the shadows of the shed, Daniel and 'Becca shifting uncomfortably beside Pap, back to Miss Lila who's holding her new tree man at bay. "Good seein' you again, Lila," he winks.

Miss Lila's shaking mad. "Leave," she hisses, "before I get a gun and shoot you myself!"

"I am but the humble servant of my constituency," he says softly, then opens his door, slides into his seat and, with a big, jabbing crowd wave, drives away.

7

Goddamn sonofabitch! Lila Hightower stands in the grove yard, hands on her hips, back to the others, and wills Kyle DeLuth off the property. *How* dare *you, how dare* you, *of all people, try to pull your shenanigans on* me*! As if I didn't know what a raggedy-ass fool you were from the first day you came here, licking at Louis's heels like some overgrown stray in search of our table scraps. The old man spent years trying to teach you some manners*—"Kyle, you're a goddamn bull in the butler's pantry!" he'd say. "Gotta learn to apply the oil, boy. Guy like you needs to apply the old oil profusely!"

But, in the end . . . She squints as his car stops at the far-off end of the drive, then wheels left onto Old Dixie. *In the end, Kyle had no manners at all. But he sure had the Judge's mannerisms— his arched brow, his ingratiating grin—down pat. It was uncanny. And Louis's . . . When Kyle hooked both thumbs into his belt, hoisted it up to straighten his pants' creases and shot his cuffs in just the way that Louis always did . . .* Lila presses her eyes, presses back the memory of Louis shooting his cuffs. Louis, who had more grace in his little finger than Kiss Ass has in his whole hulking body. Louis, who was her life's touchstone. Whose death changed everything.

Behind her, shuffling feet, a nervous cough, remind her

she's not alone. She drops her hand, opens her eyes, notes that the autumn moon, a pale disk, hangs weakly between two storm clouds. *The moon,* Lila thinks, *sheds no light, has no heat of its own. Just like Kyle, it can only reflect a more powerful sun.*

Wearily, she feels the weight, the needy pull of the ragtag assembly rimming the grove yard, and turns to face them.

The Negroes, like a company of soldiers given the command "at ease," relax, lift dark expectant eyes in her direction. Franklin Dare, protective arms around each of his children, stands aside. And the children . . . The girl's eyes are downcast, chin dropped, shoulders wilted. A tear slides silently down one cheek. The boy looks on, his face a mix of anguish and exasperation that feels somehow familiar.

How many times, as a child herself, had she and Louis suffered humiliation at the Judge's hand? *But, in our case,* she thinks, *Louis was the one who took it to heart,* dissolving into tears, which only further infuriated their father. She'd been the defiant one, walking the tightrope between her father's temper and her brother's heartache, threading the needle between outrage over the aggressor and concern for the aggrieved.

Lila takes a deep breath. *Hooah.* The humid hot air leaves her lungs craving something cleaner, fresher. *It's near impossible to breathe 'round here,* she thinks. *Wonder if that's the reason the whole damned place seems brain-damaged?*

The Negroes patiently clutch their box tickets, waiting to be paid. With a hollow look, Franklin Dare yields the lead. She sighs.

"All right, everybody. The big, bad Sheriff's gone. Good riddance to bad rubbish. Nate, take the men into the barn, get started on the Pickers' Log. Franklin and I'll be there in a minute to settle up."

Relieved, the men make their way into the cool, cavernous grove barn. Through the wide door, there's the scent of fresh-picked fruit.

Turning to Franklin, she asks, "Isn't Ed Cantrell the principal of Lake Esther Elementary?"

"Yes, ma'am," Franklin says. Beside him, the boy nods solemnly.

Memories of pudgy Eddie from grade school, shy, smart, never quite in with the in crowd, but never quite out either, fly through her mind. She pictures him in high school—he'd become Ed by then—his scarlet-and-white band uniform straining at the side seams as the horn section marched past the cheerleaders on the football field; his stubby fingers surprisingly delicate on the shiny valves of his trumpet. Son of a teacher and a traveling salesman, he'd been a nice boy. She hoped he'd become a fair man.

"We grew up together," Lila tells Franklin. "I'll go to the school with you in the morning. We'll get this straightened out, get these kids back in school where they belong. Okay?"

Franklin's face floods with gratitude. The boy eyes her warily.

"Okay with you?" she asks the boy directly.

"Y-yes, ma'am," he stammers. His ears flush bright red.

"And you, sweet girl?" Lila bends low, from the waist, places a soft hand on the girl's shoulder. *Poor thing.* Frightened eyes, the color of deep creek water, glimmer between dark, tear-clumped lashes, search Lila's face. "That Sheriff has no idea what he's talking about," Lila tells her. "You have a beautiful nose."

8

It's late—the clock beside Betty Whitworth's bed shows nearly midnight—when, finally, the rain comes. *Took its time getting here,* Betty thinks, as she listens to it run off the roof and splat in the rain barrel. She shifts, rearranges the hot-water bottle under her aching hip. The pain will be less in the morning, now that the storm has broke. But tomorrow she'll have to check the ceiling under the third-floor roost. If the shingle glue hasn't held, if the pin leak's gotten worse, she'll have to beg somebody—Daniel maybe—to climb up there and apply some more.

If only Clay was here . . . It's the hymn of her days, and most of her nights. *If only Clay was here . . .* to climb up on the roof, to rewire the chandelier, to paint the stairwell, to enforce the rules, to collect the rents. The list of ways clever Clay could make her life easier was endless.

If only Clay was here . . . a visit from the Sheriff wouldn't reduce her to a babbling idiot, a brush-off by Franklin Dare in answer to her questions about the Sheriff's business with the children would've spawned a more forceful demand for the facts. Maybe she can bribe some information out of little 'Becca tomorrow. That poor child has a sweet tooth for Cora's thumbprint cookies.

If only Clay was here . . . Stop it! You're turning into a crazy old loon just like Mama. Remember how she was in the end, roaming the halls in her old gray robe and slippers, wild white hair spilling out of her hairnet, calling out, in that voice like a dull needle on a scratched record: "Henry, are you there, dear? Henry?"

What was it that had doomed her to live—a motherless child, a childless mother—in this godforsaken, falling-apart place? *Will I wind up like Mama, wandering the halls calling out like some crazy old loon? Was it this crazy old house that cursed us both?*

Built in the boom year of 1898 (the same year Betty was born), Charmwood was one of several homes her family owned: four floors, twenty-four rooms, an acre of impossible-to-maintain plantings surrounded by a half-mile of ridiculously expensive ironwork fencing that had long since rusted into ruin in the Florida air. Back then, when Papa was in commodities in Pittsburgh, the house was open only eight weeks out of the year. Oh, the parties they'd had then, in the winters, when the other wealthy families were in town, the chances she'd had to make a better match than smiling Cash Whitworth. Why had she picked him, of all people? Let him sweet-talk her into staying here year 'round? Let him borrow all that money from Papa to canal the swampland, develop home sites on Lake Esther's mosquito side? Oh, they'd had fun in the early days, before Clay was born. But when the bust came to Florida in 1926, Clay was no more than five, Cash lit out like a Canada goose, without so much as a squawk good-bye. Papa had been there for her then, to make everything okay. But, three years later, on Black Thursday '29, her poor papa had died, having failed to survive a twelve-story "fall" from his office window, and Mama went out of her mind. When all was said and done, this rich-man's folly of a house was all they had left of Daddy's fortune. *Which was more than most, so quit your complainin'!*

If only Clay was here . . . Well, he's not, now, is he? They're all gone, now, aren't they? Cash, Papa. Mama. Clay. It's just you and me, Charmwood. You with your leaky old roof and me with my creaky old hip. And sixteen mouths to feed first thing in the morning.

Betty Whitworth rolls over on her back. In the small room off the kitchen, the one once inhabited only eight weeks out of the year by her family's cook, the only room in the house un-adorned with extravagant wallpaper, carved oak cornices, or intricate, parquet wood flooring, Betty listens to the water rushing down the old rain gutter and wipes its wetness off her cheeks.

The scouts return to confirm the whispered wisdom of the Old Ones. The days of warmth and widely available food supplies are in decline. The time the colony calls The Quickening is at hand.

Outside the rim, those who gather food follow urgent orders. They move faster, go farther, and feed themselves extra in order to carry larger loads on the longer journeys home.

Inside the walls, the guards commence their careful checking and chinking against the coming chill. Those assigned to store and stockpile prepare their reply to The Quickening's central question, "Will there be enough?"

Within her chambers, She Who Decides awaits their report. All others (except the children, of course) prepare to stay or go upon Her command.

Does She, in Her wisdom, also await the potential intervention of He Who Provides? No one knows. Nor will they ask. Nor will they suggest or protest, so long as the children, their treasures, are safe.

9

"May! Got any Bufferin in your file drawer?"

Principal Ed Cantrell sits, elbows on his desk, bald head in his hands, feeling the warning signs of a really bad one coming on, spiderlike, across the whole right side of his face. If he doesn't get some relief quick, he knows, it'll wrap his entire skull in a web of pain, and he'll have to lie down on the little cot in the nurse's closet usually reserved for sick kids and humiliated, menstruating sixth-grade girls in need of their mothers.

"May!" he yells.

"Here." Miss May White appears in front of him with two Bufferin and a white cone-shaped paper cup of water. As he grabs them, he sees with a groan the stack of message slips she's slapped on his desk.

"How many now?"

"Seven so far." She purses her thin lips.

"Plus twelve at the house last night." Cantrell jerks his chin to help the Bufferin and the water slide down his throat, then crumples the cup and hurls it into his trash can. "Goddamn K. A. DeLuth!"

"Born troublemaker, that one," May agrees.

"Did you hear me tell him he could snatch those two kids

right outta class? Stir up this hornet's nest with every hothead in town? Hand out my home phone number like it was goddamn Halloween candy?"

"Of course not!"

Cantrell closes his right eye and he rubs his right temple. Squinting with his left eye at the message stack, he asks, "Any school-board members?"

"Only three," she tells him, pursing lips again.

"Goddamnit, May!" he explodes.

May White opens her mouth to reply, then snaps it shut at the sound of the front door opening onto the office lobby. Cantrell waves a weary hand at her. May turns and hurries out of his office, into her area behind the counter.

"Why, Lila Hightower, as I live and breathe!"

Damnit, Cantrell thinks, hoping the Bufferin kicks in soon.

"Hey, Miss May, how you doin'?" he hears Lila reply.

"Fair to middlin', rain this time of year kicks up my arthritis pretty bad. How's your mamma?"

"Took to her bed right after the funeral. Got Sissy waitin' on her hand and foot."

"Poor dear. What's the doctor say?"

"Oh, you know Mamma and her nerves. She'll get up when she's good and ready."

"I've been meanin' to give her a call, catch her up on all the news."

"Gossip, y'mean? She might like that. Mornings are better than afternoons. Now, Miss May . . ."—Cantrell hears the fat pause, knows what's coming—"I'm here to see Ed and *he should know*"—these words are spoken loudly for Cantrell's benefit—"I won't take no for an answer."

"Why, Lila, of course Ed's door's open to you. And to, uh, Mr. Dare, isn't it?"

"Yes, ma'am," a man's voice says.

Damnit to hell, Cantrell thinks, rising, using a flat palm to push against the pain exploding like a land mine behind his eyeballs.

Suddenly, the phone on May White's desk rings. " 'Scuse me, Lila. Lake Esther Elementary, one moment please." As Cantrell reaches his doorway to invite them in, May covers the bottom part of the receiver with a gnarled, blue-veined hand and smiles at the two big-eyed children trailing their father, who's trailing Lila Hightower, through the half door into her area. "You two like peppermint candy? Have a seat, and I'll get you some while the adults talk."

Lila Hightower lets Cantrell close the door and take his seat before she lights into him. *She's a striking woman still,* Cantrell thinks, as the fifteen-years-ago memory of her—the queen of their Homecoming Court dressed in fire-engine red with lipstick to match, looking for all the world like Scarlett O'Hara arriving at Miz Melly's birthday party—flashes through his mind. *She's thinner now,* he notes, dressed in a crisp white shirt, open at the neck and tucked into man-tailored black pants. *More Katharine Hepburn than Vivien Leigh.*

"Ed, since when does Kyle DeLuth get to think he runs the school system on top of everything else around here?"

Cantrell feels himself take the bait. "He doesn't run it, the school board does!"

"And what, might I ask, do you do?"

Hooked, goddamnit. "Lila, Mr. Dare, I apologize. Yesterday, the Sheriff just strolled in here, grinning like a Cheshire cat, and made off with two of our students, without my knowledge or permission. Apparently, after he spoke with you two, he made the rounds—V.F.W., the Elks Club, the Masonic

Temple—informing everyone in town that I've been somehow derelict in my duty."

"But, Ed, Franklin's got the kids' birth certificates right here, same ones he showed Miss May when he enrolled them. Says plain as day they're white."

"And here, right here"—Franklin Dare holds up another document—"is my marriage certificate. Says here both me and my wife are white, too!"

Cantrell shakes his pain-racked head. "I know it. But, as I've been informed by the four school-board members who called my home last night, and will, no doubt, hear again from the three others who called here this morning,"—he points to the stack of message slips on his desk—"Florida State law bars children who are one-eighth or more Negro from attending a white school. I'm afraid, Mr. Dare, the school board will be asking you to prove that all four grandparents and all eight great-grandparents are white, too."

Dare stiffens. Anger raises a sharp ridge between his brows. Lila lays a calming hand on the small man's forearm.

"Ed, this is ridiculous. You know as well as I do that this is nothing more than Kyle DeLuth's grandstanding."

"Be that as it may, Lila. Kyle's kicked up a ruckus and, at this point, there's not much any of us can do about it."

"But these children should be in school!"

"And—so long as Mr. Dare can provide adequate documentation to the school board—they will be."

"My granpap was part Croatan Indian," Dare insists, "and 'tain't no shame in that for me and mine."

"Croatan, y'say?" Cantrell repeats, dimly recognizing the word.

"How well you remember your history, Ed?" Lila asks. "Sir

Walter Raleigh, the lost colony of Roanoke Island? The word 'Croatan' carved in the tree?"

"Virginia Dare," Cantrell says softly. "You're descended from Virginia Dare?"

"Her brother, Ananais Dare."

"Well, you're right, Mr. Dare. There's no shame in that atall."

"So these children can return to their classrooms?" Lila leans forward, pressing him.

"Well, no, not exactly." As Cantrell leans back, his chair complains over the weight shift. "I'm afraid they'll have to wait until Mr. Dare here can make his case before the school board, next Wednesday night."

"And what are they supposed to do till then?" Lila demands.

"Take a break?" Cantrell smiles, hoping to lighten things up a bit. "Never met a kid yet who minded that."

"Well, I mind," Lila shoots back. "I mind this whole thing. And the Kick Ass snake in the grass that caused it."

"Oh, Lila,"—Cantrell gently shakes his aching head—"the time for minding Kyle DeLuth is long past. You got your daddy to thank for that."

10

Daniel sits on the hard wooden bench in front of ol' Miss May's desk sucking the last sliver of his peppermint candy. 'Becca's already finished hers and is casting big fawn eyes at Miss May in hopes of another.

That's what 'Becca's always reminded him of—a fawn who looks at you, shy and trusting, with those round brown eyes and long black lashes above that nose that's big for a girl but just the right size for a half-grown fawn. She even has the spindly legs, bumpy at the knees, and that delicate toe-then-heel, sort of skippy way of walking that all fawns have. She loves her sweets, same as they do. And she's skittery, too, inclined to freeze and shake at the first sign of trouble—which is what she done yesterday in the Sheriff's car, and most of the way here, today.

On Daniel's part, he's not worried a bit. Truth is, between the Sheriff not liking 'Becca's nose and his hair, and the principal not liking trouble at the school, he's hoping to get off coming back altogether. *Wouldn't it be fine to never come back? To be, like the song says, a "Free Little Bird"!*

Bored with watching Miss May answer the constantly ringing telephone—"No, ma'am." "Yes, sir. I'll give him your

message soon as I can," she tells the callers—Daniel's mind
wings off to the heavily wooded ridge up to Uncle Dolph's
place; to last fall, when he and Pap, Uncle Dolph, and Cousins
Jack and Frank caught their limit of quail and, in the soft
light of the slanting sun, made their way back for a pickin'-
and-cleanin' party. They'd released the dogs to run on home,
let Aunt Angie know they were on the way. Cousin Jack was
on point, holding his 12-gauge in one hand and his sack of fifteen birds in t'other, and he started it, in a tenor high and clear:

> *I'm as free a little bird as I can be,*
> *I'll never build my nest on the ground;*
> *I'll build my nest in the highest oak tree,*
> *Where the wild boys cain't never tear it down.*

All the rest of 'em had joined in on the chorus, their voices
finer than a choir on the rising wind:

> *Take me home, little bird, take me home.*
> *Take me home, little bird, take me home.*
> *Take me home to my mother, she is sweeter than the others.*
> *Take me home, little bird, take me home.*

Cousin Frank walked behind Jack. He'd piped in with another verse, same as the first, 'cept for changing one word to
suit himself:

> *I'm as free a little bird as I can be,*
> *I'll never build my nest on the ground;*
> *I'll build my nest in a chinkapin tree,*
> *Where the wild boys cain't never tear it down.*

After the communal chorus, it was Uncle Dolph's turn, and he chimed in with a mulberry tree. Then the chorus, then Daniel with his weepin'-willer tree. Then one more chorus—with Uncle Dolph's cabin in sight, Aunt Angie's welcoming ribbon of chimney smoke winding toward them in the wind—and Pap had finishin' rights. Pap, never one to follow the crowd, dismissed the trees altogether and, howlin' like a hound, sang:

> *I'm a pretty little star in the sky at night,*
> *A-smiling down on the world;*
> *I'll shine my light on my true-love bright*
> *And play on her beautiful curls.*

Aunt Angie, who looked enough like Mam to be her sister and was, had heard their approach and joined them for the final chorus. From the porch, her voice rang like a bell:

> *Take me home, little bird, take me home.*
> *Take me home, little bird, take me home.*
> *Take me home to my mother, she is sweeter than the others.*
> *Take me home, little bird, take me home!*

The sudden wrench of a door handle, the creak of its hinges jerks Daniel off Uncle Dolph's ridge and back to his bench in front of Miss May's desk. As he gauges the expression in Miss Lila's eyes, the jut of Pap's jaw, the wings of his wish unfold and flap inside his chest: *I'm a-free-little-bird from school today!*

Principal Cantrell, whose face looks like a setter dog that's been caught chasing rabbits, makes a big show of kindly escorting them out the little half door and into the lobby, then out the office door with maybe the intent of opening both doors of Miss Lila's green grove truck.

At the sidewalk from the office to the driveway, however, all five of them stop short. On the concrete walkway, someone's used school chalk to draw a wobbly white line flat down the middle, with the word "WHITES" and an arrow on one side, and "NIGGERS" and an arrow on t'other.

Daniel feels Pap stiffen. 'Becca freezes and begins to tremble. Inside Daniel's chest, there's a sudden explosion of feathers. Beside a furious Miss Lila, Principal Cantrell is hopping mad.

"*May!*" he yells, loud enough for her and the whole school to hear. "Get Floyd out here with a mop. *Now!*"

AGAINST PAP'S PROTESTS ("I got work to do, ma'am"), Miss Lila parks her car beside a storefront downtown. Over the door, in fancy letters, the sign says *The Lake Esther Towncrier*, with the picture of a man, one hand holding a bell, and the other cupping his mouth in a yell. Three lines of smaller letters say *Your Hometown Bi-Weekly Newspaper*, and *Ruth Cooper Barrows, Publisher, Editor in Chief*.

"You got to trust me on this, Franklin," Miss Lila tells Pap as she hustles them out of the truck and into the office, asking the skinny, yellow-haired girl at the front, "Is Mrs. Barrows in, please?"

"May I say who's askin'?" the girl wants to know.

At the reply, "Lila Hightower," the girl nods, asks them to "Please be seated," and moves through the dark wood door off the lobby.

Miss Lila turns 'round to face 'Becca and Daniel, puts a pretty hand on each of their shoulders, and bends down to speak softly to them. "You kids have been awful patient this morning. Can you wait a few minutes more while your daddy and I talk to the nice newspaper lady?"

'Becca nods her okay.

"Will you be long?" Daniel asks, not liking the strange oily smell of the place or the rapid *thrum-thrum* of machinery somewhere in the back.

"Shouldn't be long atall," Miss Lila replies.

The wooden door opens and the girl returns with an older woman who's short and squat, round-shouldered in a red-brown suit, with chopped red-brown hair flecked with gray. *Looks like a li'l ol' barn owl,* Daniel thinks. *Got the same kinda heart-shaped face, long beak, sorta hooked, and brown see-all eyes behind them black-rimmed glasses.*

Miz Ruth Cooper Barrows introduces herself in a voice raspy as a man's, shakes hands all around, then turns to lead Miss Lila and Pap into her office. *Haw! Got knocky-knees, too— just like the barn owls up home!*

11

As the striking young woman *(A real looker. Judge How-High's only offspring?)* and the small glowering man *(What the hell's a "tree man"?)* settle into her office chairs, Ruth Cooper Barrows checks the clock on the wall behind them. *Nine-seventeen. Forty-three minutes to get these two in and out and make it to the Town Council meeting around the corner.* The vote on a Highway 441 bypass, to route heavy trucks off the city's main street, away from the downtown merchants, should be a real corker.

Miss Lila Hightower—early thirties, gorgeous, heiress to the Judge's fortune, and unmarried—what's your story? Mentally, Ruth reviews everything she's heard, in the three years since she and Hugh came to Lake Esther, about the Hightower daughter. It's a file short on details, long on rumor and courthouse innuendo.

First time Ruth actually laid eyes on Lila was ten days ago, at Judge Howard Hightower's huge public funeral. Whispers and raised eyebrows rippled through the crowd at the First Baptist Church when Lila and her mother entered the rear double doors. Lila inscrutable in dark glasses and an impeccably tailored black jacket and pants ("Pants at a funeral!" the whisperers remarked behind flat, black-gloved palms), her gleaming head of auburn hair uncovered, beside her mother, Violet

Hightower, dressed and veiled in deep purple, head to toe. Rose had watched them make their way down the aisle, the daughter shoring the mother up with a determined, shoulder-to-shoulder, locked-forearm grip. Was Mrs. Hightower overwhelmed by grief or completely drunk at ten o'clock in the morning? It had been hard to tell till after the overlong service, made even longer by the Governor's rambling "Good-bye, old friend" graveside eulogy. Later, at the massive white-columned house in the middle of the Judge's grove, it was abundantly clear that Mrs. Hightower was a heavy drinker, and a bad one at that. And Miss Hightower, who'd hustled her upstairs in short order, was one cool cookie.

The family's info for the Judge's obit said only that he was "survived by wife Violet Randall Hightower, and daughter Lila, Washington, D.C." *What's the scoop on this young woman, whom courthouse wags call "the kind of W.A.C. reserved for the four-star sacks," who's suddenly appeared with a rawboned escort and two children in tow?* On instinct, Ruth launches an opening volley, meant to separate fact from local fiction.

"Miss Hightower, you *are* the prodigal daughter of Judge How-High?"

"Yes, I am." Lila Hightower lifts her chin, narrows green eyes, but the look is more amused than defiant.

Everything about her—hair, makeup, simple gold pendant (a French fleur-de-lys?), white silk blouse with covered buttons, black wool slacks—*is an elegant understatement. No doubt she fits right into the Capital, but here in Lake Esther,* Ruth thinks, *she's a dahlia in the daisy patch.* "My condolences to you and your mother," Ruth adds, and after she accepts Lila's nodding *(guarded?)* acknowledgment, lets another salvo fly across the desk.

"Come home just in time to block the Sheriff's seizure of the Golden Fleece?"

Lila Hightower laughs. Not a polite, "Why-Miz-Brown-ah-never!" tea-party titter. No. Lila's laugh is, like her voice, a throaty alto, laced with rich humor. "Guilty, as charged, Counselor," she tells Ruth with a sly grin.

"You were in the W.A.C.'s, right?"

"Still am," Lila says, straightening her spine. "On Temporary Emergency Leave."

"Really?" Ruth's mind crackles with potential questions. "So when will you be returning to D.C.?"

"Just as soon as I can."

"What can I do for you?" Ruth asks, leaning forward, arms criss-crossed.

Lila Hightower lays out the story with cool, quick precision, spiked with red-hot derision for K. A. DeLuth (*Fire and ice,* Ruth thinks): the Sheriff's uninvited visit to the grammar school at the behest of Clive Cunningham, his unauthorized removal of the Dare children from their classrooms, his accusations "based on nothin' but the narrow confines of his own mind, assuming, that is, he has one," his subsequent "stirring up of the local pea-brained pot with every race-hating hot-head he can think of, including most members of the school board," and this morning's inflammatory chalking of the school sidewalk. Ruth has picked up her pen and begun making notes. Occasionally she looks up, sometimes at Lila, sometimes in quick, studied glances at Franklin Dare, and, through the open doorway, at the two dark-haired children sitting stiffly in the lobby.

"Mrs. Barrows . . ." Lila lays an anchoring hand on Ruth's desk and leans forward. "May I call you Ruth?" Ruth nods. "I read your article last week about the Cape Hatteras light-house, got the impression you're from the Carolinas?"

"Philadelphia, actually. But I spent six years in Raleigh."

"Then you've no doubt heard of the Roanoke Colony, the arrival of Mr. Dare's ancestors on American soil?"

"Every schoolchild in the state knows the story. I've even been there, seen the pageant they put on every summer. *The Lost Colony,* it's called. Quite a show."

"Well, Franklin here is tenth-generation Dare," Lila keeps on. "And, contrary to our local Race Relations expert, part Croatan Indian."

"On my granpap's side, and tain't no shame in it, for me or mine."

Franklin Dare's dialect calls up instantly, for Ruth, the beau-tiful, uncompromising border of blue peaks that rim the west-ern Carolinas. The hooded intensity of his eyes tells her this is a man needing to set things straight.

Ruth checks the clock. *Nine twenty-nine.* "Smoke? Mind if I do?" She shakes a Pall Mall loose, taps it briskly on the desk, lights it with the flick and snap of her Zippo, and inhales greedily. "Was it your grandfather who moved up-country then?" she asks Dare gently.

" 'Twas," Dare says. The hard lines between his dark brows soften. "Granpap was a gray-eyed Indian, fought with the Confederates under General Leventhorpe. After the War, wasn't much left of Robeson County, so he took a notion to walk the state east to west. Wound up layin' train track inter Asheville. Traded mules for a while outta Tennessee. Sold one to Granmam who was a young widder with a fine ol' orchard of Winesaps just beyant Pigeon Ridge. She was a red-haired woman lookin' for a white mule to change her luck. Set her mind on tyin' up ol' Granpap who 'lowed he weren't cut out to be no woman's straight shingle, on account of his wild side. Granmam told him she'd been married to an ol' man since she was fourteen, she could do with a li'l wildin'. Tied up Granpap for good. We's all born there, middle of that same orchard."

"Still there? The orchard, I mean?" Ruth rests her cigarette in the brass, bulging-with-butts-already ashtray on her desk, picks up her pen again.

"Well . . ." Dare's eyes shift focus from Ruth's face to some faraway point. " 'Bout a year ago, Pres'dent Gen'ral Eisenhower 'nounced he's goin' to build the parkway slab through our property. Gov'ment man give us a check, and six months to move off. It was my brother Will got the idea comin' here, gettin' inter citrus. Reckon we woulda come when he did, 'cept my wife, Rachel, took sick. Will came on, found us twenty-five acre nigh 'bout the county line; good pine land drainin' into hammock, should be fine for melons come spring."

"So you're a local property owner?" Ruth asks, scribbling.

"Yes, ma'am. Will spent the spring and summer cuttin' out pine, clearin' stumps. When I hain't top-workin' Miss Lila's trees, I'm buddin' out seedlin's for a grove of our own."

"Franklin's forgot more about trees than most people know," Lila puts in.

Dare shrugs. " 'Cept for the diff'rence in fruit, trees is trees."

"And your wife?" It's a hard question to ask.

Everything about him—eyes, expression, voice—downshifts. "She passed last month."

"I'm sorry." Ruth pauses, casts a sympathetic glance at the children in the lobby. "Your brother Will have kids?"

"Three of 'em, two in the same school as mine."

"But the Sheriff has no quarrel with them?"

"They's red-haired, ma'am. Took after Granmam's Irish. We's dark-headed like t'other side."

The story is beginning to take shape in Ruth's mind. "Were you in the war, Mr. Dare?"

"Yes, ma'am. What they called a infantry sharpshooter, Second Battalion, Two Hundred Fifty-Third."

The boy, Daniel, has drifted across the lobby, listening, and now stands boldly in the doorway. "Got hisself a Silver Star, a Purple Heart and everythin'. Show 'er yer scar, Pap."

Dare turns around to eye his son into silence. Daniel retreats to his post beside his sister.

Nine-forty, the clock reads. Ruth taps the ash off her neglected cigarette, drags, and asks, "So you're a war hero, too, Mr. Dare?"

Dare shrugs. Apparently his response to any sort of compliment.

Lila lays a silky forearm on the edge of the desk. "Ruth, what we have here is a fine little family being hung out to dry by the Sheriff's showboatin'."

Ruth sends a smoke ring circling toward the ceiling before replying. "Couldn't agree with you more." She picks up a sheet of paper from her inbox and slides it across the desk. "Fellow who works for Clive Cunningham, named—let me see,"—she adjusts her glasses higher on the bridge of her nose, squints at her handwritten note—"Leroy Russell, dropped this off earlier 'with the Sheriff's compliments.' "

Both Lila and Dare stiffen before they've even looked at the paper she's placed in front of them. "What?" Ruth asks.

Lila's stare hardens. "Leroy's working for Clive now?"

"That's what he said. Who is he?"

Her eyes shine with fury. "Leroy Russell is the pussel-gutted fool I fired in order to hire Franklin!"

"When was this?"

"What's today—Thursday? It was two days ago, Tuesday."

"And on the following day, Wednesday, at Rotary"—Ruth checks her notes—"Clive Cunningham suggests the Sheriff stop by the school."

"Sonofabitch!" Lila explodes. Over her shoulder, Ruth sees little 'Becca's eyes widen. Young Daniel grins in admiration.

"So now there's at least two cooks heating up this kitchen, and, by the looks of things, three's going to make it a crowd." Ruth taps the paper on the desk.

The flyer from the Committee to Re-Elect Sheriff K. A. DeLuth invites one and all to "hear, live and in person, patriot Billy Hathaway, Founder and President of All White is All Right, this Saturday, 2:00 P.M. at the County Fairgrounds."

At the bottom of the page, the verse in script reads:

"The Lord thy God hath chosen thee to be a special people unto himself, above all people that are upon the face of the earth." Deuteronomy 7:6

"Great! So, in addition to the crazies, Kyle thinks he's got God on his side, too," Lila sneers.

Nine-fifty one. Ruth flicks her notebook closed with a snap, returns her desk pen to its holder, and considers, not for the first time, how the spiral of darks and lights in the wood grain reminds her of the swirl of truths, both secret and revealed, that surround every story. How patterns of past injuries often shape present conflicts. *Way more here than meets the eye,* she reasons. But, to see the grain, reveal the pattern, one has to make the first, all-important cross-cut.

In five minutes flat, she tells Lila and Dare what she plans to do, calls her husband, Hugh, out of the back—"He's the real brains behind this place," she explains—to snap a Dare family photo, and is out the door and on her way to the Town Council's controversial vote on the highway bypass. Which is, as she predicted, a real corker.

12

"Bitch!" Sheriff K. A. DeLuth snarls, slamming the front section of *The Lake Esther Towncrier* onto the breakfast table, causing his wife, Birdilee, who's skittery this morning anyway, to spill the warm-up coffee she's pouring into his cup.

"Oh, Kyle-honey, I'm sorry. I didn't mean . . ." Birdilee snatches a stack of pink paper napkins from the little plastic holder in the middle of the table and sops up the spilled coffee.

"Birdilee, would you look at that nose!" He stabs a finger at the girl in the family photo under the headline *American History Among Us*. "Ain't that about the Niggerest nose you ever saw?"

Birdilee wads the wet napkins into a single ball and, cupping them between her palms like a prayer, leans over and looks. "Bless her heart, it's big all right," she murmurs.

"You ever seen a nose like that on a white girl?"

"Well, now . . . there was that one, the daughter of those Greeks that had the restaurant downtown for a while, remember? And the new Queen of England; her nose is about that big, but"—she knits her brows—"not near as wide."

"Birdilee!" DeLuth shakes his head in disgust. There must

have been a time when it didn't irritate him that she was two cards short of a pair, but he couldn't remember it.

Birdilee, silenced, carries the coffee-soaked napkins to the sink, opens the cabinet door, and deposits them in the trash.

DeLuth watches her stand, back to him, and wash her hands slowly at the sink. He feels the sudden jolt of memory and remorse. This was how he'd first seen her, sunlit, dressed in white from head to toe, washing her hands at the sink beside his hospital bed. His first thought, groggy from the operation and the morphine, was to wonder was he was dead or alive? Was she real or an angel? Hearing him stir, she'd turned smiling, stretching the small satin saddle of freckles across her nose. Angels didn't have tiny tawny freckles across their noses, did they? He was alive!

His second thought—*Did we win the game?*—was harder to answer. She was a student nurse, interning at the University Hospital for final credits. She didn't follow football, had never heard of the Gators' All-American pair of quarterback Louis Hightower and his favorite wide receiver, Kick Ass DeLuth. She was the first girl he'd ever met who was immune to Louis's charms, preferred him, Kyle DeLuth, son of a piss-poor dirt farmer, to his handsome best friend, son of the power-broking judge back home. She'd made him feel like helping him recuperate from the surgery that stitched his game-torn Achilles tendon (and left him flat-gaited for life) was her reason for living, and he'd married her out of gratitude for being the first woman he'd ever been with who was not one of Louis's leftovers.

DeLuth looks again, feeling glad that Birdilee hasn't grown thick and shrill like most women her age. She's still the same little slip of a thing she was back then, her waist no wider than the span of his hand.

"Birdilee." She turns from the sink, lured by the soft shift in his tone, and smiles at his outreached hand. He pulls her into his lap, enjoying the rainwater freshness of her hair beneath his chin, and pats her shoulder in apology. "It's this woman, Ruth Barrows at the *Towncrier,* tryin' to help these part-Niggers pass for white," he says, by way of explanation.

"Won't get past you, though, will she?"

"No, ma'am, she won't," he agrees, savoring his wife's unquestioning faith in him, the sweet press of her small frame against his chest.

"What time do you have to be at the fairgrounds?"

"The rally doesn't start till two. I told Hathaway we'd meet him around noon, share some fried chicken for lunch. Might need your help with the bunting 'round the stage."

"Chicken?" she asks, sitting up to face him. "For how many?"

"Ten or twelve, I imagine. I been braggin' you make the best fried chicken in the county."

"Ten or twelve? By noon?" She jumps up in a panic. "I better tell Ceely to get a move on!"

While his wife calls up the stairs to tell Ceely, their colored girl, "Forget the beds for now, we need to fry up some chicken!" DeLuth strolls out the back door, across the dirt yard, and past the barn to check on the whereabouts of the herd this morning.

In the south pasture, he sees three of his four gray-white Brahma bulls—Ol' Ben's on loan to Clive Cunningham—and most of his two dozen cows. It was the Judge, of course, who'd suggested they go to Texas, take a gander at this odd breed of cattle from India by way of Brazil. Most of the local cattlemen had laughed their heads off at the Brahmas' looks: humpbacked, goit-necked, hound-eared, the bulls were ugly as sin.

But the laughing stopped when the beef boys learned the Brahmas could tolerate heat, with no loss of milk, up to 105 degrees; that they weren't picky as to pastureland; that their thick, droopy skin naturally repelled the blood-sucking pests that caused most diseases; that the cows could calve and bulls could serve for fifteen years instead of ten; and that, when crossed with traditional European stock, Brahma beef gave the best "cutoff" value available, with a minimum waste of fat. "He who laughs last, laughs best," the Judge always said. *Right again, ol' man,* DeLuth thinks and feels loss, like a whiff of the Judge's cigar smoke, float through his thoughts.

First Birdilee, now the Judge. What the hell's goin' on today, got me wallowing 'round like a goddamn sow in slop? DeLuth leans over, snaps a stem of sweet grass from the base of the fence post, and sucks on the sugary stalk.

It's the rally, of course. His first ever without the Judge sitting on the stage or nodding in the wings. Not that he wasn't ready or hadn't learned well what the ol' man had to teach.

Like the Judge's Number One Campaign Rule—something he called The Terrifying It: "There ain't a bit of difference between political campaigning and late-night ghost-story telling," the Judge always said. "You gotta have a first-class boogeyman, something that scares the panties off your constituents. Real or imagined, it don't make a whit of difference. S'long as it's *you* against The Terrifying It, and *you're* their only hope for getting an ounce of sleep after the election."

Their first campaign, The Terrifying It was those overproud Nigger war veterans, strutting their stuff up and down Main Street like they owned the place. DeLuth's stump-thumping promise was to "Put every Nigger in the county back to work!" either on his own volition, or, through vigorously enforced antivagrancy laws, in the Sheriff's citrus-picking chain-gang. "Hard labor, with no pay, will settle their sulking hash, but good!"

In their second campaign, The Terrifying It presented itself as a unionizing labor leader who complained that the Sheriff's chain-gangs were little more than slave camps. The Sheriff promised he'd "rid the county of these Communist Fifth Columnists!" and, on election eve, paraded his handcuffed captive 'round the polls, then personally kicked his Red ass over the county line.

In this, his third campaign, the Supreme Court had handed him The Terrifying It on a silver platter. The very idea of desegregation had everyone, from the Governor on down, up in arms. This fellow Hathaway was riding the reactionary wave with the right idea—beat back the N.Double-A.C.P. with a white-people's version. Sell memberships, donate the proceeds to prosegregation candidates. On the night DeLuth went to see him up in Jacksonville, Hathaway raised over three thousand dollars in less than ninety minutes! DeLuth can hardly wait to see what Hathaway's take will be today.

"Kyle-honey?" Birdilee's calling him from the back porch. "You wearing your uniform? Or should I air out your seersucker suit?"

13

Ruth Cooper Barrows wheels into the fairgrounds' parking lot just as Birdilee DeLuth is closing her car door, preparing to leave.

"Is the rally over, Mrs. DeLuth?" Ruth calls through her car's open window. "Didn't the flyer say two o'clock?"

The Sheriff's wife has a sunny freckled face that radiates, in intriguing contrast to her husband's, a warm and wholesome sincerity. She glances over her shoulder toward the milling crowd. "Oh, they're just gettin' started. But I . . . well, Ceely and I have things to do at home."

Ruth leans forward, sees the tall black woman in the rider's seat of Birdilee's car, and nods. "Of course."

"And, to be honest," Birdilee's tone is teasing, "politics is Kyle's cup of tea, not mine."

Ruth chuckles at the surprising confession. "May I quote you on that, Mrs. DeLuth?"

"Don't you dare!" The Sheriff's wife's freckle-stretching grin leaves Ruth wondering, not the first time, *How does a seemingly nice woman like that wind up with a bigmouthed bully like DeLuth?*

Out of her car, Ruth picks a spot in the shade, in front of the red-and-white poultry barn, and removes her thick, black-rimmed glasses to wipe the sweat off the bridge of her nose.

It's mid-October, for God's sake! she thinks, feeling nostalgic for fall in Philadelphia, the cool, crisp days, the colorful leaves of her youth. She leans back against barn wood to watch the speaker, Billy Hathaway, warm up his audience in the County Fairgrounds' center ring.

Big crowd, she notes, *four, maybe five hundred, predominantly male, all white.* In a front corner, she spots half a dozen of the county's big citrus growers, in short-sleeved shirts and string ties, chatting amiably with a number of cattlemen, dressed western, slapping big Stetsons against powerful thighs. *Interesting that the Sheriff's chosen uniform is an amalgam of both styles.* The rest of the crowd seems a cross-section of the local male population: a few suits, some ties, mostly plaid, bleached workshirts, broad suspenders, denim overalls. Was it the Sheriff's flyers that brought them out? Or, the loudspeaker-equipped crop-duster plane that spent the morning buzzing the county's small towns, blaring a come-on for today's "All White is All Right!" rally?

This guy's trouble with a capital "T," she thinks, eyeing the handsome young man who sports his dark blond hair in a close-cropped military cut, glittering blue eyes, and the kind of chiseled good looks that could sell Sunday Best dress shirts in the Sears or Monkey Wards catalog. Billy Hathaway's blue serge suit is no mail-order number, however, Ruth notes, as he strides to the edge of the stage, arms wide open in an embracing gesture.

"Folks, in my right hand here, I got the Holy Bible, the Word of God given me by my home church, First Baptist of Houston, Georgia, on the day I accepted Jesus"—*He says it "JEE-sus," just like Billy Graham,* Ruth notes—"as my Lord and Savior. I bet you got one just like it, sitting at home by your bedstead." His smiling eyes poll the crowd and they answer him with nods of acknowledgment. *Yes, yes, of course, we do.*

"In my left hand here, I got a copy of the Constitution of the United States"—*Check rolled piece of paper,* Ruth reminds herself—"given me by my ol' Drill Sargent, John Wayne Petty, when I left Camp Lejeune to fight the Commies in Korea." *Check J. W. Petty, Camp Lejeune.*

"Now, these two things I hold in my hands represent two of the three happiest days of my life. The third is the day my baby boy, Billy, Junior, sleeping right over there in his mamma's arms—Hold him up, Cassie!—was born." Baby Billy is a pink-cheeked infant wrapped in a blue-for-boys blanket. Cassie, his pretty blond mother, also pink-cheeked, shows him off proudly then sits back down beside the attentive Sheriff and two members of the local school board, also up for reelection.

"Folks, if I'd abeen here last spring, I woulda stood here before you a happy man—with God,"—He holds up his Bible—"country,"—He waves the rolled sheet of paper—"and family"—He sweeps his Bible-holding hand toward Cassie and the baby—"all, ALL in the divine order which the Good Lord intended.

"But today,"—He drops both arms and shakes his head, mournfully—"I am not happy. And, according to your good Sheriff here, neither are you! NOR SHOULD WE BE!

"My friends, the Supreme Court of our great nation has committed a sin against God and all good Christians. The judges of the Supreme Court have set themselves in judgment of Jehovah's divine plan. They seek no less than to reverse the curse of Canaan!" At this, the young man drops the rolled paper onto the podium, and forms an angry fist. Striding to the right, he brandishes his Bible high above his head. " *'Cursed be Canaan,'* the Lord says, *'a slave of slaves shall he be to his brothers'!"*

The crowd responds with a murmured rumble of agreement; the young man lowers his Bible and again shakes his head.

"My friends, the judges of the Supreme Court seek to force the children of the white race to mingle with the children of other races. Yet, God Almighty commands us clearly: *'Ye shall not go in to them, neither shall they come in unto you: for surely they will turn away your heart after their gods'!"*

At this, there's a syncopation of emphatic calls: "That's right!" "Yes, Lord!" "Amen, brother!"

"The judges of the Supreme Court have had *their* hearts turned against God! And, in so doing, they've turned their backs upon the white race!" Returning to the podium, he flips open his Bible and pretends to read: " *'The Lord thy God hath chosen thee to be a special people unto himself, above ALL people that are upon the face of the earth'!"*

The crowd begins to hoot and holler, "Above all!" "Yes!" "You tell 'em!" On the dais, the Sheriff grins.

"Now, folks,"—the handsome speaker hushes them— "I'm not making any of this up. Every bit of it's in the holy and recorded Word of God. You can look it up yourself, easy as I did. And, while you're at it, flip on over to the New Testament"—Hathaway flips over—"where JEE-sus, our Lord and Savior, commands: *'Render unto Caesar that which is Caesar's, and unto God that which is God's.'*

"My friends,"—he places his right hand tenderly on the open pages—"just like you, just like JEE-sus says to, I pay my taxes. And, like a whole lotta you out there, when my country

called, I paid two years of my life in Korea. Those slant-eyed
Commie devils cost me half a hand!" Hathaway holds up his
angry left fist and finally opens it, for all to see. The fingers
have no nails or upper knuckles. The crowd gasps. "I have rendered unto Caesar that which is his to have!" He thrusts the
ugly mitt in their faces. "But, lemme tell you,"—On cue,
Cassie stands up, steps forward, cradling the baby in her arms.
Hathaway points—"this child is not Caesar's! This child is
a child of God! And, so long as there's breath in my body,
THIS CHILD WILL NOT ATTEND SCHOOL WITH
NIGGERS!!!"

Ruth watches the blond madonna and child. It's clear the
young woman knows what's coming, her bright blue eyes
watch for it, wait for it. And when it comes—the communal
roar of paternal protection, the howl and bellow of the displaced beast unleashed—she slowly, gratefully bows her head.
As the furious men bellow their anger and agreement and intention, pretty Cassie plants a reassuring kiss on her baby's
cheek and awaits her next cue.

Billy Hathaway waits, too. Arms outstretched, he lets the
roar rise and swell and wash over him like a roiling wave off
the ocean and, as it recedes, he steps right, and tenderly helps
Cassie return to her seat.

Striding back to the edge of the stage, he leans forward,
eyeballs the crowd, and asks them, softly, "How, you want to
know, did this insanity happen? What demon, you want to
know, drove the Supreme Court away from one nation under
God? The answer is in five little letters." Hathaway holds up
his left mitt, emphasizing each letter with a jabbing thumb or
half-finger. "N.Double-A.C.P."

The crowd growls angrily.

Hathaway's catalog good looks have become suddenly too

sharp to sell Sears church shirts. His tone drips derision. "The National Association for the ADVANCEMENT of Niggers has done its job! In New York, Philadelphia, Baltimore, the local school boards have done the Supreme Court's bidding and let the Niggers in! Let 'em in, I tell you! The question is, will YOU? Will YOU let the Niggers into YOUR local schools?"

"NO!" the beast rises up and roars.

"No, you say? No?" Hathaway's contempt cracks like a bullwhip above their heads. "Well, lemme tell you, folks, a lot of parents in Baltimore said no, too. But their local school board, their local Sheriff said yes, and, since September, they've let the Niggers in!"

"NO!" the beast bellows.

"My friends, in two weeks' time, you get to choose. In America, we call it a vote. And, make no mistake about it, every single vote from here on out—whether it's for school board, or Sheriff, or Senator, or Governor, or President—is a vote either for, or against, segregation. It's a simple choice really. Do you let the Niggers in? Yes or no?"

"NO!"

"Then cast your votes carefully, my friends. Choose the candidates who'll say no when it counts." At this, Hathaway makes a sweeping gesture to Sheriff DeLuth and the two other men on the dais. The three of them stand as one and nod confidently to the crowd as if to say, "Trust us—we'll say no."

The crowd yells and applauds their own: "Yeh!" "Kick Ass'll say no!" "Give 'em hell, Kick Ass!"

Hathaway nods to the candidates, who nod to the crowd then sit, serious, in their seats. "And, what shall we do with those who turn against us?" His tone cracks the whip. "How

shall we deal with the turncoats, the Commie Fifth Columnists who take up the side of the N.Double-A.C.P.? I'll tell you
what we'll do—we'll follow the example of JEE-sus with the
money changers in the temple. We'll cast 'em out! We will
CAST THEIR ASSES OUT!"

"YES!" the beast bellows. "CAST 'EM OUT!"

"But that, my friends, takes work, takes organization," he
advises, wiping sweat, eyeballing them into silence. "It takes
leadership and membership and airplaned announcements to
get out the vote. Now, I don't mind takin' on the leadership
role—I'm doin' it as much for Cassie and little Billy as I am
for you—but to build a national association, All White is All
Right, A.W.A.R.—and make no mistake, this is *a war* for the
soul of this country—we need MEMBERS! And, folks, it
don't take much to be a member." Hathaway holds up a small
white card. "Just five little dollars and you're full-fledged! Can
you do that, folks? Can you spare five bucks to help us fight
the war against desegregation, CAST THE NIGGER-LOVERS
OUT?"

Ruth Barrows watches as the many-legged beast roars its
"YES! YES, WE CAN!" She draws a ragged breath as it
reaches into its many pockets and wallets and waves many
five-dollar bills high above its many heads.

Catalog-handsome, mitt-handed Billy Hathaway whips a
cardboard box out from behind the speaker's podium. And,
with the help of blue-eyed Cassie carting baby Billy to the
front, with Sheriff DeLuth and the two prosegregation school-
board candidates, Billy Hathaway feeds the beast four, maybe
five hundred little white membership cards, five bucks a head.

14

Sixteen miles south of the County Fairgrounds, in the hammock part of their property, Daniel drops to his knees beside his father. He watches Pap steady a short green stalk of root stock in one hand and, wielding a sharp knife in the other, make the small, smooth vertical cut. Flipping the blade horizontally, Pap cuts a second slit at the base of the first, creating the shape of an upside-down "T."

Working quickly, Pap grabs a piece of loose budwood, expertly slices off a single bud shield, and slips it gently off the knife into the T-shaped slit. "That'll do 'er," he murmurs, picks up a strip of white muslin soaked in grafting wax, and wraps the graft with surgical precision.

"What's it gonna be, Pap?"

"This whole batch'll be the sweetest bunch of tangerines you ever tasted. We'll plant 'em next to the house so we kin pick a fair apron-full whenever we take a mind to."

The words "fair apron-full" were Mam's favorite way of saying "plenty." Many's the time she'd sent Daniel out to the orchard for a fair apron-full of Winesaps, which, if measured, meant enough for three apple pies. A fair apron-full of eggs made eggnog for the whole hollow. And a fair apron-full of strawberries kept their family in jam for weeks. Now, the words hurt Daniel's heart to hear them. And he drops his chin, hastily, so Pap won't see.

Behind them, Daniel hears Uncle Will hammering split shingles onto the roof of the smaller cabin that will be theirs in a few weeks. On the rise above them, he hears the squeals and squawks of the girls—'Becca, bossy Minna, lisping Sara-Faye, and baby June—as they pick and poke their way through the pea cover in search of four-leaf clovers. In her garden, its rows as neat and tidy as Pap's root-stock seedlings, Aunt Lu chops collards for their supper. Daniel can hardly wait to sop up the juice, pot-licker green, with a hunk of Aunt Lu's skillet-baked cornbread.

He closes his eyes and, for the briefest moment, this strange flat land feels almost like home. But the picture won't hold. The air's too thick, the sky's too close, the lacy gray moss that hangs off the live oak is too strange to hold it. Other strange things, too, push against his innards. And, without warning, as if a giant hand reached into his gut and ripped them out of his own private hollow, he hears his words flung into the space between them. "Pap," he hears his own voice asking, "was Ol' Granpap part Nigger?"

Pap, squatting, rocks back on his heels, turns his gray hawk eyes to get a bead on Daniel's face. "I don't rightly like that term," he says. "It's a mean word, nasty, sorta like the words 'dumb hillbilly'; meant to make one fella feel less than 'nother. There's folks that'd call ever'body ye know up home 'a dumb hillbilly.' And, I'm asking ye, are they? Do ye know any 'dumb hillbillies'?"

In Daniel's mind's eye, he sees the face of ol' Jack McKenna, which can turn plum silly on a jar full of 'shine. Most Saturdays, ol' Jack's a pure, blamed fool, but dumb? As a fox.

"No, sir."

"I'd just asoon not hear either of those words outta yore mouth, ever again."

"Yes, sir."

"But, ye got a question, son. And, considerin' what ye been through, ye got a answer comin'."

Daniel sees Pap rock back off his heels and onto his hind end. He closes his grafting knife with a well-oiled click, slides it into his shirt pocket, then twines his hands together around one knee.

"Oncet, when I was 'bout yore age, I asked Ol' Granpap how come his skin was so dark. He had gray eyes like mine but skin darker than most Cher'kees. He told me then, and I'm tellin' ye now, I don't know. He said the Croatans, his Indians, were tender-hearted folk—had to be to help out a bunch of blamed fool Englishmen who had no business bein' there in the first place. We's lucky, he said, that Ananais Dare was jus' a boy. It wasn't in them Croatans to let the children starve, he said. Or, after that, to turn away runaway slaves who weren't of a mind to let their fam'lies be sold off like cattle and treated worse. Ye come with me to Robeson County, Ol' Granpap said, and ye'll see Croatans come in all colors, from pale as hominy to pot-burnt molasses. But seein' a man, and knowin' what he is, are two diff'rent things." Pap looks up to watch a hawk circling high above their heads. "Ol' Granpap useter make big talk 'bout his 'wild side.' But, truth is, he was the kindest, gentlest man I ever knowed. He had goodness in his blood, and God knows what else. But"—Pap leans forward, giving Daniel the eye—"whatever 'twas, 'tweren't no shame in it, boy. Not one single drap."

Daniel nods and sees Pap's gaze wander back to the row of root-stock seedlings. He wonders if their talk is over.

"Y'know, Daniel," Pap continues abruptly, "not up home,

but in most places, the Nigra was the root stock onter which th' whole South bloomed. Everythin' ye hear about th' Gran' Ol' Confed'racy happened because Nigras sank their arms elbow-deep, their legs thigh-high in the dirt and let things bloom on their back. That there tangerine bud couldn't grow by itself anywhere near here. But, ye graft it on the roots of a rough lemon and ye get yoreself a mighty fine tree. Thing I hain't never understood is the way some people, grafted here from somewheres else, resent the very root that helped 'em grow. This meanness from whites onto Nigras, or anyone who looks like they might have a drap or two of Nigra blood— Well, I reckon, it's 'bout the most ignorant thing I ever seed. Miss Lila says not ever'one 'round here's as ignorant as that Sheriff. Think we'll see for ourselves next Wednesday night, get ye and 'Becca back in school where ye belong."

At that, Pap rocks forward, quickly up onto his heels, fishes out his grafting knife, grabs a stalk, and gets back to work.

Standing, Daniel feels somehow both lighter and heavier. He looks around—at the girls, Aunt Lu, Uncle Will—and decides to climb up on the new roof, lend Uncle Will a hand with the shingles. But suddenly, something way off yonder, moving out of the uncleared pine woods, catches his eye. He lifts a hand to shade his face against the slanting sun. Walking their way is the biggest, blackest human being he's ever seen. And, from this distance, it appears he's carrying something shiny, golden, in his hands.

"Comp'ny comin', Pap." Daniel says it quietly, and points at the dark figure crossing the field. The girls, startled by the stranger, scoop up baby June, and run to the garden to hide behind Aunt Lu. Pap folds and stows his grafting knife and stands, hand on Daniel's shoulder, to watch the big man walking lightly, just like a Cher'kee, into their clearing.

He's dressed in a simple homespun shirt, some kind of ancient military pants tucked into tall boots, and a dark hat with two crossed metal arrows on the front of its crown. His face is pitch black, broad and flat across the cheeks, his hair and beard cottony white. *Up close,* Daniel thinks, *he looks even older than th' Ol' Cher'kee, which folks up home'd say t'aint possible. They say Ol' Will Wolf's the oldest thing on two feet. But,* Daniel thinks, *this 'un's got 'im beat.*

"How do," the man says to Pap and, seeing Aunt Lu and the girls, gently tips his hat. "Name's Sampson. Brung you some honey."

"Mighty nice of ye," Pap says and offers up his hand. "Franklin Dare."

When the old man holds out the jar of honey, Pap takes it with his other hand and continues to offer up a handshake. Sampson stands still, mute.

Pap's open hand indicates Daniel. "This here's my son, Daniel. Up-air on the roof's my brother Will. His wife, Lu, and the girls, 'Becca, Minna, SaraFaye, and baby June."

With a slow grin, the old man nods all around and, finally, accepts Pap's grip. "Seen your field full of peas," he says.

"Cover crop," Pap tells him. "Hopin' to help out the soil so's we can plant our trees next spring."

"Got bees," Sampson says. "Peas're good for bees in winter. Pay you in honey."

"Fine by me. Reckon they'd be good for the garden, too. What y'think, Lu?"

"Reckon they'd be fine. I like bees." Lu's smiling wide inside her sunbonnet.

"Need some help gettin' 'em here?" Pap asks.

Sampson shakes his head. "Got a cart. Bring 'em over next week?"

"Anytime ye want," Pap tells him, smiling.

"Orange blossom, heh?" Sampson points to the jar of sunlit honey.

"Never had it but we'll give it a whirl."

"Good. Be back soon."

"Thank ye, Mr. Sampson. We'll keep a lookout fer ye."

Sampson nods his silent good-bye, lifts his hat to the females and, as hushed and light-footed as he'd come, he's gone. Daniel watches the tall dark figure slip across the field and into the far line of woods, which seem, for a moment, to leap with the flames of the fiery red sunset.

15

In the dead of Saturday night, in the small, unadorned room just off the kitchen of the Charmwood Guest House, Betty Clayton Whitworth dreams of her other life. In 1918, she was twenty, the pretty, eligible daughter of one of Pittsburgh's wealthiest families, and, like Isabel Amberson, heroine of that year's most popular novel, she wore nothing but silk or velvet. Her dream of that life is not unlike the opening sequence of Mr. Welles's 1942 film of Mr. Tarkington's novel. In fact, although the dream's images are personal—of her family's great brick Gothic mansion, her father's black silk stovepipe hats and gray frock coats, her pink parasol cocked over her pink silk shoulder—in her mind's ear, she hears, as if just for her, Orson Welles's opening narration of the popular film (she saw it seven times):

"They had time for everything," Mr. Welles intones. *Yes, yes, we did.* She smoothes her skirt, adjusts her matching pink parasol, and smiles prettily. "Time for sleigh rides, and balls, and assemblies, and cotillions, and open house on New Year's, and all-day picnics in the woods, and even that prettiest of all vanished customs: the serenade."

Yes, Betty smiles in her sleep. But, unlike the fictional Isabel—who rebuffed the advances of the wild rogue Eugene, to marry dull, passionless Wilbur, and thereby received her comeuppance—twenty-year-old Betty, in a naïve interpretation of the popular story, chose dashing and more-than-a-little-drunk Cash Whitworth. The logic of Mr. Tarkington's tale was unmistakable: marry the daredevil instead of the dullard and live passionately ever after. Betty tosses uncomfortably in her sleep, not wanting the pretty pinkness of her dream to fade into the eventual gray of her present state. But the truth of her life is inescapable: she and Isabel, through entirely opposite routes, arrived at a similar, unhappy end.

The sudden ring of the telephone beside her bed snatches her awake. Relief at having the dream-turned-nightmare interrupted gives way to wondering concern. The man's voice at the other end is oddly familiar.

"That you, Miz Betty?"

"Yes, who's this?" she asks.

"Outta respect for Clay, ma'am, we're callin' ahead. This ain't about you, it's about them Nigger Dares. You gotta cast 'em out. Y'hear me, Miz Betty? You gotta cast them Niggers out!"

Somewhere, out of the bottom of Betty's groggy brain, a name swims up to her. A friend of Clay's from long ago.

"Leroy? Leroy Russell, is that you? What's this all about?"

The caller clicks off. And, in the widening silence that follows, Betty hangs up the phone and shakes her head, trying to clear the confusing jumble of thoughts.

What was that about? Unable to make sense of things in the dark, Betty turns on the light to think. *Why would Leroy Russell—I'm certain that's who it was—call me now, in the middle of the night? "Outta respect for Clay," he said—and "Cast them Niggers out!" Didn't the story in the* Towncrier *explain they were part Indian? And, besides, they have references—Lila Hightower, the Judge's own daughter, after all!!!!*

Just as Betty's about to dismiss the whole thing as a young man's craziness—*God knows my Clay did worse things*—the ring of metal hitting metal sings outside the house. It's another sound that swims up to her from the faraway past, when Cash was posting For Sale signs at the drained swamp lots on the other side of the lake. It is, no doubt, the song of a post-hole digger forcing its way through the dense clay hardpan just beneath the earth's sandy surface.

Betty pulls on her pink robe and, hand on her hip, crosses stiffly through the darkened kitchen—*No need to disturb the first-floor tenants*—to peer out the dining room's big front-facing windows.

The scene on the lawn sends her hand, clutching thin cotton, to her throat. Outside, in a ghostly circle, ten, maybe twelve, men, dressed head to toe in white robes, hold fiery orange torches above their heads. The air reeks of flaming kerosene. In their center, a man wields the singing post-hole digger up, then down, then jams it in the earth, then yanks up two dark shovelfuls of dirt. At his signal, two other men hand off their torches and join him. Something like a huge hammer rises high above their heads, then straightens, then drops with a wooden thud into the hole. Betty feels fear, like cold metal, the taste of copper, on her tongue. She sees the sudden sweep of torch, the flash of vertical flame, the streak of yellow fire. She recoils in horror at the blazing, crackling fifteen-foot cross before her. One of the men turns, lifts his torch toward the house. "Cast them Niggers out!" he yells. "Or, next time, we'll burn 'em out!" Panic balloons inside her chest, bursts in a high screeching howl as Betty faints and falls onto the diamond-patterned parquet floor.

*   *   *

WHEN SHE COMES TO—thanks to smelling salts thrust beneath her nose by old Mrs. Wexall of Minneapolis, Room Four—she grasps the woman's papery arms and attempts to haul herself up screaming, "Fire! The house! On fire!! Help me, PLEASE!!!"

"Calm down, Miz Betty!" Bunny Collins, the young manicurist from Room Five, tells her. "It's all right!" But, stumbling outside, she must see for herself. The men in white have vanished into the night. And the men of the house— welder Tim Wallace, winter fishermen George and Henry Howell, regional sales manager Graham Firth, frail Mr. Wexall and his brother-in-law Mr. Lindstrom—have organized a bucket brigade from the side yard's big cistern. The flaming cross is mostly extinguished, sputtering sparks into the shadows.

She runs to them, weeping. "Has anyone checked the roof? The house! It's all, ALL I have left!!!"

"It's okay, Miz Betty. Look!" they tell her, sloshing buckets. "See for yourself!"

By the light of the moon, she sees Charmwood—all that remains of the dream and the nightmare that has been her life— stands unharmed.

THEY CROWD AROUND HER at the big dining-room table, oddly out of their accustomed places. Betty sees them as if from a distance, as if she were somehow outside herself.

On her right, in the spot normally reserved for Mr. Wexall, on account of his "good ear," sits a twitching, walleyed Bunny Collins, bobby pins poking every which way off her head. Next to her, a dark-eyed Graham Firth appears almost pirate-like for want of a shave. Beside him, the poor displaced Wexalls and their in-laws, the Lindstroms; all four of them, usually pale, gone pasty gray over the evening's excitement.

On Betty's left, in 'Becca's place, sits Sara Chambers, the third-grade teacher who practically missed the whole thing taking time, while the others rushed outside, to wash her face and comb her hair. Beside her, in blue overalls pulled hastily over plaid pajamas, is a lock-jawed Tim Wallace, his powerful welder's hands clasped rigidly on the table in front of him. Next to him are the fishing Howell brothers, George and Henry from upstate New York, who, always unkempt, look most like themselves. Beyond them, the five remaining empty chairs sit silent witness for Mr. and Mrs. Colkannan, who drove to Daytona for the night, and the three Dares—'Becca, Daniel, and their father—who normally spend weekends "working out at their property."

"What's this about a phone call?" Graham Firth's demanding to know. Betty hears herself explaining as best she can.

"Your son's friend, you say?" George Howell asks. At his elbow, his brother Henry mutters, "Some friend."

Beneath glowering black brows, Firth's eyes narrow to a fierce flicker.

"I—I thought it was a prank. He and my Clay—well, they were always . . ." Betty loses her train of thought. She looks for it in the faces around the table.

Tim Wallace continues to stare down at his clenched hands. "Leroy's a little old t'be pullin' pranks."

A distant memory darts like a swallow across Betty's mind. Wallace had a big brother, Frank, who was Clay and Leroy's age, joined the Army same time they did. Except Frank Wallace never made it home. *Corregidor, wasn't it?* Betty wonders.

"Could've burned the house down!" Mr. Wexall attempts

outrage but his reedy-thin voice falls short of it. He turns watery eyes onto Graham Firth.

"Fascists!" Firth hisses, glaring around the table.

"It's all that Sheriff DeLuth's fault," Sara Chambers says. "He's got the whole town in an uproar over whether or not the Dares are part Negro."

"But the paper explained all that; they're part Croatan!" Bunny Collins is fond of 'Becca and was the first in the house to see the article and show it around to the others.

"Those men said if you didn't turn 'em out, they'll burn 'em out," Mrs. Wexall murmurs, her face fearful. "I heard them, didn't you?"

"They should be shot," Firth says. "Lined up against the wall and shot!"

"Who?" Bunny says, eyes wide.

"Those men, whoever they were, who did this thing, said those things about *children*!" Firth tells her.

"Thank God the Dares weren't here to see it! Poor little 'Becca would've been scared to death," Bunny agrees.

"But, of course, they must move." Everyone turns in surprise to old Mr. Lindstrom who rarely says anything. "You can't let them stay."

"But, what—I mean, what if—how could I?" Betty hears herself stammering.

"And let the Fascists *win?*" Firth turns dagger-sharp eyes onto Mr. Lindstrom, but the old man holds his ground.

"This house, it's all Mrs. Betty has. You heard them say they'll burn it down. A house like this would catch like matchsticks. And all of us with it."

"But, surely, they're just bluffing," Sara Chambers stammers. "They wouldn't really—"

"Hard t'say." Tim Wallace shakes his head. "Enough time, enough 'shine, these ol' boys are likely to try anythin'."

"Oh!" Betty's beginning to feel faint again.

"Which is why they must go." Mr. Lindstrom casts a shaming glance at the still smoldering Graham Firth. The older man points his chin, prickly with white stubble, in Betty's direction. Beside him, pale as a specter, Mrs. Lindstrom nods her timid encouragement.

Around the table, the others, one by one, all but Graham Firth and Bunny Collins, nod their agreement in Betty's direction. Betty Clayton Whitworth, watching herself from somewhere else, hears again the silent, searing wail of her soul: *If only Clay was here——If only——If——*

One way and now the other, the colony is moving.

The Old Ones recall that this has happened before, that She Who Decides, whose wish is law, may change Her mind. The others, younger, mask their worries behind a more careful attention to their daily duties. And keep their eyes open for anything.

It happened this way: First, upon answering The Quickening's central question, She Who Decides decreed a Divergence. Preparations began immediately to provide for the safety of those who would go and, more important, those who would stay. She even went so far as to select Her successor and that initiation was begun in earnest.

Then, the unthinkable happened. He Who Provides arrived at eventide in a web of smoke, redressed Her chambers, wrapped a wire net around their ramparts. And She announced the dangerous Divergence was off! The Quickening is complete. Above all, the children, their treasures, will be safe.

16

Ruth Cooper Barrows, former reporter for the *Raleigh Observer,* former feature writer for the *Philadelphia Free Press,* supposed Publisher and Editor in Chief of *The Lake Esther Towncrier,* is on to something.

The feeling—*Billy Hathaway is a big, fat fraud*—hits her just below the breastbone; her reporter's site-specific itch that must be scratched by the facts.

"Fact number one," she tells her husband, Hugh, over their Sunday-morning coffee, "according to the operator, Hathaway's home church—First Baptist of Houston, Georgia—does not exist."

Hugh looks up from the stack of five newspapers he drove all the way to Hylandia, early this morning, to collect: Friday's *New York Times* and *Washington Post* (their two-day delay "the price one pays for hieing to the hinterlands," he says), today's *St. Pete Times* and *Miami Herald* ("the only rags in the state—besides ours, of course—worth reading") and *The Hylandia Sentinel* (which he calls *The Slantinel* for its way-to-the-right leanings).

Reading glasses halfway down his nose, a double ditch of concentration between his brows, he's several columns deep into the *New York Times's* lead story—"JUST A MOMENT,

SENATOR!"—about the Select Committee's surprising repri-
mand of Senator Joe McCarthy and their unexpected recommendation that Tailgunner Joe be censured for "conduct contrary
to the august traditions of the United States Senate."

It's old news. But given Hugh's history—his refusal, as managing editor of Philly's *Free Press,* to sign a McCarthy-inspired
loyalty oath, or, on principle, to ask his reporters to do so either; his "sign-or-leave" resignation, and listing, without cause,
as an unemployable "fellow-traveler" in *Counterattack,* the Red-
baiters' Bible; all of which compelled their makeshift "retirement" to Florida—he can't get enough of what he calls "the
impending demise of that dimwitted demagogue."

"Listen to the adjectives they used in their report." His eyes
twinkle above the flat, horntop of his glasses. " 'Contumacious,
contemptuous, insulting, unworthy, denunciatory, vulgar, un-
justified, inexcusable, repreHENsible!' Who knew the old boys
had that many teeth in their heads?"

She doesn't begrudge him his glee. But, for the moment,
it's too soon, too hard, too potentially painful to buy into the
idea that Joe McCarthy may be on his way out. *He's been chal-
lenged before and fought his way back. In the meantime, I've got a
story to write.*

"Hugh?" Had he lost his old Editor's ability to read one
thing and hear another at the same time?

"No First Baptist?" he muses. "How about a plain old
Houston Baptist?"

"Got the number this morning, but,"—Ruth checks her
watch—"it's too damn early to reach the pastor. No doubt,
he's standing in the pulpit this minute, offering up the Sin-
ner's Invitation."

Hugh squints at his own watch. "Third, maybe fourth
verse of 'Just as I Am, without One Plea'?"

"Fact number two: the Provost Marshall at Camp Lejeune, who claims to know every Drill Sergeant ever since '22, never heard of one John Wayne Petty."

"Or?" He's reading again and, at the same time, raising a single inquisitive eyebrow.

"Or, incensed by our hero's claim, one Billy or William Hathaway."

He looks up, grinning. "You got him to crack the Camp files?"

"To expose a pretender to the pride of the Corps? Semper Fi!"

"Pretty contumacious yourself, aren't you? Anything else?" he asks, moving on with relish to *The Washington Post*.

"Not until after the Benediction at Houston Baptist." She checks her watch again.

AN HOUR LATER, Pastor Ted Bascombe confirms, "Sister Grace Hathaway's been a backbone member of our church for close to forty years."

"And Billy?"

"Well, Billy senior was a wild one. How a good Christian woman like Miz Grace wound up with the Devil's own hind end is beyond me. Wild Bill, they called him, died young, running bootleg whiskey into Chattanooga."

"So Billy Hathaway's their son?"

"Now you're talkin' Billy the Kid, thorn in his mother's side since the day that boy was born."

"But he did join your church?"

"Billy the Kid? Not hardly."

"So you never baptized him? Gave him a Bible for being a full-fledged member of Houston Baptist?"

"Only congregation that boy ever b'longed to was the Church of Charlie's Pool Hall. Or the Clinton County Corrections Facility. You want the whole story, Miz Barrows, you best be talkin' to Sheriff Jim Tatum. Let me get you his home phone number."

SHERIFF JIM TATUM CONFIRMS that young Billy was indeed "a sliver outta Wild Bill's quiver."

"Claims he was a war hero in Korea."

Tatum snorts. "He does, does he? Was that before or after he did two and a half in County Corrections?"

"You tell me. I saw him show a crippled hand to a crowd of four, maybe five hundred people, claim it was the Commies in Korea that did it."

Tatum gets a rich belly laugh out of that one. "Miz Barrows, you ever been to Memphis?"

"Not in years," Ruth admits.

"Sawed-off paws like Billy's mean only one thing in Memphis."

"What's that?"

"Somebody tried to outhustle the wrong pool shark, and got himself caught. It's Beale Street Bubba's trademark for makin' sure the cheater never holds a cue again."

"Billy Hathaway lost half his fingers for cheating at pool?"

"You bet. What's his scam now?"

"Membership in All White is All Right, A.W.A.R., five bucks a head."

"Wouldn't Wild Bill be proud!"

"Sheriff Tatum?"

"Ma'am."

"What was Billy in for? In the County Jail, I mean."

Tatum chuckles. "Oh, a li'l car theft, bad checks, moonshinin'. Ol' Judge Shaw jus' decided that boy's mamma needed a rest from worryin' 'bout where he was every night. Tell your local Sheriff—if he wants a list—to give me a call."

"Sure," Ruth says, the irony of Sheriff K. A. DeLuth calling anybody for help with Billy Hathaway lost on jovial Sheriff Tatum from Houston, Georgia.

RUTH LIGHTS A PALL MALL and blows slow, spinning smoke rings at the ceiling. *Trouble with a capital "T,"* she thinks. So far, it had proved easy to discredit the messenger, but what about his message?

Obviously, Hathaway played loose and fast with the facts of his own history. Were his Biblical interpretations equally bogus? But, the crowd had swallowed his racist rant wholesale. What would it take to expose the lies as thoroughly as the liar? As Ruth begins to make a mental list of local clergymen who might care to comment, the big, black phone on her desk rings.

"Ruth?" It's the no-nonsense voice of Lila Hightower. "You heard about the cross-burnin' at Charmwood Guest House last night?"

Half an hour later, Ruth checks the address in her notes once again, *147 Elm Street,* and scans the old house, a mansion really, for corresponding numbers. *Nothing there.* But the three empty nails on the wood above the wide, once-white porch show where they probably belong.

This place must've been something in its prime, she thinks, realizing that although she's been on this street a half a dozen times, or more—for receptions at the Mayor's house, an interview with the President of the D.A.R., a meeting of the

Ladies' Historical Preservation Society—*I've never even noticed it before.* Of course, the house sits opposite one of the grandest of the old Victorians in town. *Guess I've always been looking the other way.*

She looks again. The four-window bay, the prominent castled turret, the broad front and side verandahs are oddly familiar. *Of course:* This house was a much larger, grander version of her parents' home in Philadelphia's Powelton Village— *where Mama tried to wrap Poppy's bootlegging in Baring Street respectability.* It didn't work. *Prohibition or not, speakeasy or saloon, Poppy was an unabashed barkeep with a blatant irreverence for polite society.* "*Them and their airs,*" *he'd snort,* "*as if their whiskey don't wash in and out the same holes as everybody else.*" *Poor Mama. Between the two of us, she never had a chance.*

Ah! In the front lawn, Ruth spots a large round hole showing dirt, grass heavily trampled all around, and, to the right, at the base of a giant elm, a long, burnt black log with two smaller ones beside it. *This is the place.*

Ruth flips her notepad closed, slips it in the side pocket of her camera bag, hooks her right thumb on the bag's shoulder strap close to her hip, and enters the walk.

Midway up, she stops to study the hole. *Too bad they took the cross down,* she thinks, despairing of her hoped-for photo. The sudden screech of a door hinge, the appearance of a pert young woman, blond with bright, passion pink lips and sweater, draws Ruth's attention to the porch.

"Oh, hi!" the young woman says, covering surprise with friendliness.

"Hello, I'm Ruth Cooper Barrows, *Lake Esther Towncrier,*" Ruth calls from the walk. "Heard you had some excitement last night."

"Oh, Miz *Barrows!*" The blonde—scarcely more than a

teenager, Ruth realizes, close up—bounces down the steps, holds out a hand. "I read your *article* about the Dares, 'Becca and her family. Showed it 'round to *all* my customers, too! I'm a manicurist down at Lucille's LaMonde Salon. *Oh,* I'm Bunny Collins," she adds, pumping Ruth's tobacco-stained paw.

"Miss Collins, were you home last night for the cross-burning?" Ruth extracts her hand from the girl's eager grip, reaches into her bag for notepad and pen.

"Oh, *yes!*" Bunny's eyes appear, like shiny shallow mirrors, to reflect far more than they absorb. "It was just *awful*! We all thought Miz Betty had *died* of *fright*! Don't know *what* we would've done without Miz Wexall's smelling salts!"

This should play well at the LaMonde Salon, Ruth thinks. "Did you see anyone out front, the people who lit the fire?"

"The *Klan*? Oh, *yes!* But they were getting in their *trucks* by the time I got up. But Miz *Betty,* poor thing, she saw it *all*!"

"Did you recognize anyone?"

"Oh, *no!*" *Whenever she says "Oh!" or "No!" her eyes and lips form perfect round circles, like that cartoon character Betty Boop,* Ruth thinks. "They were wearing their *sheets,* y'know. All I saw was a bunch of white *shapes,* pointy at the top, gettin' in the trucks."

"How many men? What kind of trucks?"

"I don't *know*. Oh! *Pick*ups! *You* know, like all the men 'round here drive."

"How many trucks? Did you happen to note what kind?"

"No. I don't know. Miz Betty was *laying* there on the *floor*! I was just so *terrified* that she had *died*!"

"Thank you, Miss Collins." Ruth glances at her watch. "If you'll excuse me, I have an appointment with Mrs. Whitworth. . . ."

"Oh! Of *course*. She's in the kitchen, poor thing. The door's just over there, around the side."

MRS. BETTY WHITWORTH, a stocky, graying woman who appears nervous by nature, has indeed suffered a terrible shock.

Like her tenant Bunny Collins, Ruth discovers, Betty Whitworth's account of the Klan's cross-burning is short on details of the event, long on description of its emotional impact. Worse than that, the woman seems incapable of completing a sentence.

"The flames!—Mrs. Barrows, my father built this—all I could *think* of—flames so close to the eaves—can you *imagine?*"

"It must have been horrible for you. How many men did you say you saw outside, erecting the cross?"

"Horrible??!! Mrs. Barrows, you've no—I mean, this is a respectable—We've never had any—not in *this* neighborhood!—Why, my father was one of the town's most distinguished—of course, everything was different back—and my son, Clay, Mrs. Barrows—Fought with *Patton*! Africa to *Berlin*!—Like to see his medals, Mrs. Barrows? A real hero, my Clay . . ."

"How many men, Mrs. Whitworth? Did you recognize any of them?"

"Clay!—If only Clay was here—Well, if Clay, this would never—I mean—Leroy Russell!—they wouldn't've dared!"

"What's Leroy Russell got to do with this?"

"Well, he—well, I—well, no, I can't be sure—I'd rather not—no!"

"And the Dares, Mrs. Whitworth. I understand they weren't here. Have they returned?"

"The Dares?—Well, of course, I hated to—but, the others,

my *other* tenants, they don't want—and I can't afford—*Really!* Like I told Miss Hightower—they've gone."

At the end, Ruth's notes are as jumbled as Betty Whitworth's brain. She got answers to *who?* (Klansmen), *what?* (cross-burning), *where?* (Charmwood), and *why?* ("Cast the Dares out!"). *But I knew that before I came.* Although it was chilling to hear from Betty that the Klansmen had echoed the words of Billy Hathaway in yesterday's speech. ("Cast 'em out!" he'd said.) The answers to *when? how? how many?* and any other significant facts were lost in the mental fog of the only eyewitness. *How in the world does this woman run a boardinghouse?* Ruth can't help but wonder.

Two things, however, stand out—she'd underlined them— among the rambling references to Alexander Clayton, town pioneer, Clay Whitworth, war hero, General Patton, and Cash Whitworth, lakeside developer: the vaguely familiar name of Leroy Russell, and the fact that the Dares had been asked to leave.

Where did they go? "Check w/Lila HighT," her notes say. *And who is Leroy Russell? What's his connection to Betty Whitworth, her son, Clay, and, if I remember right, to Franklin Dare and Lila Hightower?* Ruth muses, as she shoots a close-up of the burnt logs with her Kodak, and a wide-angle view of the dirt hole in front of the pale, peeling face of once-glorious Charmwood.

17

In the busy First Baptist parking lot, K. A. DeLuth, dressed in his crisp Sunday seersucker and signature white hat, squires Birdilee to the rider's side of their ranch truck.

Charm bracelet jingling, Birdilee puts one hand on his arm, the other on her own small linen-and-net Mamie Eisenhower hat, and hoists herself up and onto the big bench seat with a quiet "Thank you."

Rounding the hood to his side, DeLuth notes with pleasure the number of cars bearing red-white-and-blue "RE-ELECT SHERIFF DELUTH" bumper stickers. Quite a few folks wave in his direction. As he waves back, he sees a pair of local boys grin and mimic his jabbing salute. He stops, squares his shoulders, and gives them the evil eye. With secret delight, he watches the silliness slide off their faces, their eyes widen. He holds them in the clench of his gaze a moment longer then, suddenly, winks broadly, shakes a pointing finger in their direction. They shiver in relief and shoot off to find their families.

"Kyle," Birdilee chides him, "you terrified the poor things!"

"Learned 'em a li'l respect is all," he replies, inserting the key, pressing the starter.

At their usual Sunday supper at the Lake Esther Inn, the colored waitresses and busboys treat them like royalty, and the local whites either eye them in hushed, nodding recognition or saunter over for an exchange of pleasantries. Privately, DeLuth enjoys the discomfort of his inferiors, interprets their sliding-away glances as the regard he considers his due. Beside him, Birdilee makes no such distinctions. She smiles prettily, nods pleasantly, asks kindly after this one's mother or that one's son who she has attended in her role as the local hospital's chief Pink Lady volunteer. Birdilee has what most people call "a good heart." Her ability to draw people in, tease a grin out of even the grumpiest or most seriously ill patients—leave them feeling lighter somehow, less weighed down—has always worked to DeLuth's political advantage. As the Judge often said and, DeLuth assumes, most people think: "K.A., you're a hard-assed sonofabitch, but anyone married to a sweetheart like Birdilee can't be all bad, can they?"

"What's so funny?" Birdilee asks him.

"Nothin', darlin'," DeLuth says, stifling himself.

After lunch, DeLuth and Birdilee once again board the truck and head out Route 441 to the Cunningham Groves and Ranch.

"Didn't see any of 'em at church this morning," Birdilee says, adjusting the bird-wing window on her side. "You sure this is a good time?" Although Birdilee rarely admits to disliking anyone, DeLuth knows that coarse-talking horsewoman Sarah Cunningham is not one of her favorite people.

"I told Clive we'd drop by for a few minutes. Want to make sure Ol' Ben's doin' us proud," DeLuth tells her. "Gettin' good and warmed up for his trip to the Governor's in January."

The Cunningham place isn't near as grand as the Judge's. The entrance road through the big navel orange grove is washboard clay and gravel. The house under the oaks is a sprawling single-story ranch, not a thing like the courthouse downtown. But the parking yard in the back opens onto cattle pastures instead of more groves. And Cunningham's cash-on-the-hoof crop of prime Hereford beef makes him, now that the Judge is gone, the richest man in the county.

As DeLuth wheels the truck into place, the screen door on the back porch bangs open and stringy-built Sarah Cunningham, all bones and angles, emerges, crowing, "Oh, Birdilee! I've been stuck in the house all damn week with a bunch of sick brats! Come in and give me something to talk about besides green vomit and runny poop!"

Birdilee smiles out the window, turns to DeLuth with a wry, "Don't be long now," and lets herself out of the truck.

Across the yard, one foot up on a fence rail, big Clive Cunningham waves DeLuth over. Cunningham's not especially tall, but he's broad as a boulder, with a shining bald head atop a mass of shoulders, chest, belly, and hips, too solid to be called fat, with a big booming voice. "Over here, K.A!"

"How's our boy?" DeLuth asks, nodding at the big Brahma bull inside the fence.

"Ol' Ben's been puttin' on quite a show! And, by the way he's smellin' that heifer, you're just in time for a matinee!"

The men turn and watch the brooding all-white bull nudge the big, brown female's behind, his great white wattle swaying beneath his chin. The female swishes him with her tail, takes a few mincing steps away.

"You talked to him yet?" DeLuth asks quietly.

"Thought we'd do it together." Cunningham pivots to bellow at a ranch hand entering the barn. "Dwayne, tell Leroy to get his butt out here!"

The big bull bumps the heifer again, this time laying a heavy head on her rump. He rises up to ride her but, again, she skitters away.

"Go, Ben!" Leroy Russell applauds, as he swaggers across the yard, his hat pulled deeply down against the sun.

"Slow start this mornin'?" Cunningham booms at his ranch hand whose looks are pretty-boy. Overlong blond hair curls around his ears and onto his shirt collar.

Leroy Russell wags his head and rolls his eyes in that way that says "hangover," then, lifting a pointy chin at the two big men, asks, "What's up?"

"Heard you and the boys lit a li'l bonfire last night," Cunningham says, soft.

"Well," Leroy laughs, "had us some hundred-proof panther piss, one thing led t'another."

DeLuth has turned profile, his attention deliberately on Ol' Ben. Without looking at Leroy, he asks, "How long you been livin' in this county?"

"All my life, Sheriff, you know that."

"And, at any time, in that entire life, can you recall a cross-burnin' on any one of the tree streets downtown?" DeLuth's tone is without warning loaded, like he spotted something over yonder and is taking aim.

"Can't say as I can." Leroy's turned cautious.

"Downtown's a white section, boy. The Mayor lives there. The President of the Daughters of the American Revolution lives there."

"My mother lives there," Cunningham adds.

"And"—DeLuth turns to face him full-bore—"a little ol' hen in a big boardinghouse lives there, practically dead of fright this morning."

"C'mon, now." Leroy laughs nervously. "We's just havin' a li'l fun."

"Fun's for East Town, boy." DeLuth says it sharply. "Or

down by the river. Or out in the woods. But there ain't no fun on Elm Street. *Ever!* You got that?"

"But, we's jus'—"

"I know what your lousy ass was tryin' to do. And, I told you to leave him alone, I'll settle his hash. This here's a Law 'n' Order county—I'm the law and you had your orders. You cross me again, you'll be choppin' weeds in chains for life. Understand?"

Leroy's Adam's apple bobs up and down in a hard swallow. He drops his eyes and chin in a silent nod.

"And lay off the panther piss," Cunningham adds. "Nothin' worse than a chef gettin' fat off his own cookin'."

"Yessir," Leroy mumbles.

A sudden, surly snort draws the men's attention to the field where Ol' Ben, top lip cocked back, has reared up in earnest, one thousand pounds of male intention on hind hooves. His big red dong, the size of a baseball bat turned backward, sways briefly above the heifer's hind end then, with a savage jab, thrusts deeply home. The heifer, shaken, locks her fore-legs in front, struggles to stay steady as the great bull covers her. His heavy front hooves paw the soft hide around her hips, raise raw pink crescents which weep bloodred tears. His huge head strains straight up, groaning, teeth bared, eyes wild and rolling. His big fatty neck hump jerks, the sagging white wattle jiggles. Then, almost as abruptly as he got on, Ol' Ben grunts and slides off. The heifer, with a low, ragged whimper, shudders head to toe and wobbles weakly away.

DeLuth averts his eyes from Ol' Ben's dong (drooping wearily now, spent) and looks right, past Cunningham, intending to tell Leroy that he could use a haircut. But the young man's gone, disappeared into the barn, or one of the other ranch buildings.

"Like I said," Cunningham nods, "quite a show. And, he ain't shootin' blanks neither. Got all but ten of my heifers in calf production already, 'nother week and . . ."

While Cunningham rambles on about his herd, DeLuth's mind sticks on the words "shootin' blanks." It's loaded terrain, primed by the very public fact that, despite ten years of marriage, he and Birdilee remain childless. Of course, the public word is some sort of female problem on Birdilee's part but his wife, a schooled nurse, has always sidestepped details. Then there's the additional matter of Lynette Thompson, the seventeen-year-old who, back in '43, the year he and Louis made All-American, got an all-expenses-paid trip (courtesy of the Judge) to the doctor in Jacksonville who took care of such things. Publicly, DeLuth got bragging rights but, privately, he knew he'd never touched the girl or impregnated anyone.

". . . sure wish I could talk you into selling him," Cunningham's still going on about Ol' Ben.

"Sell Ben?" DeLuth turns to Cunningham, flashing his you-know-me-better'n-that grin. "Ol' Ben's like family to me, Clive. Love that bull like a brother."

18

Daniel presses flat to the floor of the unfinished cabin, playing possum. His eyes are squeezed shut but his ears are wide open, straining to hear Pap and Aunt Lu talking softly on the dark porch.

"She didn't say *any*thin'?" Aunt Lu's wondering about Miz Betty, their boardinghouse lady.

"She tried to smile purt, like nuthin' was wrong, but her face was all puffed up and worried like. When I thanked her for the stay, she teared up considerable, couldn't talk atall. I told her I knowed she's a good-hearted woman and we hain't carryin' no grudge," Pap says.

"And Miss Lila?"

"She's rared up like a polecat fixed to spit."

"Will says there's bad blood 'twixt her and that Sheriff."

"They go back; that's for dang shore."

"Franklin, maybe I ortn't say it, but these younguns don't belong in th' middle of somebody else's fight."

Daniel hears the scratch, flare, and draw of Pap lighting his pipe. The creak of wood tells him Aunt Lu's decided to rock awhile.

It's shore been a quare day, Daniel thinks, what with Miss Lila showing up outta nowheres in her big green field truck and asking for a word, private like, with Pap.

Pap and Uncle Will driving off with her—with nary a word of what for—and, a few hours later, coming back with all their things from the room at Miz Betty's boardinghouse, and the big storage barn out back.

Somebody had added a sack of Cora the Cook's thumbprint cookies "for the children," and, boy, were they good! And there was a note to 'Becca from Miss Bunny Collins saying "good luck" and she was "going to miss having y'all around the house."

While Daniel helped Pap and Uncle Will unload the truck, Aunt Lu had got busy tacking up oilcloth over the open windows of their unfinished cabin and had the girls sweep the floor free of sawdust "so's to make it more homelike." Together, they set up Mam's chester drawers, the plank-board worktable, the hardwood chairs, the sleeping pallets, and the hickory-seat rockers on the porch.

Except for the back wall, which still needs chinking, and the roof, which is nearly done, the cabin's just fine. At least for him and Pap. 'Becca remains across the way at Uncle Will and Aunt Lu's place, tucked in between the girl cousins.

After the sun went down, and the air turned chill—maybe Floridy has a fall after all—Aunt Lu cracked open Mam's big cedar chest and hauled out Daniel's wool coverlet from up home. The coverlet smells of cedarwood and the wildflowers Mam used to jar by the window and hang off the rafters to dry by the fire.

Like it was yesterday, Daniel remembers the day last fall Mam called him out to the porch to admire the valley view.

"Ain't Mother Nature spread out the purties' coverlet ye

ever saw? Reckon I could try and make ye one in jus' them colors. Ef ye'd like me to, that is," she'd said.

The very next day, she had Pap set up her big loom right in the corner. And the rest of the fall and winter had been filled with her careful spinning and dyeing of the wool, her squint-eyed mumbling over the lines and numbers on her pencil-drawn pattern, the setting of the woof, and, for nights on end, the back and forth song of the shuttle and tramping of the treadles. His memories sting bittersweet. The taller that bright red, orange, and yellow coverlet grew on her loom, in the intricate pattern she called Jacob's Ladder, the smaller Mam got until, at the end, she tweren't hardly more than a shrunken shadow, all eyes and teeth and knobby fingers, tying off the knots.

On the porch, Aunt Lu stops her rocking. "Franklin, tell me that thing the Sheriff said 'bout 'Becca's nose."

"He said he didn't fancy the shape of it."

"That's all?"

"Yes, why? She hear somethin' diff'rent?"

"Who knows? She hain't talkin'."

"What d'ye mean?"

"That girl hain't said a word for days. I seed it on Friday and figured it'd pass. But, it's been three days now and nary a word, not even to the girls."

Pap's answer is the slow deliberate creak of his rocker.

"T'other thing is, she's taken to coverin' it and squeezin' it on the sly, like she's shamed and tryin' to make it smaller."

Pap's rocker stops. "I'm shamed to say I hain't noticed none of it." *Me neither,* Daniel thinks, feeling the awful twinge of his promise to Mam to "look after yer sister." Pap takes a deep draw on his pipe. "I'll speak to her tomorr' mornin'. I 'preciate your help, Lu. These younguns—"

"Miss their mamma." Aunt Lu finishes it soft. "We all do." Daniel hears her stand and step lightly off the porch. " 'Night now," she calls.

Outside, Pap's rocker creaks in mournful thought.

Inside his brightly colored coverlet, Daniel sees the humped-up grave on the broom sedge knoll up home. He worries over the effect of the October rains and wonders if the dark earth's sunk in on itself yet. He expects that, if it has, the sunken spot is filled up with red, orange, and yellow leaves from the autumn hardwoods. With all his heart, he hopes that poor Mam rests peaceful and easy, under "the purties' coverlet ye ever saw."

19

Another goddamn stack of them, Lila bristles as she seats herself at the giant mahogany desk that dominates her father's study as surely and surly as the old man himself.

He's been dead and buried two weeks now. When will the constant, irritating stream of condolence cards and letters end? Wasn't it enough she'd had to endure the funereal coronation of the old sonofabitch by everyone from two U.S. Senators to the Governor on down? Now, like Chinese water torture, comes the almost daily drip-drip-drip of sugary cards, fawning letters, and flowery tributes.

Lila snatches open the desk drawer, recoils from the smell of old cigar, grabs the Judge's silver letter opener, emblazoned with the seal of the Great State of Florida, and, one by one, slits the spines of the offending envelopes. The condolence cards go first. They're acknowledged most easily by her own preprinted message cards—"The family of Judge Howard Hightower thanks you for your kind expression of sympathy in the untimely event of his death."

Untimely, my ass. Not a minute too soon's more like it, Lila thinks as she licks and sticks three-cent stamps and wonders, for the millionth time, whatever possessed her to return to this godforsaken place after she'd vowed *for years* not to.

It certainly wasn't mother love for the shrill Daughter of the Confederacy who chose now, of all times, to have yet another "nervous breakdown" and retreat to her bedroom with a case of bourbon "for medicinal purposes." *When was it,* Lila wonders, *that Mamma's drinking became "nerves," and her out-and-out bingeing a "nervous breakdown"?*

It wasn't some silly Scarlett O'Hara yearning for the fertile soil surrounding the old homestead. There was no strength to be drawn from *this* Tara. It wasn't even greed. Didn't she have everything she could possibly want up in Washington? *Well, not exactly. But as soon as Jazz gets his divorce from Kitsy, I will!*

What brought her back, she remembers, was Sissy, the colored woman who's ruled the Hightower roost forever, and her pleading request to "come home, settle your daddy's affairs, and keep Kyle from walking off with everything whole hog."

Affairs! Lila snorts, recalling the Judge's surprise assignation of fifteen thousand dollars apiece to three mystery women who, coincidentally, lived in each of the three surrounding counties. *The old bastard!*

And Kyle. She relished the fact that her simple presence had been enough to deliberately, summarily thwart Kyle DeLuth's smug ascension to Daddy's property and preeminence as the most powerful S.O.B. in the county. Not that they didn't deserve each other. Truth was, Daddy and Kyle were cut from the same lean and hungry cloth. She'd seen it years ago, when she and Louis would complain about their father's heavy-handedness, his apparent disregard for anything that smacked of sentiment, his ruthless dispatch of one character-building high-school coach for another more in tune to the team's win-loss record. At every turn, with every issue, even then, ol' Kiss Ass had taken the Judge's side. And—like Cassius to Brutus—hung around for a bite of Louis's leftovers.

Louis. Her twin brother was the only fine and true thing the Judge ever produced. And the old man spent the boy's lifetime attempting to remake Louis's perfection after his own power-grubbing image. *But Louis . . . well, Louis wasn't capable of becoming Daddy's kind of man. But he certainly died trying, didn't he?*

"Jesus H. Christ," Lila mutters as she opens the official proclamation from the State Legislature rechristening the county's main thoroughfare the Judge Howard Hightower Memorial Highway. There'd been talk of it at the funeral. The state's big men openly envied the way Judge How-High had bullwhipped this county out of its malarial malaise into a marvel of citrus, cattle, and tourist-industry production.

That was Lila's most persistent memory of the old man—Hav-A-Tampa cigar in full, jaw clenched flare, his left thumb hooked casually in his belt loop while his right hand flicked the rattlesnake bullwhip with pinpoint accuracy at the hind end of a reluctant steer, the back of a thieving Negro or, in Louis's case, the legs of a soft-hearted, daydreaming boy. *The bastard.*

Lila hears the Westminster chime of the front door, checks her watch, and listens as Sissy hobbles to the entryway and admits her guest. As steps echo across the hardwood hall, Lila sweeps the rest of the envelopes into a pile beside the phone and, at Sissy's knock on the study door, rises to greet Fred Sykes.

"Miss Hightower, it's a real pleasure to meet you," Sykes says, shaking her hand a bit too heartily. "You got a real nice place here." As he drops into a leather guest chair, his eyes skim the room with the deft economy of one accustomed to evaluating property. Lila watches him take in the deep mahogany shelves flanking the windows with floor-to-ceiling leather-bound books, the wall of dark paneling behind her with its certificates, awards, and proclamations, including the framed headline: "Hightower and DeLuth Named All-Americans." This revelation, just over her left shoulder, brings his eyes suddenly back to her. "Though I have to admit I'm surprised to be here."

"Why's that, Mr. Sykes?" Lila asks, smiling. The man is about her age, with the sort of firm-chinned, nicely combed, not-from-around-here good looks that she might, under other circumstances, find attractive. He smelled good, too, freshly showered with a discreetly spiced aftershave.

"Well, like that headline says, the names Hightower and DeLuth are fairly tight around here. And I'm obviously not a fan of the incumbent Sheriff."

"But that's precisely why you *are* here, Mr. Sykes. I can't stand Kick Ass any more than you can."

Sykes's eyes flicker surprise.

"I *had* to know," Lila continues, "what possessed you to run against him in the first place?"

"Well, to be honest, I lost a bet."

The man's got a great grin, Lila thinks, admiring the slow, sly parting of Fred Sykes's lips, his confident display of square, white teeth. *And a rather shiny gold wedding ring,* she notes.

" 'Scuse me?" Lila asks.

"A bunch of us were down at the Board of Realtors one day, complaining about the Sheriff and some of his high jinks— like running a legitimate labor organizer out of town barefoot and in handcuffs. There's a flood of folks moving into Florida just now, a lot of them Northerners and fairly liberal. We're competing with half a dozen other counties, you see, and the Sheriff—well, he's just plain bad for business. So, one fella says, 'It's hard to get rid of somebody who runs unopposed.'

And another fella says, 'Yeh, we need somebody more modern-minded and friendly.' Well, one thing led to another and, before you could say Jack Robinson, we were drawing straws. And I lost."

"So, what are you doin' to win? I haven't seen any bumper stickers, heard any speeches."

"Well, I haven't had much luck with fund-raising. And a lot of folks tell me they're happy with the way things are."

"A lot of folks are scared to death. Do you want to win, Mr. Sykes?"

"Well, yes, I guess so. I mean, it's not like he's got a lot to do. This is hardly a hotbed of crime, is it?"

"Not in the traditional sense, no," Lila answers. "But, if you're serious about this, I could help you win."

Sykes sits back, his handsome face a blank. Lila studies him carefully. Her years—as her father's daughter, as one of the first women admitted into the Army's Command General Staff School (the one they called Suicide School because every class had at least one man blow his brains out), as Special Assistant to Major General Jasper P. Atkinson, S.H.A.E.F. Intelligence—had taught her the art of instigation: You toss a man a challenge and wait; if he's up to it, he'll volunteer. If he's not, he'll quibble. At which point, you find yourself another man.

Sykes drops his eyes to study, for a moment, his nails cut short and straight across. He frowns. Then, with a single movement, he lifts hands, starched white cuffs, broadclothed forearms onto the desk and, with a determined blue-green gaze, declares, "Show me how."

Lila chuckles. She opens the leather address book on the desk, bracing herself against the sudden smell of cigar that permeates every thing that was her father's, and dials the number.

"JoLee, this is Lila Hightower, is Hizzoner the Mayor in? . . . Thank you. . . . Well, hey, Jimbo, catch any fish this weekend? . . . You don't say, what'd you use? . . . Really? Imagine that. Now, Jimbo, the reason I'm calling is to tell you I'm a friend of Betty Whitworth's, and to ask you what kind of Law 'n' Order allows a cross-burnin' in the town's best neighborhood? . . . I know, I know. . . . Well, course if Daddy was still around, there'd been hell to pay. . . . Now, Jim, I'm just wonderin' if you've had a chance to sit down and talk to Fred Sykes . . . Sykes, Jim, running against Kyle for Sheriff? . . . Real estate . . . Well, I just had a meeting with the man. He's got some fine ideas, progressive, thought you and the other mayors might want to at least give 'im a listen. Y'all still have that Third Monday meeting? . . . Tonight? What time? . . . I think you'll be impressed, Jim. . . . Thank you, I'd love to, soon as I find my tackle around here. . . . Bye now."

Lila hangs up the phone, jots down "Mayors' Meeting, 7:30 tonight, Dixie's Coffee Shop," and hands the note to Sykes.

"Every mayor in the county'll be there. Lean heavy on Kyle being bad for business, on things gettin' outta hand around here—you know about the cross-burnin'?"

"I heard a rumor, didn't know whether to believe it or not."

"Oh, you can believe it. Four doors up from the Mayor's house, too. Think about introducing yourself as Fred Sykes, the future Sheriff, talk about how you're focused on the future instead of the past. The war's long over, the whole country's movin' forward, and this county can't afford to be left behind. How's that sound?"

Sykes gives Lila an admiring nod. "Sounds great."

Lila smiles and dials another number.

"Why, Lloyd Green, got the boss man himself answerin' the phone today? . . . You still head of the downtown Chamber of Commerce? . . ."

Three phone calls later, Sykes holds a handful of appointments with the key small-business groups around the county. Noticeably missing are the elite citrus men and cattlemen clubs which, Lila says, "will no doubt back Kyle for another term."

"This last one's a little tricky," she says, dialing. "Big Nick there? . . . Tell him it's Missy Lila. . . ." At this, she shoots Sykes an ain't-I-cute look. "Nick? . . . Nick, I sent you a note but I wanted to call you in person, tell you that bouquet you sent to the funeral was the biggest, most beautiful one there. . . . Meant a lot to me, Nick . . . yes, yes, he was . . . Thank you. But, Nick, well, this is kind of hard, but, you know that I know 'bout the arrangements you and Daddy and the Sheriff have on Friday nights. But, maybe you don't know that, ever since Daddy died, the Sheriff's been keepin' Daddy's share . . . yes, yes, he has . . . You're right, ain't right atall. . . . No, no, I'm not askin' that, I'm askin' somethin' else. The Sheriff's up for reelection, Nick, and there's a man, a real good man named Fred Sykes, runnin' against him. Now, if you were to have the runners spread the word to vote for Sykes, and if Sykes got elected, I could promise you a much better deal than you got now, considerably better, Nick. . . . Something like that, Nick. . . . Sure . . . My word on it good enough? . . . So you'll spread the word? . . . Two weeks from tomorrow, November fourth . . . Thanks, Nick, Daddy always said you were the smartest businessman in the county. . . . I will. Bye-bye."

"Miss Hightower, did you just cut a deal with Big Nick the Bolita King?" For the first time, Sykes appears distinctly ill at ease.

Lila grins. "I sure did."

"But, Miss Hightower, I couldn't possibly—"

"Win without his help? You're absolutely right."

"No, I mean—"

"Mr. Sykes, I couldn't care less what you mean to do after you get elected. The goal here is to get you into office. Afterward, if you want to collect the Sheriff's share of Big Nick's bolita money or, if you want to shut down every Friday-night numbers game in town—it makes not one goddamn bit of difference to me. As I recall, your words were 'Show me how.' *This*"—Lila has unscrewed the cap of her father's ebony fountain pen, written and signed the check. She blows the ink dry and hands the check over—"Mr. Fred Sykes, future Sheriff, is how it's done. Now, get yourself some buttons, bumper stickers, and placards. I suggest the slogan 'I LIKE SYKES!' Worked for Ike, y'know."

20

Ruth Cooper Barrows sits facing the typewriter table beside her desk, lost in the rapid clack of the keys, the slap and slam of the carriage. *Almost there, almost there,* she promises the sharp craving for a cigarette, as her stubby, new-ribbon-and-tobacco-smudged fingers fly across the final paragraphs to the "—30—" finish line.

Done! Ruth yanks the sheet out with one hand, pats her coat pocket with the other. *Where the hell did I put them?* she wonders, then spots the pack of Pall Malls and her lighter stacked on the far side of her Underwood. She lights up, inhales greedily, and checks the big clock (a gift from the guys in the Raleigh newsroom) on the wall in front of her. Just enough time to proof the story before Hugh returns to threaten, for the last time, he's going to press without it. Ruth smokes and reads quickly:

A Tale of Two Bible-Toting Billys

WITH apologies to Mr. Dickens, it is the best of times and the worst of times when two men named Billy can read the same Good Book and come up with entirely different interpretations, one appealing to man's baser instincts, one approaching the higher good.

One Billy, named Hathaway, visited our county last weekend carrying a Bible purportedly given to him by his home church (although the pastor of the Houston, Georgia, Baptist church disavows Hathaway's claim to membership). Hoisting the Good Book high above his head, Billy Hathaway preached a sermon demeaning the U.S. Supreme Court and espousing white racial supremacy (although, according to his mother, he is not an ordained minister). Hathaway also claimed to be a war hero, injured in service to his country (although the U.S. Marines have no record of him, and his local sheriff states that the only uniformed service Hathaway may legitimately claim is two and a half years in Clinton County Corrections). There was, of course, at the end of Hathaway's sermon an invitation, not to accept the love of God, but to join a club of hate.

Compare this story with that of another Billy, named Graham, who was graduated and ordained by our state's own Florida Bible Institute, who has prayed with three Presidents, preached to thousands from coast to coast, and hosts the popular "The Hour of Decision" radio show. This Billy, in a recent article in *Life* magazine, disagrees with Billy Hathaway's message of hate. Billy Graham says that those who "apply the Old Testament to justify racial discrimination" miss the point. "Again and again, through the law and the prophets, by

His warnings and by His judgments, by His action and by His word, God worked to impress two lessons: 1) that the standards of lasting and constructive fellowship are religious—not racial; 2) that the purpose of the separation He commands is for service—not superiority." To this, Billy Graham adds, "Then came Christ. Jesus broke down the barriers." In his extensive article, Graham argues that Christ gives us "the commandment and the power to love thy neighbor as thyself," and that "Jesus put no color bar on the Golden Rule." "Jesus made it clear," Billy Graham warns, "that what we shall have to answer for is the way in which we have treated our neighbor" and reminds us to "remember the sobering words of our Lord: 'As you did it not to one of the least of these, you did it not to me.' "

Whose interpretation is correct? The unordained, unchurched minister of white supremacy, Billy Hathaway? Or the leader of Billy Graham's worldwide Crusade for Christ? As laymen, we must all thoughtfully, prayerfully search our hearts for the appropriate answer.

Editor's Note: In preparing this article, we contacted ministers from Lake Esther's seven local churches for assistance or comment. All refused because, as one pastor put it, "My congregation is a long way from resolved on this issue." Special thanks to Dr. John Leighton, President of the private Clark Christian Academy, who did direct us to the *Life* magazine article by the Reverend Billy Graham.

"Well?" Hugh drawls from the doorway.

"Done," Ruth reports, holding the sheets up and out to him.

Hugh's eyes drop from her face down to the double-spaced lines of copy in his hands. He reads intently, knitting bushy brows, but does not, she notices, reach for the pencil perched above his right ear. At the end, he looks up. "Thought your plan was to discredit the messenger," he says quietly.

"Had to take on his message, too, Hugh. It's more dangerous than he is."

Hugh frowns.

"What?" she asks him.

He steps into her office, closes the door behind him, then sits down, holding her copy between them. "This Hathaway's a huckster, no doubt. But he's also a shill for our esteemed Sheriff, is he not?"

"Yes," Ruth says, wondering where he's going with this.

"Correct me if I'm wrong. But wasn't it a head-to-head with the Sheriff over the last election that cost our predecessor his life's savings and enabled us to pick up this paper for a song?"

"Ye-es," Ruth replies.

"We've got this Hathaway piece, plus the photos and story on the cross-burning at Charmwood, plus some editorial outrage over the Dares' forced move, plus the statement in support of Fred Sykes, the opposing candidate. Any chance we're hitting the Sheriff a trifle hard this week?"

"A trifle hard for whom?"

Hugh shrugs. "You're the one picking this fight. You prepared to see it through—win, lose, or draw?"

"You asking me to back off?" Ruth feels her face flush. "If we don't take a stand, who will?"

"Who indeed, my dear?" he echoes with a searching look,

then stands to go. "Fighting hellfire with brimstone, little lady," he tells her. "We who bear our battle scars vainglorious salute you." He turns on his heel toward the door.

"Thanks," she calls after him.

Hugh's silent acknowledgment is a single wave of the rolled pages in his hand.

21

Daniel squats on the roof ridge, hammering the last batch of shingles into place. It's hard work under the hot sun, but he likes the roiling scent of cedar rising off the shakes and the satisfaction of finishing up his uncle's job.

In his head, he can hear Uncle Will's voice telling him just what to do: " 'Fore you get holt of a shingle, get yer nails ready." Ready means put two nails in your mouth, clamp the warm metal tips 'twixt your teeth. "Then, lay yer shingle down flat, halfway up t'other. And line 'er up nice 'n' straight." Nice 'n' straight means side by side, a finger's width apart. "And don't go switchin' fingers on me; use the same one ever'time." Now, "set up yer first nail, two fingers from the side, a hand's width down from the top." *The hammerin' is the best part.* "Then set up t'other one same way, straight across."

Roofin's man's work, Daniel decides, hitting the second nail squarely into place, *and a heap more fun than any ol' schoolwork.* It's been turnin' on three days since he, Pap, and 'Becca moved out here permanent and, to Daniel, it's felt like heaven and halleloo. *Haven't missed ol' Miss Burch or any of them flinty-eyed schoolkids one bit,* he thinks. *Nor ol' Mr. Wexall, snorin' up a storm in the room next door at the boardin'house, nuther.* It was fine to sleep in a cabin again, nothing but the chime of field crickets, the chuckling of the hens, and the chitter and caw of wild birds from the pine woods yonder to break the peace.

Each morning, before Pap and Uncle Will lit out for work— Pap to Miss Lila's groves, Uncle Will to the lumberyard— they'd given him his jobs to do. Then, while Aunt Lu, 'Becca, and baby June walked Minna and SaraFaye to the school bus stop at the crossroads, and later on, while the baby napped and 'Becca and Aunt Lu busied themselves in the kitchen, Daniel had hit it hard. Monday, he'd finished chinking the back wall of the cabin, inside and out, and cleaned out the chicken coop. Yesterday, he'd hoed the corn rows, then chopped and piled more stove wood than Aunt Lu said she could use in a month. And, this morning, after an evening's worth of asking, Uncle Will had allowed that he could finish up the roof.

Daniel had surprised them, and himself, with the amount of work a boy bent on proving himself a man could get done in a day. But, try as he might, he hadn't fooled Pap into thinking he was man enough to quit school altogether. Fact was, before Daniel had even got 'round to bringin' it up, Pap had squashed it.

"I 'preciate the help ye been, boy. But I promised your mam you'd get your schoolin'. Soon as we get this meetin' outer the way, you'll be climbin' on that school bus, same as your cousins."

The school-board meeting was tonight, but Daniel had no notion of what to expect. Pap said they were to hook up with Miss Lila and that Yankee newspaper lady, Miz Barrows, outside the Courthouse at seven o'clock. Beyond that, it was a mystery and a misery so Daniel had let go thinking of it.

Hammering the last nail in the last shingle, he squats back on his heels to admire his work. And to scan the clear blue horizon, wishing for some rain clouds. *Y'all come on now any time,* he thinks with pride, *this roof's ready for ye.*

As Daniel gathers the half dozen extra shingles, the hammer, and the tin of nails into Uncle Will's work sack, stands, and steps downhill toward the place where the ladder leans against the side eaves, something—movement, a flicker of color—pulls his attention to the tree line.

Got hisself a trail, Daniel thinks, seeing Ol' Sampson emerge from the woods at the exact spot where he'd disappeared the other day. *And what's that?* he wonders, squinting at the strange contraption the giant black man pulls behind him.

Looks like a cross 'twixt a wagon and a Roman chariot, like in the history books, but small enough for a man to pull with a wide diagonal leather strap across his chest. It has three wheels on it, one up front plus another on each side. A framed wood floor floats on braided green ropes, the color of palm leaves. And it is, Daniel sees, the perfect size for moving six big beehives from one place to another.

Daniel drops down the ladder quickly, stows Uncle Will's tool sack on the porch, and runs out to meet him. Sampson is dressed in the same military britches, boots, and hat as the other day, but today he sports a shirt with colorful horizontal stripes and a red kerchief knotted at his neck, its long ends dangling down to his belt.

Daniel's bursting with questions. "Them our bees? You live in them woods? You make that-air cart? Is it hard to pull? Kin I try it?"

The old man appears to eye Daniel sternly, as if he has no time for a lonely boy's eager questions. But then the ancient face cracks, showing teeth as gray and pointy as an old picket fence.

"Bees off first, heh?" he tells Daniel in a deep voice that rumbles from his chest.

Daniel trails the old man and the strange cart across the flat and fragrant pea field to a spot some hundred yards from the cabins. Stepping out of the harness, Sampson circles to the back and eyes Daniel again. "Help me?"

"Sure." Daniel steps forward, then, hearing the angry buzz from inside the hives, scoots backward, afraid of being stung.

Sampson points a patient finger to the hive's opening, wrapped with a tight wire mesh. "Bees in, air out," the old man tells him and, grasping one side of the hive, waits for Daniel to take the other.

The wooden hive is three boxes high and heavy, but together, the old man and the boy shoulder it off the cart—"Easy, easy now," Sampson says—and gently onto the ground. A vent hole in the upper back, Daniel sees, has been stuffed closed with a wad of cotton cloth.

Like the first, the other five hives vibrate with the thrum of angry wings. "What're they so het up about?" Daniel wonders, helping set the last of the hives into what has become an outward-facing circle.

"Don't like moving," Sampson replies, then, eyeing Daniel, "any more'n you."

How does he know that? Daniel feels a sudden, bewildering exposure, like a rabbit caught out of its hole. He steps back as the beekeeper pushes a pair of boards under each hive to raise it up and off the ground. He watches Sampson return to the cart, pick up a thing that looks like a big watering can with small bellows attached. The old man lights a match, drops it into the can, and, using the bellows, pumps a smoke stream out the spout and in Daniel's direction. The sweet scent of burning pine needles curls through the air.

"Smoker," Sampson explains. "Bees can't hear. Use their eyes 'n' noses instead. Smoker tells 'em everythin's all right, th' chil'ren are safe."

"Children?"

"Hive's just a big bee family, doin' for their chil'ren." He holds the smoker's spout to the bottom hole of the nearest stack. Gradually, the hive's angry thrum shifts to a more peaceable hum. Gently, he removes the wire mesh. In the back, he pulls out the wad of cloth blocking the vent hole and smokes that as well.

"Happy now," Sampson reports, moving on to the next one.

"Ain't they got a queen in there?" Daniel asks.

"Queen's every bee's mamma."

"Who's their pap?"

"Think I am."

"How you know what bees think?"

Sampson shrugs. "Do."

That's it, Daniel decides, watching the beekeeper smoke his way around the circle of hives. It's not only that this Sampson's more ancient than th' Ol' Cher'kee. It's that other thing, too. The feeling that, somehow, he knows more than any ord'nary human ort to.

"You part Indian?" Daniel asks.

"Yat'siminoli."

"What?"

"In English—Seminole. Means free people, unconquered."

"But, you're . . ."

"Part African? Part Slave-For-A-Day."

"You were a slave?"

"Oh, ho! No!" The old man's howling laugh erupts from somewhere deep in his belly. "Slave ship brought grandfather from Africa to St. Augustine. Escaped from boat docks next day. Seminole name meant Slave-For-A-Day."

"Indians took your granpap in?"

"Yes." Sampson looks up from the last hive.

Daniel stands in the hives' center, surrounded by the hum of a hundred thousand reassuring wings.

"Indians took in my ancestors, too," Daniel tells the old man quietly.

"Yes," Sampson says.

He knows that, too, Daniel thinks.

The Seminole—*a black Indian older than th' Ol' Cher'kee!*—nods, floats a small cloud of pine-sweet smoke into the heart of the humming circle. Daniel sniffs. The perfumey smell works its way up his nose and down into his chest.

Like medicine, or magic, it salves the pinky-white, prickly tight scars that hang, like scabs, upon his heart. For the first time since Mam got sick and died, since Pap packed up everything and left their home hill, since that big bear of a Sheriff made 'Becca feel bad about her nose, for reasons he can't begin to understand, Daniel, encircled by six beehives, feels—somehow—safe.

22

Principal Ed Cantrell checks his watch. Again. *Seven twenty-three! Where the hell's that goddamn Kyle DeLuth?* he fumes, as the school-board members drone on about the cost of putting a new asbestos roof on the high-school auditorium.

Normally, he's excused from attending these things, gets everything he needs from the minutes published the week after. Well, truth is, he has his secretary, May, read the minutes and tell him whatever he needs to know. But this business about the Dare children demands his personal attention.

Seven-thirty! Lila's gotta be fit to be tied, he thinks. When she'd called to insist on coming ("I'm not about to let Kyle DeLuth railroad these kids outta their schooling," she'd declared), he'd assured her they'd be first up on the agenda. And when, at the board's request, he'd asked her and the Dares and that newspaperwoman, Ruth Cooper Barrows, to wait in the hall, outside the courtroom where the meetings take place, he'd promised them entry "just as soon as the Sheriff shows up."

So where the hell is he? Cantrell wonders, putting a hand inside his coat pocket, feeling the two Bufferin his wife, Alice, slipped in "just in case." But, of course, the water fountain is out in the hallway where, no doubt, Lila sits, jiggling her Capezio-clad foot in angry impatience.

You'd think with all the time they'd spent together in high school—Kyle and her brother were best friends, hardly ever saw one without the other—they'd have figured out how to get along. But, Lord! The fire in her eyes at the mere mention of his name is enough to singe your eyebrows. Cantrell chuckles. *These board members have no idea what they're in for.*

Just then, the door behind the dais opens and DeLuth strides in, having let himself in the back way, through the Judge's chambers.

"Sorry, boys, got caught up in a call from the Governor," he says, grinning, pretending he's oblivious to the fact that he's stopped them, midvote, in their approval of the new roof expenditure.

The seven men seated at the long table facing the empty courtroom nod their hellos and finish their vote quickly.

Rather than take a seat next to Cantrell, DeLuth continues to stand, holding a book and a newspaper relaxed at his side. At the sound of the gavel—"Motion passed!"—Cantrell stands, too.

"Mr. Chairman, if you don't mind, I'll get the Dares now. They're waiting in the hall."

"Now, Ed, that ain't necessary." DeLuth's tone is like the indulgent mother of a spoiled child. "Mr. Chairman, this whole thing'll be over in two shakes." He rocks back on his boot heels to address the entire panel. "All y'all know I removed those kids from Lake Esther Elementary, on account of they don't belong. Now, maybe y'all saw the Saturday paper, same as me? Exhibit number one is their picture. Is that a Nigger nose or what?" DeLuth shows off the photo and shoots Cantrell a reproachful look.

It's best, Cantrell realizes, *the children don't hear this.*

"Right here," DeLuth points to the text, "is the father's own admission that the family's Croatan." He tosses the paper onto the table in front of Zeke Roberts, School Board Chairman. "Now, what the hell, you might ask—I certainly did—is a goddamn Croatan? I don't know what you did, but I pulled out my Webster's dictionary and looked it up! In exhibit number two, Mr. Noah Webster says . . ." He opens the blue-bound book to his marker—*A blank parking ticket,* Cantrell notes. DeLuth holds the dictionary like a hymnal, and glances up, as if to make sure all present are suitably impressed by the eloquent simplicity of his presentation. "Mr. Webster defines Croatan as 'a mixture of white, Indian, and Negro blood'!" He snaps the book shut and grins. "As plain as the nose on that pickaninny's face. Case closed?" he asks, softly.

Without hesitation—*Prearranged?* Cantrell thinks—Chairman Roberts says, "All in favor of barring these kids from Ed's school, say aye!"

The chorus of ayes tells Cantrell it's unanimous. His heart sinks. And the expectant eyes all around make it clear that he's dismissed to deliver the bad news to the people waiting in the hall.

Pain beats against his temples like a drum. "But, they've got two cousins in school, too. Redheaded with blue eyes," he protests.

"Also Croatan?" DeLuth asks.

"Also barred!" Roberts decrees, pounding his gavel.

Cantrell is speechless. One by one, he eyes the men at the table to make sure he's not mistaken. One by one, he sees their icy, unspoken message—*Get on outta here and get rid of 'em.* He turns, awkwardly, and carts the big bellowing bass drum that is his brain away from their unfeeling faces, past the empty chairs, and out the door into the hall.

"WELL, IT'S ABOUT GODDAMN TIME!" Lila says, rising, then turns quickly to the youngest Dares. " 'Scuse me, children."

Most of the Dares—brothers Franklin and Will and the boy, Daniel; Will's solemn-eyed wife, Lu, with the baby girl on her hip—stand anxiously to greet him. The three girls in flowered pastel dresses—dark-eyed 'Becca, freckle-faced Minna, and little SaraFaye, missing both front teeth—flank newspaper-woman Ruth Barrows, who's got them involved in some kind of word game using her notepad.

"It's over," Cantrell tells them.

"Over?" Lila repeats. Between the drumbeats of his head-ache, Cantrell can feel the heat of her disbelief. "But Kyle—" She falters.

"Slipped in through the back and rigged the vote," Cantrell tells her.

"Without seeing any of the evidence? Without any sort of hearing at all?" Ruth Barrows is dumbfounded.

Cantrell squeezes the top of his nose ridge between his eye-brows, hard, hoping to block the pain's advance. "The vote was unanimous. Mr. Dare, your children are barred from at-tending our school." 'Becca stands, moves toward her aunt, who slides a comforting arm around her shoulders without taking her eyes off Ed. "And, yours, too, I'm sorry to say," Cantrell tells Will Dare and his wife. Their girls sit back, stunned.

"This is ridiculous!" Ruth Barrows is up, wrenching the doorknob into the courtroom, finding it locked.

"And goddamn illegal!" Lila blazes.

The beginning of a major migraine marches up and over Cantrell's skull. "The Sheriff's the law around here."

Lila bursts into full flame. "The Sheriff's become a goddamn Nazi and this is *not,* by God, the Rhine!"

"In this country, the law is the law. People are entitled to due process." Ruth Barrows nods vigorously.

"And, by God, these kids are going to get it!" Lila vows.

Ed Cantrell surveys the two of them—tall, fiery Lila Hightower beside the short, smoldering Ruth Barrows—surrounded by a semicircle of Dares, young and old. His head's become a pounding parade ground of pain, but somehow he hears it, the whispered echo of his earlier thought: *They have no idea what they're in for.*

23

After reassuring Franklin Dare—"This school board's nothin' but a bunch of fools. They won't get away with this, I promise you!"—Lila Hightower strides down the hall and mounts the stairs, two at a time, to the second-floor office of District Attorney Wade Hampton Berry.

Just outside his open doorway, where a rectangle of light planes across the wooden floor, Lila stops short. *How the hell am I going to do this?* she wonders. Ever since she returned to Lake Esther, she'd been avoiding him, sidestepping all but the most formal of exchanges. *Now, I'm going to waltz in unannounced? As if I had the right? As if all that went wrong between us . . .* Lila shudders. In the after-hours hallway, memories creep forward, call out like street beggars for her heart's spare change. *Stop it! This isn't about us. It's about those children, and the school board's ridiculous, closed-door charade tonight. Hamp will understand that. He's got to!*

Lila, struggling, straightens her shoulders, levels her chin. And with as much confidence as she can muster, steps into the light and calls through the small reception room, "Too late for cocktails?"

In his office, Wade Hampton Berry reclines, tie loosened, sleeves rolled up above his wrists, the soles of his Florsheim

Imperials crossed on top of his desk. He looks up from a cut-glass tumbler of amber liquid and, after the briefest pause, smiles—eyes brightening, mouth curling slowly into Hamp's old, gotta-great-joke-to-tell-ya grin.

As if my walking in here was just the most natural thing in the world, Lila thinks.

Berry shifts his feet to the right and, with the lazy grace of the gifted dancer she knows him to be, slides open the drawer on his left, extracts another glass and a half-empty bottle of rich gold liquid. Squinting at the familiar black-and-white label, he drawls, "Whadya say, Jack? Bar still open for the prettiest girl in the county?"

"Pretty is as pretty does," Lila says. As Hamp pours, she leans in, tips the bottleneck a little steeper, for three fingers' worth instead of two.

"Rumor is you do quite well." Berry salutes her with his drink. He'd been a handsome young man—trim, sandy-haired, athletic—but the years of rural lawyering, buoyed, no doubt, by a sea of Jack Daniel's, had begun to blur the fine chisel of his cheeks and chin, round out his waist and ribs.

"You know better than to lay stock in rumors around here, Counselor." Lila takes a seat in one of the two leather chairs facing his desk.

"Shall we call it conventional wisdom then, Judge?"

God, how quickly we fall into the old ways—he the charming lawyer, me the ever-evasive judge, Lila thinks, embarrassed by her slip into the intimate banter of their college years.

"More like massive stupidity, if you ask me," she tells him tartly, sucking in the bracing burn of Tennessee's finest whiskey. They'd been best friends in high school, eager but awkward lovers in college. *If we'd married, as everyone expected, would we still be together by now?*

"Hmmm." Hamp eyes her over the rim of his glass. "Shall we get down to whatever business brought you here, or shall I torture myself with the fantasy that you've come to see me?"

"Oh, Hamp, I am not the girl you remember."

"Obviously not, my dear. You're a gorgeous, full-grown woman now, with a slew of many starred-and-striped pelts on your belt. Or do my sources misspeak?"

"You have no sources on my love life, Hamp."

"None but my own eyes and an abiding, bayonet-sharp understanding of the male animal in the presence of such a desirable female."

Lila inhales raggedly. The air had gotten too close to carve out a proper breath. "Oh, Hamp, I'm not here to joust. You're too good at it and we both know I hate to lose."

"Better to leave the worthy adversary choking in your dust, right?"

The whiskey is working against her resolve. "Okay, Hamp." She surrenders wearily. "You deserve your pound of flesh. I was an ass. And I am truly sorry."

"Sorry is as sorry does, my dear." Abruptly, he swings his feet onto the floor, leans forward and, now all business, asks her, "How can I help? That what you're here for . . . help with the ignorant masses?"

"That and a certain imbecilic Kiss Ass."

ONE HOUR and the rest of the Jack Daniel's later, Lila emerges from Hamp's office with her marching orders in hand. First up is a personal appeal to Tallahassee, aimed at getting the Governor to direct Hamp's office to investigate the Dare children's appropriate legal classification, their denial of due process.

"The statutes are extremely clear," Hamp had said. "If those kids are not one-eighth or more Negro, they're entitled to attend the white school. What kind of proof do they have?"

"Birth certificates, marriage license, the Family Bible. Far as I can see, the whole family's Blue Ridge Scotch-Irish except for Old Granpap."

"A great-grandfather? And he's . . ."

"Part Indian, Croatan, descended from Sir Walter Raleigh's Lost Colony, fought for the Confederacy."

"In a white regiment or colored?"

"I don't know, Hamp."

"Find out. While you're at it, why not contact one of your four-star swains in Washington and suggest the F.B.I. investigate possible violations of the family's federal rights? That'll set Kick Ass's bacon to burnin'."

"Any chance we can wrap this up in the next nine days? I'm due back in D.C. November first."

Hamp winces. "I thought the Belle of the County was back for good." He doesn't bother to hide his hurt look.

In the end, as she thanks him, he stops just short of asking her to dinner. *Thank God!* Lila thinks. *He's old business. Badly finished. But definitely over and filed for all time.*

Outside, Lila's surprised to see Ruth Barrows. The older woman leans against the hood of a station wagon parked beside the sidewalk, within the bright pool of street lamp that illuminates the Courthouse exit. Against the black backdrop of the nearly empty parking lot, she appears patiently on guard, cigarette in one hand, notebook in the other.

"So far, the school board's a unanimous 'No comment,' but"—Ruth nods toward the doorway—"I've got one last board member to ambush before I leave."

As Lila outlines Hamp's suggestions, Ruth, cigarette hanging off her lip, jots a few notes. The harsh street lamp gives the lined surface of her page, the gold tube of her pen, the small white cylinder of cigarette an otherworldly glow. *As if we're the odd ones,* Lila thinks, *outside the bounds of the prevailing craziness.*

When Lila mentions Hamp's idea about involving the F.B.I., Ruth looks up sharply, yanks her cigarette out of her mouth. "The F.B.I.?! Surely, if you can get the Governor, we don't need the Gestapo!"

"Well, no," Lila says. "I guess not."

"Sorry." Ruth drops her cigarette on the sidewalk, grinds it out deliberately with her foot. "I am not a fan of Mr. Hoover. So . . ."—she looks up, smiles—"you'll take on Tallahassee and the District Attorney's office, while I work the court of public opinion?"

Lila chuckles, holds out her hand. "Deal," she says.

BACK AT THE HOUSE, Lila wheels the truck into the big grove barn. As she crosses the yard to the porch, she sees the small brown figure rise from the kitchen table, grab a tall glass from the cupboard, and turn, calling out, "Glass uh tea?"

"No thanks, Sissy. Sweet tea on top of Jack Daniel's sounds terrible." Lila extracts a squat glass from the cupboard, pours herself a nightcap.

"You drink like yo' daddy," Sissy pouts, returning to the table. Disapproval puckers her face like a prune.

"Better him than Mamma, huh?" Lila says darkly, sliding into the chair opposite her.

"Since when they serve Jack Daniel's at a school-board meetin'?" Sissy wants to know.

"Meetin', my fanny!" Lila huffs. "Kyle back-doored the school board while we were waitin' out front. We never even got inside."

"Those chil'ren get to go back t' they school?"

"Not yet. But I talked to Hamp Berry and he's goin' to help."

"Hamp?" Sissy's taken aback. "G'wan t'help *who* do *whut*?"

"Well, for starters, he helped me kill a bottle of J.D. He's also lookin' into takin' Kyle and the board to court."

Sissy shakes her head at Lila's smirk. Her tongue makes soft *tut-tut* noises against the roof of her mouth. "Shoulda married Hamp Berry when yuh had th' chance," she says, mournful.

"Think so? Given up my shot to rub shoulders with the Army's top brass? Dodge the buzz bombs in Bushey Park? Follow Ike into Paris and Berlin?" Lila's bristling.

"Ain't nobody rubbin' yore shoulders now," Sissy says slyly, "far as Ah see."

"Damnit, Sissy. You can't really see me married, with a husband like Hamp, and a screaming passel of kids, can you?" *The old fraud.* Everyone knew Sissy's history with husbands was "three away—run away, put away, and passed away." It was after Henry, "the good and last one," died that the Judge added rooms for Sissy to the back of the house, where she received "callers," but pointedly refused all proposals.

Sissy's eyes, her whole face, softens with genuine affection. "No, Missy, course not. But I shore would give anythin' tuh see you happy."

"Aw, Sissy." Lila swigs deeply, feeling the whiskey expand her growing sense of melancholy. "Happy stood me up years ago. You know that."

"Well," the old woman's false teeth show abruptly, wide and white. "Ah remember you happy once or twice. When you and Louis wuz little, leapin' and croakin' 'round here, like uh couple pond frogs!"

"We drove you crazy, I know."

"And the night they made you Queen of th' whole school, and yuh looked like one, too."

"And Mamma made me wear that ridiculous red dress, and Hamp and Daddy had to hold her up on the sidelines, cause she was so soused she couldn't climb the steps to the parents' section?"

Sissy refuses to take the bait. "And the day they named Louis All-American. Yore daddy so proud, he 'bout bust a gut!"

"And the night Louis lit outta here?" Lila says it quietly, staring into her empty glass. "And the day that stranger in a uniform delivered the telegram? 'We regret to inform you . . . sincere gratitude for your great sacrifice . . .' "

"Tha's th' Jack talkin', girl," Sissy says sharply, rising, clearing the table. "Ain' no happy there."

"Or *any*where 'round here, far as I see," Lila retorts. She stands, refills her glass, and moves toward the door. "G'night, Sissy," she says without looking back.

Upstairs in her room, she resists turning on the light. Too many memories reside in the pink rosebud wallpaper, matching chenille bedspread, her teenage vanity with its pleated satin skirt and twin fitted drawers jammed with prom tickets, play programs, fading photographs and, in the back, the small ribbon-tied stack of college love letters from Hamp. She sets down her drink in the dark, removes her shoes, drapes slacks and shirt on the back of her bedside chair; slips off the sheer French lace and silk underthings that are, since Paris, her private indulgence; and slides into bed. She sips the remaining whiskey, awash tonight in painful wavering images: Louis's flag-draped coffin with its bayonetted body missing a hand; Hamp's bloated, unhappy face; and Jazz, candlelit in her apartment, pulling her out of bed to dance with him, naked, to Lady Ella's smoky "Night and Day." Jazz, who would soon be all hers forever, but who—*for what reason?*—had not, for three days now, returned her call. *His lack of response means something*—all his actions are artfully calculated—*but what? That he's asked for the divorce? Or not? That our own plans are on? Or off?* That her private ache for an open, legitimate life, too long delayed, so recently promised, is . . . ? Lila drains her glass, wincing at the Jack's hot descent down her throat.

She lays back, sinking into the whiskey's warm embrace. For a few hours at least, it frees her from further thought.

With the loss of but a few of the Old Ones, who spent the last of their lives wisely reminding others that all of life is uncertain, the move is complete.

Once again, by the grace of He Who Provides, food is plentiful. And, with the exception of one startling bit of news, life in the colony returns to normal.

The news, unexpected yet, in retrospect, not surprising, is that He Who Provides appears to have widened his net of care to include a young one of His own kind. In return for the move to a more plentiful dwelling place, the colony is to accord this Young One the same mindful protection provided each of their own.

She Who Decides has decreed it. The Young One has been marked with His scent, as surely as She has marked each of them with Hers. Despite his size, the Young One remains a sentient child. And children, of all kinds, are to be protected, at all cost.

24

Daniel sits on the porch with Pap watching Uncle Will cross the twilit clearing 'twixt his cabin and theirs. Midpoint, in front of the big woodpile, Uncle Will stops, scoops up a small chunk of pine, and, turning it in his hand as if it were a tender robin's egg or a sparkling piece of feldspar, seats himself in the empty rocker next to Pap.

The boy watches as Uncle Will, without a word, unfolds his pocketknife and peels back the rough bark to reveal the pearly white pinewood with a knotty streak of red running through it.

Pap draws on his pipe. And Daniel waits for Uncle Will to tell how Aunt Lu's faring with Minna and SaraFaye. The girls, after hearing they, too, were barred from school, had howled broken-hearted all the way home from the Courthouse. And how was silent 'Becca, who'd hidden her face and darkened the front of her dress with fat tears rolling like raindrops off her cheeks?

Years before Daniel was born, the old men up home, who spent half of any given day warming their backsides at the potbelly stove in Hart's General Store, had nicknamed Will "The Puzzler." "Give ol' Will enough time and he'll puzzle his way outta jus' 'bout anythin'," they'd tell Daniel and his

cousins, voicing grudging respect for the man who'd been un-
beatable at sodapop-top checkers since he was six years old.

"Ol' Will's a puzzler all right," they'd say, tossing back another piece of root-beer candy. "Steady and slow like that-air
turtle in the tale, 'Th' Tortoise 'n' th' Hare.' Not atall like his
brother Franklin, who's as hare-headed as can be," they'd add,
squinting their eyes at some recalled instance that proved, to
them at least, that Pap and his brother were as different as
night and day.

Slowly, Uncle Will slices off the wood's odd corners, its
sharp edges, till it's the size and shape of a large potato. Then,
turning the streak of red topside, he begins to carve.

"Minna 'n' SaraFaye are sleepin'," he says without looking
up. "Pore 'Becca's jus' sittin', woe-eyed, by the fire."

"That blamed Sheriff!" Pap jerks his pipe out of his mouth
and stabs the stem into the air. "I shore God should a-laid him
out, the day this trouble first come up."

"Now, Linny . . ." Uncle Will, the only person in the world
'lowed to call Pap that, gives his brother a black look. "That-
air Sheriff's like a wild b'ar hog. It 'ud take a whole huntin'
party, an' a pack of prime dogs, to lay that man out. And, I
reckon yer 'ware, we's slap outta good dogs."

Pap jabs his pipe back into his mouth and sucks hard.
Daniel sees the tobac in the bowl glow like a piece of coal, col-
oring the tip of Pap's hawk nose an angry red.

"Ain't the crook of it," Uncle Will asks quietly, shaving
wood, "that this-here Sheriff's the king of Clark County?"
He's rounded the red part and, eyeing it carefully, begins to
shape the white wood on either side. "And, over there,"—he
points casually with his knife blade to the tidy rows of Aunt
Lu's vegetable patch—"somewheres 'twixt Lu's taters and the

scarlet runner beans is 'nuther county altogether. Reckon they got schools over there, free as water? And a Sheriff who ain't K. A. DeLuth?"

Pap leans forward, peering through the haze of smoke, his pipe clamped tight on one side of his mouth. "Tangerine County," Pap whispers, as if somethin's suddenly risen up yonder, out of the corn rows, beyant the beanpoles.

"How 'bout you 'n' me take off work early tomorr', go on down there to Opalakee, get these kids back in school where they b'long?" Will asks softly.

Daniel rocks back, caught between the seeping dread of another new school, another passel of squinty-eyed strangers, and the rushing joy of recognizing the cock of head, the slant of tail of a robin redbreast, 'Becca's favorite bird, taking shape in Uncle Will's patient hands.

"Tomorr', then," Pap says, settling back in his rocker.

"Tomorr'." Uncle Will nods, adding delicate detail to the robin's beak, using the blade tip to tenderly outline a round, expectant eye.

25

It's past nine-thirty, the back of the newspaper office entirely dark except for the night-light on the loading dock, when Ruth opens the gate and wheels into her parking spot.

Beside her car window, Gordon, the black-and-tan Doberman that is their office watchdog, wags his nub of a tail in welcome. Gordon and the gate became necessary last year when local teenagers adopted the paper's hidden-from-the-street parking area as a late-night party spot. The gate is a nuisance, but, like Hugh says, "less trouble than picking up broken beer bottles every morning."

"Good dog." Ruth pats Gordon's silky black head, and allows him to follow her up onto the dock, through the silent press and production rooms and into her office in the front.

Her first call is to Hugh at home. "How'd the hearing go?" he asks. When she gives him the update, his response is a soft, round whistle of disbelief.

"I know I promised you I'd never say this, Hugh. But, God, I wish we were a daily!"

"Yeh, with daily ad, editorial, and delivery headaches?" he slings back.

"It's just that today's paper's already trash and Saturday's edition—"

"—goes to bed in forty-eight hours," he chides her. "If you're hot to get the word out, you could try the wire to St. Pete. But you'll have to hurry. Clint calls the ball on the morning edition at eleven-fifteen."

"Okay—" Ruth's eyes fly to the clock. *Hour and a half. No problem.*

"While you're at it, call Charlie in New York. He's got till midnight. This thing is right up his alley."

Ruth hesitates. Their old friend Charlie runs the national desk at *Time* magazine. For the past three years, since their "retirement" to Florida, she and Hugh had kept a deliberately local profile.

As if reading her mind, he says, "Use your old byline. Charlie will be fine."

"But, Hugh—"

"Sed quis custodiet ipsos custodes?" Who watches the watchman? Hugh considered it the Reporter's Creed.

"All right. If you're sure—"

"And don't forget to padlock the back gate," he tells her by way of good-bye.

"Aye-aye," she replies and turns, smiling, to light a cigarette, look up Charlie's number, and jam paper into her Underwood all at once.

CHARLIE SAID, "Send me four good graphs, op-ed—quick." And Clint had promised to "squeeze 'em in somewhere." So the race was on.

She slaps the return twice and begins:

> IF you're a parent, look no farther than the face of
> your own child to feel the horror of what's happening

in Lake Esther, Florida. Pick out a familiar feature on that face—the curl of his hair, the curve of her nose—and imagine a six-foot, six-inch Sheriff arriving at their school and pronouncing his hair or her nose unacceptable.

Imagine your children enduring the curious stares of their classmates as he carts them away in his squad car. Imagine him publicly accusing them of being something they're not. As parents who know better, would you not be outraged? Would you not demand an official hearing to clear things up?

Now, imagine that the school board, having promised you a hearing, denies it; and, having considered only the Sheriff's unsubstantiated opinions, votes to bar your children from their constitutionally guaranteed public schooling. Imagine the shock of a unanimous vote. Surely there would be one rational person among the seven who would care to at least question the Sheriff's stance?

Parents, look to the face of your own child and imagine that face falsely accused and punished in a town where nobody, not one person, cares. Not for Franklin Dare and his children, curly-haired Daniel and sweet-faced Rebecca. Not this week in Lake Esther, Florida.

Ruth rocks back in her chair, ponders suggesting the headline— "Nobody Cares"—adds it quickly above the byline: Ruth Cooper. Jerking the text from her typewriter, she moves to the wire desk keyboard in the production room. As she completes both transmissions, just under their joint deadlines, the phone rings on Hugh's desk.

Expecting it's him, she answers, "Just finished!"

"Hardly," the man's voice on the other end drawls. "This Miz Ruth Cooper Barrows?"

"Yes?" she says, puzzled. The voice has a familiar twang.

"Miz Ruth Cooper Barrows, you got a big fat mouth."

"Who is this?"

"This, Miz Ruth, is the man you chose to defame in your newspaper today."

Of course. "Why, Billy Hathaway. You in town?"

"No, ma'am, but I'll be dropping by soon to accept your retraction of this piss-poor pack of lies."

"I check my facts extremely carefully, Mr. Hathaway."

"How dare you defame me, a decorated veteran with a war injury!"

"Come off it, Billy. Shall I publish my interview with Beale Street Bubba? He's got a very clear memory of how you earned your 'war injury.' And his bartender, as I recall, has pictures. What do they call it over there—Bubba's Wall of Shame?"

She can hear Hathaway sucking air between his teeth. "Lady, you're picking on the wrong guy. I have powerful friends in your town."

"Do tell, Mr. Hathaway." *Damn,* she thinks, *wish I had this on tape!*

"Your Sheriff's on the board of directors of my organization. When you insult me, you're insultin' him."

"If you checked *your* facts, Mr. Hathaway . . . if you read the entire paper, you'd see I consider it my journalistic duty to insult Sheriff DeLuth."

"Sheriff ain't the only one around to help me settle your hash!"

"May I quote you on that, Mr. Hathaway?" Ruth asks, with a bravado that feels, suddenly, more than a little false.

"Lady, you've pissed off the wrong guy," Hathaway hisses and breaks their connection.

Ruth stands frozen, then, pursing her lips, returns Hugh's receiver to its cradle.

"Here, boy," she calls to Gordon, who pads in obediently from the lobby, panting. She pats her pockets for her cigarettes, lights up, and draws comfort from the dog's confident lope around the room. "Let's lock up, shall we?"

The Doberman trails her as she double-checks the locks on the front door and several windows, turns out lights, and dead-bolts the back door on the loading dock. She stands on the top stair watching him. In the dim light, she sees the dog run his usual route along the perimeter of the back lot, long nose sniffing, head oscillating, all senses alert to any intrusion upon his territory. When he returns to the steps, wagging his stub with a happy all-clear, she makes her way quickly to the car.

At the gate, she secures the padlock, reaches in to pat him good-bye, then watches him disappear, his shiny coat shimmering silver like a fish swimming off out of the shallows. The drive home to Hugh is brief—it's a mere two miles to their subdivision—but this close to midnight, with the menace of Billy Hathaway's threats scrolling through her inner ear, it feels infinitely longer.

26

"Sheriff DeLuth?"

"You got 'im, who's callin'?"

"Sheriff, this is Clint Patterson from the *St. Petersburg Times*. I'm calling about your barring of the Dare children from Lake Esther Elementary?"

These damn reporters, always talkin' in a rush. "If you're lookin' for a quote I ain't givin' you one."

"Why's that, Sheriff?"

"In the first place, I didn't bar 'em, the Lake Esther school board did. In the second place, you Fifth Columnists never get it right anyway."

"Sir, are you calling me a Communist?"

"See right there? There you go!"

"Sir, didn't you act independently? Didn't you remove those kids before the school board even knew they were there?"

"I'm sworn to uphold the law."

"So your action did precede the school board's directive?"

"If I do not respond to my constituents, I could be cited for failure to do my duty."

"The family claims they're Irish-Indian, sir. What makes you so sure they're not?"

"You ever raised a chicken, son? Or a sheep or a cow? Any 4-H schoolkid knows you breed a Indian red with a white, you get somethin' lighter, not dark. And definitely not kinky hair. Everybody knows Indians have long straight hair, not a curl, one."

"You a board-certified ethnologist, Sheriff?"

"Go to hell!" *Goddamn Ruth Barrows, got the Pinko Press cawin' over this like a buncha goddamn crows in a cornfield.*

"Who in the world was that?" Birdilee looks up from her magazine, eyes quizzing him over her reading glasses.

"Some goddamn reporter from the *St. Pete Times*."

"Kyle-honey," she says with a small frown, "what's raisin' chickens got to do with those poor Dare children?"

"Goddamnit, Birdilee, don't you go jumpin' on that 'poor children' bandwagon with me! Those kids have Nigger in their blood, plain as day!"

Birdilee blinks at him. She removes her glasses, bites her lower lip in thought. When she speaks, her tone is soft, airy, as if she's puzzling out a problem and in need of his help. "Funny thing, honey. I've been volunteering at the hospital ten years now, seen every skin tone you can imagine, coal black to paper white and near everything in between. Funny thing is, underneath, every one of 'em bleeds the same color, not one bit of difference atall." She frowns again, then adds, with a shrug, "Course, I've never raised chickens. So I wouldn't know 'bout them."

DeLuth glares at her. "Confound it, Birdilee." He shakes his head in disgust. "Sometimes you don't have a brain, one!"

27

Lila drums her fingers on the green suede blotter atop her father's desk. *Ring, goddamnit,* she wills the big black phone in front of her. She'd called the Governor's office over an hour ago. And his secretary, Gert, after the obligatory condolences, had promised, "I'll give the Governor your message just as soon as he's off the phone, Miss Hightower. Shouldn't be too long atall."

Lila had smiled then. There was something deliciously full circle about using her father's name to gain access to the Governor's ear so she could initiate the downfall of Kyle DeLuth. But now, the Governor's delay had become an irritant, a signal, perhaps, of some resistance and, she guessed, murkier waters than she'd hoped for.

Lila picks up the heavy, black Bakelite receiver, then quickly puts it down. *Too soon to call again,* she decides and jumps at Sissy's knock on the office door.

Sissy shakes her head, rolls her eyes upward signifying that what she has to say springs from the upper bedroom where Violet Hightower reclines against her velvet headboard, cussing over the morning crossword puzzle.

"Now what?" Lila asks, dropping into the co-conspirators'

tone she and Sissy use whenever they're forced to deal with her mother.

"She need tuh see you."

"She does, does she? What for?"

Sissy shrugs. "Could be anythin'. Coffee too strong—though Ah been makin' it the same way for thirty-seven year—pillow too soft, mattress too hard. Or, mebbe, she g'wanna 'pologize for bein' the mizrables' human bein' on God's green earth, and fuh spendin' ever' blesset day makin' ever'body else mizrable too!"

Lila laughs. Sissy's humor had always been the light that had gotten her through the dark tunnel of Violet's mother love. "Oh, Sissy, without you, I'd've either killed Mamma or gone crazy myself by now."

"Either way,"—Sissy's grin crinkles her whole face—"I'da been there to change the sheets."

Caught between baby-sitting the silent phone or answering her mother's summons, Lila eyes the clock. It's twenty till twelve, the magic hour when Violet Hightower allows herself the first of many bourbons that will send her from prickly to passed out just after sunset.

"Sissy, I've got a call in to the Governor's office. If he calls back before I'm done with Mamma . . ."

Sissy waves her on, out of the room. *Wouldn't be the first Governor she's talked to,* Lila reminds herself as she mounts the carpeted stairs. *Sissy'll handle him as well as she's handled all the others.*

Midway up, Lila stops, one hand on the mahogany banister. On good days, she found dealing with her mother a challenge. But today, with the weight of a hangover bearing down behind her eyes—*Hooah*—she'd have to be careful. She grasps the rail, lifts one heavy foot, and then the other, trudges slowly uphill as though waist-deep in water.

She and Louis were ten when their parents decided to build the "Big House" in the grove. From the onset, she remembered, the principal bone of contention was the size and shape of this staircase. Lila had sided with the Judge, who wanted something solid and straightforward. But Louis, poor Louis who could never see through anything or anybody, had sided with Mamma whose vision was "something more Twelve Oaks than Tara," heavily carved, elegantly curved.

"The Wilkeses of Twelve Oaks," she'd say, as if that fictional family actually existed, "were true gentry like my family, the Randalls. Not bootstrap Irish like Gerald O'Hara, or, for that matter, your father." The wrangling over the final design went on for weeks, until, finally, the Judge brokered a peace: Mamma could have her way—the design Daddy called "Violet Ascending"—if, and only if, she agreed to give up her daily stream of afternoon sherries. She did. Then quietly switched to bourbon over ice with a sprig of mint, which she insisted, fooling no one, was "only a watered-down julep and what of it?"

Upstairs, turning the French porcelain doorknob into her mother's bedroom, Lila forces a slow, measured breath. The sight of her mother ensconced in the ridiculous thronelike, violet velvet bed—as close to Vivien Leigh's red one in *Gone with the Wind* as local upholsterers could get—floods her with dread. What new level of craziness would they reach today? The competing scents of crushed mint, Jim Beam bourbon, and her mother's all-pervasive Violettes de Nice perfume could, if she wasn't careful, make her retch.

"Mamma, why are you wearing a hat in bed?"

"This is not a *hat,* Lila. It's an Empress Eugenie *creation,* in my signature color, of course." Violet reaches up and pats the

turned-up felt brim, higher on one side than the other, caresses the dyed-to-match egret feathers at its peak, and smiles,
coquettish, beneath her reading glasses. "Besides, it helps me
think." Bright pink lipstick and liberal face powder attempt
to hide the long-term effects of Kentucky bourbon on her
mother's once good looks. But, no amount of makeup can dis-
guise her watery, red-rimmed eyes, the bulbing of her nose, or
the sagging of her jowls into a jiggling double chin.

"Well, for my money, it makes you look more Blanche
DuBois than Scarlett O'Hara," Lila says, drawing first blood.

"Both Oscar-winning performances, my dear," Violet croons
back. "And, you needn't remind me whose money is whose,"
she adds acidly.

"Sissy says you need to see me?"

"Not *need* to, *want* to. There's a difference," Violet pouts.
"Lord," she sighs, clasping her hands, gazing heavenward,
"she has my eyes but she cannot see."

*God, now she's Joan of Arc in a feathered hat and satin bed
jacket.* "Your point, Mamma?"

"My point is, Missy," Violet brightens, "I want to give a
party and I'd like your help."

"A *what?*"

"A party, silly. Everybody knows I've been laid low, my
nerves absolutely shot by your daddy's death."—Violet feigns
hurt at Lila's sudden intake of breath—"Well, they *do*! It'd be
a sort of combination celebration, y'see, my coming out and
your coming home!"

"No," Lila says quietly.

"Oh, just a small thing at the Citrus Club—"

Lila interrupts. "The two-letter word for absolutely not."

"It would be *fun*!"

"It would be absurd," Lila says stiffly, between her teeth.

"Nobody in their right mind gives themselves a party to celebrate the end of their supposed nervous breakdown. And, besides, I've not 'come home,' I'm merely passing through."

"Oh, c'mon, honey. We haven't had a nice party 'round here
since . . ." Violet trails off, suddenly aware she's on shaky
ground.

"Since the night Louis nearly killed Daddy then ran off and
joined the Army. You're right, Mamma, that was a swell
time."

"But it was your daddy that spoiled that one," Violet says,
recovering. "And, obviously, he won't be able to make *this*
one."

"No, Mamma. And neither will you. Because there's not
going to be a party."

"Good God Almighty, you're as selfish and unreasonable as
he was! Can't you see I need a *reason* to get outta this bed? Or
do you expect me to sit up here and waste away *forever?*"

Lila pauses,—*Careful now*—locks steady eyes on her mother's,
and says, in a very calm voice, "I gave up expecting anything
from you, Mamma, years ago."

Violet retreats behind half-lowered lids. "Oh, it's all my
fault, is it?"

Lila's hands have begun to tremble. She hides them,
clasped, behind her back. "Get outta bed, or don't, Mamma.
Frankly, I don't give a damn."

"Really?" Violet's slow smile stretches her lips into a pink-
rimmed slit. "And, I was so hopin' we could invite your general and his pretty wife." Her hands, shaking, toss the folded
front page to the foot of the bed.

Lila tenses herself, to stop the trembling, and casually—
she's determined not to appear forced—leans forward, picks
up the newspaper, and scans the headline: "Ike Taps Taylor

Army Chief, Atkinson to Assist." The photo below hits her like a fist. In the center, Ike, grinning, flanked by the two generals: Jazz, lean and level-eyed—*sporting a third star!*—and handsome, intense General Maxwell D. Taylor, pumping Ike's hand. Behind them, two matrons: pert, proud Lydia Taylor, and thin, startled-looking Kitsy Atkinson. *Damn you, Ike! And, Jazz—Assistant Chief of Staff? Oh, Jazz—how could you?*

"She's a looker, that one," comes the sly, dangerous taunt from the bed. "Lousy in the sack, I imagine. Not atall like *you.*" Lila shivers, feeling nakedly exposed to her mother's drawling insinuation. She cannot, will not, meet Violet's awful eyes. "Quite the vixen *you* are—with your fancy silk panties and French lace bras—"

"Mamma!" Lila cries hollowly. (She'd taken great pains to hand wash and hang dry her underthings in the supposed privacy of her own bathroom. Obviously, the Lady Violate's been up to her old tricks.)

"Bet you take it any way he wants, then sit up and beg for more!" Violet sneers.

From somewhere far away, the peal of a ringing telephone sails like a life preserver into the space between them. "If you'll excuse me"—Lila clutches the paper, summons the strength to walk, weak-kneed, to the door—"I have an important call."

SHE'S BREATHLESS, from the news about Jazz, from her mother and the stairs, as Sissy hands her the phone and exits the office.

"Governor, how kind of you to return my call. How are you?" Lila sits in her father's chair, drops the newspaper on the desk blotter in front of her, stares at the familiar face. *Oh, Jazz, how could you?*

"Not bad for an old lame duck. How're you? And how's your mamma?" Governor Big Jim Yates booms from the other end. Lila pictures him towering over everybody but Kyle at her father's funeral, white-haired, heavily jowled, with a constant, concerned scowl.

"Got herself a new hat, perked her right up!" Lila says, her eyes skeetering up to the ceiling, in Violet's direction. *Though, of course, this is all Ike's doing. Prissy old bastard.*

"Well, she's been through a lot these last few months, hasn't she?"

"Haven't we all?" *This isn't the first time Ike sniffed divorce and wagged another star in Jazz's direction.* "And, Governor, that's just why I'm calling. You know how Daddy liked to keep everything and everybody on a short leash?" *Just like Ike, come to think of it. But, damnit, Jazz . . . we had a deal!*

"He was a master at it, darlin'."

"Well, I'm havin' the devil of a time finding a good grove manager to take over the reins around here." *What am I gonna do now?*

"Sorry to hear that."

Not half as sorry as I am. "I've got a great candidate—best tree man you ever saw, and a firm hand with the picking crews, but—"

"But, what?"

"But, Kyle DeLuth's decided my man's children can't attend the local school. They've got a little Indian blood in 'em, not much, but Kyle's decided he doesn't like their looks. So he's barred them from attending school." *God, I'm surrounded by sorry bastards.*

On the other end, Lila hears the creak of wood, Big Jim shifting his enormous weight in the Governor's chair. When he speaks, finally, his tone, she notes, has turned guarded. "What's your school board have to say about that?"

"Well, they promised the family a hearing. But, Kyle talked 'em out of it. I spoke to Hamp Berry and he's willing to look into this, set things straight. All he needs is a nod from you." *Goddamn ol' boy network!*

Another chair creak. "Well, Lila,"—she hears the hedge in his voice—"you know K.A. and I go back 'bout as far as your daddy and I do." *Same damn thing every-damn-where I go!*

"Of course, Governor. But, it was Daddy who made Kyle what he is today. And now that Daddy's gone, Kyle's running roughshod over some innocent schoolkids. He's just flat-out wrong on this. And I'm not the only one who thinks so."

"I hear you. But, Lila,"—*creak*—"you're your daddy's daughter so I'm gonna give it t'ya straight, same as I'd do for him. You know my term's up first of the year. I got ninety days left then I'm heading home to the panhandle. Got me a good-size ranch and . . . well, darlin', K.A.'s promised me the use of his blue-ribbon bull soon as I get there."

The Governor's blatant self-interest flaps like laundry hung on the line between them. *Sold out! For a blue-ribbon bull. And a third star!*

"Any suggestions for me, then?" she asks, trying to hit the mark between sober political allowance and sincere feminine distress.

"Well, now," his tone is suddenly magnanimous, "the quickest way out is to elect yourself a new Sheriff."

Lila gasps. "But the election's not till November fourth, and I'm due back in Washington the end of this month!"

"Well, if you need some strings pulled to stay a little longer, darlin', you let me know. In the meantime, you could call Lamar Rawlings. He's on deck, y'know, with no connections to K.A. that I know of."

Lila shakes her head. The governorship of Florida had been passed like a baton between mostly panhandle partisans ever since Reconstruction. And would continue to be until the rest of the state raised enough hell to effect reapportionment. If Lamar Rawlings was "on deck," it was a given he'd be Florida's next governor.

"Matter of fact," Big Jim was adding, "Lamar's from Jacksonville. And I doubt he's charmed by K.A.'s speechmaking at some blamed fool White People's rally over there last month."

He'd thrown her a bone. Lila knew she was expected to be grateful. "Thank you so much," she tells him. *Self-serving son-ofabitch!*

"My pleasure, darlin'. And, when you and I are done, I'll have Gert get you Lamar's home phone number."

"Could Hamp start something on his go-ahead?" she presses.

"I don't see why not."

"May I tell him you said so?" *C'mon! Give me this, at least!*

"If you need to, honey. Will that 'bout do it then?"

Game over. "Yes, sir. Thank you."

"Take care, darlin'. My best to your sweet mamma, hear?"

The bastards win—Lila jabs a finger at Ike's photographic chest—*again.* Sadly, slowly, she traces the resolute jaw, the handsome cleft chin of Lieutenant General Jasper P. "Jazz" Atkinson.

Oh, Jazz. The weight she'd felt earlier, behind her eyes, had shifted to the back of her neck, spread across her shoulders and, now, pushed heavily on her chest.

The photo in the newspaper is black-and-white. Her mind

fills in the colors: the dark blue sheen, the quiet whisper of worsted wool, the winking gleam of brass and gold, the flare and pop of the reporters' cameras, the subtle spice of General J. P. Atkinson's aftershave. "The General" was only one of his characters—the one she'd met first and liked least—sly, controlling, sardonic. "General J. P. Asskisser," he'd say, clicking his heels sharply, snapping a crisp salute. She preferred "Jasper," the shy Ames, Iowa, farm boy who'd bring her flowers, bump into furniture, fumble over buttons with a quiet "Beg your pardon, ma'am." And, above all, she loved "Jazz," the free-spirited sybarite who'd leap into her bed and announce that, tonight, he was the incomparable Art Tatum and, head to toe, she was his piano.

Oh, Jazz. How did this happen? When? And why? But, of course, she knew—she KNEW—that it was Jazz who'd promised the divorce from Kitsy, a honeymoon in Paris, a quiet retirement to Virginia. But, when the phone rang—*was it Ike or his old friend Max Taylor on the other end?*—it was, of course, The General who'd taken the call.

"Oh, Jazz," she sighs hollowly, out loud, and leans back limp against the chair. This was her private nightmare come true: that The General would never give up his grip, his eager grasping for more and always more power and prestige. And Jazz—

A memory flickers across her closed eyelids, vividly sharp. They were in New York, at a tedious official conference all day, and afterwards, anonymous in their civvies, the cramped jazz club where Tatum was rumored to play. The piano great never showed, but the performing quartet was quite good and, in between sets, the hulking young man, introduced as one of the "new beat poets," assailed the crowd with his biting, off-the-cuff rhymes. His method was to pick someone out and, after a brief squint, spout his poetic pronouncement. He chose Jazz and, in the dreariest of couplets, declared:

*"Pursuers of power make lousy lovers,
Hooked on the high of screwing others, they must,
eventually, fuck themselves!"*

Afterwards, seeing that she and Jazz hadn't joined in the crowd's embarrassed hoot of laughter, he'd boldly shrugged. "Sigmund Freud, man. Look it up."

With a spine-long shiver, Lila pushes herself up, out of the chair, and moves toward the silver tray, the cut-crystal decanters on her father's sideboard. Her arms and legs feel separate, detached, their sole purpose to carry the chill weight, the heavy ballast of her heart's sinking pain.

She pours hastily, drinks quickly. She feels the whiskey burn a hot path down her throat into her stomach. But it does not, it cannot warm her. She studies the glass, stares into the amber liquid and sees, for a wavering instant, the shifting features of her reflection. Thirty-two and now, more than ever, alone.

I am adrift—she shudders—*in the sea of my own choosing.* She drops the glass onto the silver tray. It hits with a heavy thud, tilts, overturns, and spills, pale gold gilding sterling, spotting the mahogany sideboard.

On their own, her knees tense then begin to buckle. Her hands grasp and let go of the sideboard. She feels herself, her heavy center, sliding past, leaning against, clinging to the bottom shelf that anchors the walls to the roiling floor, anchors her against the sobbing waves of old, unspeakable sorrow.

28

The trip to Opalakee—with Pap, Uncle Will, Aunt Lu, and baby June squinched up front; Daniel, complaining Minna, lisping SaraFaye, and a silent, thumb-sucking 'Becca bouncing in the back—had not gone well. Daniel never thought it would.

The Opalakee school principal, a tall drink of water with bushy black eyebrows, had scowled over their papers, had even gone so far as to say, "Yes, yes, everything appears to be in order," but, shaking his head, had informed them, "Superintendent Hawkins, down in Hylandia, has the final say."

Back at the truck, squinting into the early-afternoon sun, the adults had leaned against the tailgate, studied the principal's directions to the County Superintendent's office. Finally, Uncle Will sighed and said, "We come this far, might as well see it through."

Superintendent Hawkins had kept them waiting outside his office for over two hours. His secretary, nowhere near as friendly as that Miss May at their old school, had *clicketty-clacked* away on her typewriter without even offering them a piece of candy or a drink of water from the cooler in the corner.

When he did come out, the Superintendent, a fleshy man sweating heavily in a short-sleeved white shirt and brown string tie, had promised Pap he'd "look into this and get back to you next week." But he had the lowered chin and rocked-back-on-his-heels stance, Daniel decides, of someone not square with the truth.

On the ride home, the girls curled beside him asleep in the heat, Daniel watches the sky cloud up, cluster, and begin to stream off dark rain in the distance. The storm, heading north, same direction as Pap's truck, appears to be chasing them out of Tangerine County, back to the cabins that Daniel still refuses to call home. *I hope it ketches us,* Daniel thinks. A good rain might take the lid off whatever it was that had been pressing on him all day, making it hard to breathe. The sky, now as flat and black as a frying pan, sits atop the orange groves that line both sides of the road, as orderly and uninteresting as egg cartons. The eyes of the people, in cars and along the road, seem flat, too, and their unfriendliness rankles him, making him want to shout, "Hey, I'm worth a nod, at the least!"

When they arrive at the clearing, Daniel leaps out of the back of the truck, calling over his shoulder, "I'll be back 'fore full dark."

"Sooner ef it rains," Pap yells back.

Free of the truck, and the adults, heavy in their disappointment, Daniel runs headlong across the field, toward the tree line and that place where he's certain there's a footpath.

He finds it easily enough, a sandy trail not much wider than he is, and follows it into the longleaf pines, their fragrant needles fingering his arms and hair. He runs, with no direction or intention other than "away," away from the flat, flinty eyes of unwelcome, the shaking-no heads, the hands too heavy or too white for waving, so different from his upbringing and experience. Up home . . .

It's a pure waste of time to compare ever'thing here to there, he thinks, chest heaving. *Besides—home, as I knowed it, hain't there anymore.* Hadn't Pres'dent Gen'ral Eisenhower's highway builders bulldozed the old homeplace by now? Wasn't the chestnut beside the porch long pulled? The patch he'd helped Mam plow and harrow ever' April he could remember, the spring house hung with hams, the trickly creek with its downy ducklings, its prickly buckberry bushes, its brooding brown-speckled trout—gone, all of it lost to him forever? Covered up with concrete and blacktop, cars rolling over what had been a good and peaceable life, lived with nary a thought that it might not last?

Prodded by the scuffle of wildlife in the underbrush—*skunks, most likely, possums mebbe*—and the rustle and chatter of squirrels in the canopy of live oaks, Daniel runs on, squinching his eyes against the tears, scraping a forearm across the wetness on his cheeks. He stops just short of a batch of hand-shaped footprints, large and small, sharply nailed, a family of raccoons on their way toward water, and looks for the dark arc of a magnolia tree, its broad green leaves, velvety brown underneath, the woodsman's signal that there's a spring or river nearby. Magnolias like to get their feet wet, he knew that as well as anybody, and he bounds down the path in search of the smell of wet grass and rotting leaves, the murmur of lapping water. His heart leaps with the thought: *Where there's water, there's fish, and wouldn't it be fine to find myself a fishing hole?*

Running flat-out on the loose sand trail, he trips over a hidden tree root, and, falling into the bushes, finds himself slip-sliding down a dense bank, toward the dark green gleam of deep-woods water.

It takes him a moment to right himself, to let his eyes grow used to the leafy gloom, and make out, a fair piece ahead, the shape of a beached boat, a kind of canoe carved out of a single tree trunk.

It's his'n, I bet. Daniel scans the sandy banks. "Hallooo?" he calls, "Sampson? Hallooo?"

The response is instant, the whistle of an almost whippoor-will, good enough to fool a body not born to the woods. Daniel whistles back and, picking his way toward and around the dugout, sees the big man, chest deep, downriver.

Sampson nods at him, eyes twinkling, and holds the finger of his left hand to his lips for silence. His right hand and arm is wrapped, elbow to fingertips, with the bright red scarf that he normally wears around his neck; a corner of the cloth hangs, like a little flag, off his fingertips. Turning, he dives underwater between the widespread knees of a cypress tree.

What's he up to? Daniel stands mesmerized on the sandy shore. At first, there's nothing to see. Then, suddenly, the sur-face of the water churns like a boiling kettle. Sampson shoots up, laughing, his right hand and forearm disappeared inside the ugliest fish Daniel's ever seen; his left hand clamped on its large lower jaw. With a snatching twist, Sampson hurls the fish off his arm and onto the sand at Daniel's feet. Its head, atop a mottled brown body, is huge and flat; long strings of flesh hang off its snout, whiskerlike. Daniel judges its size at thirty pounds, *mebbe more!* And he looks up, in wonder, as Sampson emerges from the river, water running off his back onto the sand.

"Got 'im! Done grabbled Ol' Goblin out of his haunt hole!" Sampson tells Daniel, gleeful. Then, raising the fish, "Got you, big monster! Done bit off Ol' Sampson, more'n you could chew!"

"What kinda fish is that?" Daniel asks.

"Ol' Goblin? Flathead catfish. Too smart to take a hook, too mean t'turn down a fight."

"What you goin' to do with 'im?"

"Eat 'im, boy. Plenty for ever'body!"

"You can eat that thing?"

"Oh, yeh!" Sampson shows his picket-fence smile and slips a bit of wire and a knife from his belt. Daniel marvels as the old man runs a round of wire through the flathead's lower lip, then strings it up and over a nearby tree limb. On the ground underneath, he digs a hole with the heel of his boot. Then, hoisting his knife, he slices the tail just above the lower fin. As the big fish bleeds into the sandy basin below, he fetches two leather pouches from the dugout canoe, and fills them with river water.

The next cut's a circle just under the side fins, then straight down the belly and the back, on either side. With nimble fingers, he spirals off the skin, top to bottom. Working belly to spine, he slices slabs of meat and stows them in the two water-filled pouches. "Taste too strong to eat till tomorra," he says.

Eyeing the huge head hanging off the tree limb, Daniel says, "He's goblin-lookin', all right."

"Meanest ol' fish there is. Eats up ever' other fish in sight."

"How'd you catch 'im then?"

"Grabbled 'im! Put mah fist inside his hole, shook the tip like it was a tongue. And, Ol' Goblin, he bit like he born to do! Opened his big mouth and gobbled mah arm. 'Cept once I's inside, I opened mah hand, y'see?" Sampson shows the spread fingers of his huge hand. "Caught 'im from the inside, jacked open his lower jaw, and flung 'im on the bank!"

"What you gonna do with the rest?" Daniel asks as Sampson unhangs the head, kicks sand over the hole below.

"Cathead stew! Mah fav'rite," he says, dropping the head inside the second pouch. He walks to the dugout, pulls on his shirt, and spreads the red scarf out to dry.

Daniel feels an intruder to the old man's privacy, suddenly shy.

Sampson looks up. "Good to be in th' woods again, heh?"

Daniel nods, with the odd sensation that, once again, the Ol' Seminole had read his mind.

"Wonderin' what took yuh so long," Sampson says.

"You, uh . . ." The words come out in a rush. "You teach me to fish like that, Indian style?"

"To grabble? Ain't hard. Start small, heh?" Sampson holds his palms facing each other. "Work your way up?" He spreads them apart to Goblin size.

Daniel's delighted. He wishes he could start right now. But the old man's eyeing the sky.

"Dark soon," he predicts. He scoops up the first pouch, the one without the cathead, and hands it to Daniel. "Tell your auntie, change the water, fry 'em up tomorra, heh?"

"But . . ."

"Way out's over there . . . less'n you want t'dive through th' bushes again." The ancient eyes dance.

Daniel's sorry to leave. But the Ol' Seminole's right. It'll be dark soon and he promised Pap.

The boy turns but Sampson's voice calls him back.

"Dan'l?"

"Yes?"

"Woods is woods," the old man says quietly, then smiles, holds up a huge hand, and waves good-bye. "Find your way back, heh?"

After the rain, the intruder comes slowly, on quiet feet.

The guards at the gate, lulled into laziness by the quiet hum of the colony's internal activity and the soft, soaking-in silence of the outside world, are caught completely unawares.

Their first sight, a long slender white snout accompanied by a clever, clawed paw, is also their last, as the intruder snatches them and, head to mouth, sucks the husks of their bodies dry.

Other guards rush forward in swift reinforcement with the certain knowledge that, at this range, the intruder cannot be repelled, but merely fed. Wave after wave of guards present themselves outside the gate, hoping to draw the intruder, who carries her own children upon her back, away from the now vulnerable nursery chambers.

The pile and scatter of sucked-dry husks mounts until, satiated at last, the intruder departs, leaving the rest to celebrate their survival, and mourn its cost.

29

Fridays, the day Ruth and Hugh put the weekend edition of the *Towncrier* to bed, start too early and end late.

Five-fifteen, the clock on Ruth's side of the bed shows. But she needn't have looked. Greenwich could set their bells by Hugh's movements at this time of the morning: Five A.M., out of bed and into the kitchen to start brewing the coffee the way Ruth likes it—"darker than dirt and thicker than mud." Five-ten, shave. Five-fifteen, shower. Five-twenty, out of the shower and back into the kitchen to pour the first of the three cups that it takes to get Ruth out the door and on their way to the office.

"Rise and shine," he says quietly, handing her the steaming mug. In a fog, she sits upright and takes it, watches him don undershorts and shirt, then return to the foot of the bed to put his socks on.

Most other mornings, except Tuesdays, the day they wrap up Wednesday's paper, Ruth sleeps in. But, Fridays are somehow worse. "Rain?" she asks, squinting at the window.

"All night," he tells her, buttoning his shirt. Their pre-coffee conversations rarely involve complete sentences. Precaffeine, he believes, she's functionally illiterate. Or is it literally ill-functioning? *This time of day, who the hell cares?*

"All right," she grouses, tossing back the covers, padding to the bathroom with mug in hand. By the time she's out of the shower, he's refilled her cup and the fog has begun to lift. By six o'clock, gulping down the last of her third cup, they're on their way.

The rain has stopped. But the streets of their subdivision are shiny wet; the drainage ditches, on either side of the black-top into town, glittering with runoff.

Familiar pub-day tasks lie ahead of them: While typesetter Walt VanZant punches out the linotype, Hugh will be hunched over the makeup bench, assembling the chases for pressman Joe Stephens and the big flatbed press that will run through midnight. Ruth's role is to prep the last-minute ads, classified and otherwise; assemble the local social notes into the column "Tidbits from Around Town"; proof the initial pages off the proofing press; and, for the rest of the day, fend off unnecessary phone calls so the guys in the back can work uninterrupted.

"Thank God it quit raining," Ruth says.

Hugh nods. Rainy days play hell with the newsprint, jam the presses, slow down the process.

"Donny's gonna have to bag, though," she says. The ground is too wet for the home-delivery guy to get by with rubber bands.

"Supposed to be sunny later," Hugh suggests. "Might dry out."

Ruth squints out at the relative wetness of the roadside, al-ways more cynical than he is. "We'll see. Beats the hell out of snow, I suppose."

"I don't know, Ruthie. Sometimes a good snowstorm can warm the heart . . . feed the soul . . ."

"Ruin your life?"

He shoots her a sly wink. "I think not, my sweet."

Ruth feels herself flush—*like a goddamn schoolgirl!*—over Hugh's oblique reference to the night the boys in the Philly newsroom called "The Big Thaw." When a freak snowstorm stranded the famous muckraking reporter turned crusty editor, then in his late fifties, and the tough-as-nails feature writer and confirmed careerist, in her late forties, both never married and not looking, in the City Room overnight.

Somehow, after hours of verbal jousting, she and Hugh discovered they shared a passionate love for hard work, high principles, rare books (especially those by Elbert Hubbard's defunct Roycroft Press), and each other. Upon their marriage, a fellow reporter quipped, "They say stranger things have happened. But I don't know any."

In minutes, Hugh wheels up to the back gate of the office. Ruth gets out, keys in hand, and undoes the padlock. "Gordon, here boy!" she whistles. *Where's he gone off to?* she wonders, expecting the Doberman to appear, tail stub wagging, any second.

Hugh drives in. Ruth closes the gate behind him then whirls at the screech of tires, the slam of car door, as Hugh runs forward.

"What is it?" she calls.

"Oh, God," he says, dropping to his knees in front of the car. "God!"

"What's wrong?" She strides toward him, then sees the dog. "Did you hit him?"

"Of course not, but look at him. God, would you look!"

On the ground in front of them, Gordon lies twitching in a puddle of vomit, lips drawn hideously back, exposing his teeth. His sleek black body jerks in violent convulsion, his spine twists in a spastic backward arch.

"Gordon!" Ruth cries, dropping down to lay a comforting hand on his heaving ribs. Instantly, he recoils and cries piteously, a high keening whine of intense pain and distress.

"Get Doc Denby over here!" she shrieks at Hugh. The town vet lives on Chestnut, just two blocks away. "We don't dare move him!"

But Hugh is already up and running, taking the steps to the loading dock two at a time, fumbling for his keys to unbolt the back door.

"Poor thing," Ruth croons, her eyes clouding with tears. "Poor, poor thing. Oh, what can I do for you?" She scrambles up, ransacks the car for something, anything, to slip beneath his head, soothe his pain. She settles for an old newspaper to cover up the vomit. But, once again, the dog keens horribly at her touch.

Hugh reappears, his face lock-jawed, and moves to reopen the gate.

In another minute, Dr. Charles Denby, pajama top tucked into his trousers, drives in and drops down beside her. One look and he shakes his head. "Strychnine," he says in quiet anger and disgust. "Sprinkled over raw meat. He'll be dead within an hour, maybe two. Unless"—the vet looks from Ruth to Hugh—"I put him out of his misery now."

Hugh nods, grimly. The doc rises wearily to retrieve his bag from his car.

"Poison? Somebody poisoned him?" Ruth is unbelieving. "Who would do such a thing?"

"No doubt"—Hugh's voice is ragged—"the same folks who painted a couple of big, bloodred K.K.K.'s across our front windows."

"Oh, Hugh, no," Ruth whispers, in horror. And then, as if

from the bottom of a deep well, she hears the chilling echo of Billy Hathaway's threat, "Sheriff ain't the only one around to help me settle your hash."

TWO HOURS AND A PACK OF PALL MALLS LATER, Ruth is still shaken by the numbing revulsion of Gordon's poisoning, and the pained relief of his final, labored breath at Doc Denby's hands. Her first inclination, after the vet removed the body for burial, after she saw for herself the large red K.K.K.'s on the front windows, was to grab razor and paint solvent and scrape the place clean of the vandals' graphics.

"No," Hugh told her quietly. "We'll leave it up, at least for the weekend."

In the center of the lobby window, they hung a poster, on top of the Klan's red paint, in big, black-on-white type: **Sheriff DeLuth: This Is Law and Order?** In the other window, in front of her own off-the-lobby office, Hugh had added the Page One headline from the *Towncrier*: **KKK Vandalizes Free Press, Poisons Guard Dog.**

Standing on the sidewalk, admiring the effect, Hugh turns to her with an old City Editor's gleam in his eyes. "Now!" he tells her, "we'll see what this town's made of."

Ruth wants to, tries to, match Hugh's fervor. But worry presses on her like a vise. This is not the day to show him the stack of subscription-cancellation notices piling up in her bottom-left desk drawer. So far, he hasn't noticed the drop-off in display-ad inches. And God bless Lila Hightower for keeping the print shop busy with Fred Sykes's political flyers, brochures, and bumper stickers. But, soon, very soon, there'll have to be a reckoning.

30

It doesn't take long—twenty minutes, tops—for word of the *Towncrier*'s challenge to reach the ears of Sheriff K. A. DeLuth, holding court at the Sit-A-Spell coffee shop off Old Dixie Highway. It's cattleman Mac Grubbs, a late arrival to the usual Friday-morning gabfest, who tells it. And the Sheriff, not by nature a thinking man, merely winks broadly 'round the table, then, after a time, makes his excuses and leaves early to "have it out with the Pinko Press."

As he parks, smack-dab in front of the *Towncrier*'s door, he's certain it's Ruth Barrows's mousy little face—owl eyes filling black-rimmed glasses—that appears briefly in an unpainted patch of the window. Her expression makes him smile, as he checks his teeth in the rearview mirror. Of course, there was no mistaking the rumble of his souped-up gray-and-green Chrysler squad car—*fastest car in the county. Ain't a moonshiner in three states can outrun this baby.*

Taking his time, he unfolds himself out of his seat, retrieves his hat, straightens his string tie, and stands on the sidewalk to, in his mind, *admire the boys' handiwork.*

After a while, giving Miz Barrows time to, no doubt, collect her husband from the back, he strolls into the newspaper-office lobby and grins at the golden-haired girl at the desk.

"Mr. and Miz Barrows in?" he asks.

"Of course, we are." Ruth Barrows says it curtly from the open door of her office. "Please come in."

"Miz Barrows." DeLuth smiles and arcs off his hat. "Mister," he adds, nodding to the gray-haired, stoop-shouldered husband—*a weak-looking intellectual type*—who stands beside her.

Ruth Barrows—*hippy little thing*—quits the doorway to move behind her desk. As DeLuth takes his seat on the opposite side, Hugh Barrows quietly closes the door and rounds the desk to lean against the bookcase beside the wife. Both watch him with angry eyes.

Inwardly delighted, DeLuth places his hat on the empty seat to his right, leans back lazily, and says, "Got your invitation," nodding at the painted and postered front window. "Your party," he concedes, amiably giving them the floor.

The woman, brown eyes unblinking behind those ugly black glasses, speaks first. "Sheriff, two nights ago I received a threatening phone call from Billy Hathaway. He was upset by my telling the truth about his bogus military record. And he warned me that an insult to him was an insult to you, that his local friends would, quote, 'settle' my 'hash.' Last night, somebody maliciously poisoned our dog. Hamburger laced with strychnine, Doc Denby says. They also left their calling card all over our storefront. Care to comment on your connection to these events?"

"Didn't know about the dog. And, as you know, my initials are K.A., not K.K.K." DeLuth drawls and gives them a grin.

"Is this your idea of Law and Order?" she demands.

"Well, no, ma'am. I'd never condone the destruction of private property. But, a little paint solvent oughtta do the trick."

"Is that your *official* response?!" she slings at him, acid in her voice. Her husband lays a quiet hand on her shoulder.

"Sheriff," he says, "what's the game here? Children yanked out of school with no recourse. Crosses burned. Businesses vandalized. Constitutional rights trampled right and left. This is hardly the way to campaign for reelection in a political democracy."

"Whoa, ho!" DeLuth throws back his head and chuckles. "Slow down. Any minute now you goin' t' accuse me of throwin' the switch on those Rosenberg traitors, too? Which I'd've gladly done, by the way, given half a chance. But, did I burn a cross, poison your dog, paint your windows? Course not! I do, however, freely admit to removing those mule-otto children from the white school. And will, most assuredly, stand beside our Governor against that Jew-blinded Supreme Court and their asinine attempt to abolish States' Rights, destroy the U.S. Constitution, and ruin the White Race! Yessirree-Bob, you can count on that!"

DeLuth watches the two of them exchange disbelieving looks. This was his favorite backroom stump speech, herding the unknowing into the corral of Truth. "What you people in the press forget is this: In a *real* democracy, majority rules. And, in this county, the majority of white people don't hold with some Marxist idea of mixing the races, which, of course, is nothing more than Jewry's plot to mongrelize the rest of mankind!"

"Excuse me?" the little hen sputters.

"Good God! Don't you see what's happening? This ain't about a couple of half-breed schoolkids. We're talking the future of the White Race here. In all God's creation, is there any other creature that disobeys the divine law of segregation? Does the lark nest with the sparrow? The goat go at the sheep?

The bull cover the mare? Course not! The Jews know that. They got their own laws about mixing blood. But, that don't stop 'em from trying to mix ours. They know the White Race is God's chosen people. They've known it ever since the Garden of Eden when Eve lay down with Satan to create Cain, and with Adam to create Abel. *We, the Adamites,* are the ones made in God's image. And *they're* descendants of the Devil, don't you see? *They're* the ones who laid down with the animals to create the other races. *We're* the ones who God Almighty gave dominion over the earth!"

The husband turned ashen. "You can't be serious . . ." he says, scarcely above a whisper.

DeLuth stands, drops both fists, straight-armed, onto the desk. The little owl jumps. He leans forward and lowers his voice to make it clear that this next point is the most telling of all—"Dead serious. Whether you know it or not, there's a war going on, for the very soul of mankind. It's us against the Hebrew Communists, who preach race-mixing and the ruin of miscegenation. Either you're with us or against us. You *need* to *choose.*"

The little owl-eyed woman, the bushy-browed man stare at him with tight lips, their breath shallow, and, he'd bet, the backs of their necks prickling.

Set them straight, didn't I? he thinks. "Sorry about your dog," he says. "Casualty of war." DeLuth retrieves his hat from the nearby chair, bows his good-bye, turns on his heel, winks at the pretty girl in the lobby, and is gone.

SATURDAY MORNING, DeLuth drops his wife, Birdilee, off at Lucille's LaMonde Salon de Beaute for her weekly appointment ("See you at noon, darlin'.") then heads toward Lake George for his usual post-Friday-night exchange with Big Nick Pop-a-Dop, the Bolita King.

Along the way, he squints in his rearview mirror at the hind ends of several passing cars bearing green-and-white bumper stickers for "I Like Sykes, Our Future Sheriff." *More this week than last.* Would they make any difference in the ten-days-away election? *Not a chance,* he decides.

Off Lake George, at the outskirts of Big Scrub, DeLuth enters the old logging road and pulls into the clearing of the abandoned camp. Just ahead, Big Nick—short, stocky, wavy-haired, hook-nosed, the color the locals call high yaller—leans against his shiny new Mercury coupe, waiting.

Everybody in town, colored and white, knows the racy story of Big Nick's parentage: The colored Baptist preacher's daughter visiting her aunt outside Ybor City; seduced by a handsome Greek sponge exporter from Tarpon Springs; secretly married, spurned by her Orthodox in-laws and, eventually, her husband; returned in disgrace to raise the boy whose last name nobody could pronounce, something like Pop-a-Dop, which is what it became. A smart child, he grew into a savvy young man, possessed of both his Baptist grandfather's way with words and his Greek grandfather's skill with money. Early on, he established himself with the Tampa Cubans as the county's most reliable numbers operator for the popular game out of Havana. Ten years ago, when the last Bolita king turned up mysteriously dead, Nick was the natural next in line. His ascension to prominence in the colored community had, almost exactly, paralleled DeLuth's on the white side, both under the expert tutelage of Judge How-High. Nick ran Bolita, private game rooms in the backs of half a dozen county jooks, and two whorehouses, popularly called fun houses, down by the river, one each for coloreds and for whites. Big Nick's and

DeLuth's mutually beneficial relationship was, for the most part, cordial. Though both would balk at the term "friends." Especially today.

"Mornin'." DeLuth takes in Big Nick's crisply tailored suit, his gleaming shoes, the diamond pinky ring that winks on his manicured right hand, as Nick, arms crossed, remains against his car. DeLuth, the son of an unruly, forever-falling-down drunkard, favored neatness, practiced orderliness in every detail of his personal appearance, and appreciated it in others. "Nice suit." He nods.

Big Nick nods back, dropping impassive eyes from the Sheriff's face down to his gun belt. It was unusual for DeLuth to come to these meetings armed. DeLuth was making a point. And Big Nick had taken note.

"How'd we do this week?" DeLuth asks.

"Not as good as we might've." Big Nick purses his lips. On Thursday night, the night the boys had visited the newspaper office, they'd also swung 'round the game room behind Number Five Jook and busted up the slot machines, card booths, and the big green-felt crap table in the back. "Why'd you do it?" Big Nick asks quietly.

"Well, I'll tell you, Nick." DeLuth rocks back on his own gleaming heels, crosses his arms, and leans against his own shiny car. "My wife, Birdilee, heard from our maid, Ceely, who heard from her hairdresser, Hattie, who got it from the barbershop next door, that the Big Bolita Man's backing the wrong man for Sheriff."

"Not true," Big Nick says smoothly.

Those damned, hooded eyes of his, DeLuth thinks, *never give up a thing.* "That's exactly what I told Birdilee. But, then, I heard the same thing from the boy that shines my boots downtown, who got it from the cousin of one of your bartenders."

"Not true, I say," Big Nick repeats, straightening up off his car, squaring his shoulders for emphasis.

"Well, y'know, Nick. I'm real glad to hear that. I'm sure the boys didn't mean to do any serious damage. Just wanted to be in on the game, that's all. You don't discriminate against white boys playin' a little craps, d'yuh?"

"Of course not, Sheriff. Your friends are welcome anytime. Though it's less expensive for both of us, if they behave themselves." Big Nick, a full head shorter than DeLuth, looks up innocent-eyed, with a rueful grin.

Goddamn Greek Nigger's got balls, DeLuth thinks, and finds himself grinning back. "See the receipts?" he asks.

"Of course." Big Nick's already reaching into his backseat for the bulging paper sack. "Not a bad week, all things considered."

31

Lila Hightower sits on the floor surrounded by the stacks of file folders pulled from her father's cabinets.

"What in tarnation you lookin' fuh?" Sissy asks, setting her tray on the desk, hoisting the coffeepot to pour Lila another cup.

"Hmmm—" How could she explain the eerie sense that she was the survivor of a family shipwreck, that, before she could move on, these files, her father's flotsam, *had* to be sorted out? "I'm not exactly sure," Lila says, snapping the file in her hand shut, dropping it on the "looked-at" stack to her left. "Guess I'll know it when I see it," she adds, reaching for the steaming cup. "Thank you."

"Welcome." Sissy crosses her arms and waits. "Sheriff had hisself a busy week," she says flatly.

"You mean the newspaper office downtown, killing that poor dog and all?" Lila's flipping through the next file.

"No."

Sissy's tone, quiet, insistent, draws Lila's eyes to her face. "What then?" Lila asks, trying not to sound impatient.

"Ah mean sendin' them Klanners to tear up the back of one uh Big Nick's jooks."

"What?"

"Number Five Jook, out Sandy Hill Road toward Lang-horn? Klanners come in just 'fore midnight, scared ever'body ha'f to death, tore th' game room to hell and back."

"Good God!"

"God ain't got nuthin' to do with this, Miss," Sissy says, her look and tone accusatory.

"Sissy, what *are* you tryin' to say?" Lila snaps.

"Ah'm sayin' the Sheriff got wind of somethin' he didn't like, 'bout Big Nick and that Mistuh Fred Sykes who wuz here t'other day. Ah'm sayin' . . . *somebody* 'bout to open up Pandory's Box, and there'll be hell to pay for the folks on t'other side."

"You sayin' that somebody is me?" Lila demands, point-blank.

Sissy pouts; her old eyes flash angry. " 'S one thing to med-dle in white-man's politics. Call up th' Mayor, sweet-talk th' Guv'nor. Judge did it all th' time. But, pullin' in Big Nick, Missy. You startin' somethin' mah folks kain't finish."

"But how in the hell did Kyle find out?" Lila asks, rising to her knees.

"Lordamercy, girl!" Sissy explodes. "You know better than to think all the cullud's on the same side. They's black fools, same as white!"

The truth of Sissy's statement sends Lila, sinking, back to the floor. *Goddamnit! Now the hell what?*

"If yuh'd ast me, Ah'd atold you," Sissy huffs, stands up straight, and retrieves her tray. "Big Nick and Kyle two peas in a pod, same as yore daddy. All of 'em raised feelin' *small*. Spend the rest of they lives tryin' to *puff* theyselves up, bigger than the rest of us!" The heavy office door slams behind her.

Peas in a pod. Lila stares at the closed door. Like everything else in the room, and the house, for that matter, it's mahogany—that wild Brazilian wood—tamed by local carpenters into perfectly mitered, raised, and receded panels. Their repetitive orderliness (in sharp contrast to the disarray of the files on the floor) reminds her of a platoon in parade formation, recalls, for her, life in Washington. Days disciplined by the protocol of military life: Chain of Command, Rules of Engagement, Standard Operating Procedures. In the Army, a renegade like Kyle DeLuth would've been thrown in the stockade, busted to Buck Private, maybe even booted out as dishonorable deadwood.

But thoughts of her days in Washington begged her to remember her nights. And, just now, nights in Washington were entirely too painful to contemplate.

Of course, he'd called the afternoon after the story broke.

"Hooah, HiLi! What d'you think?" At The General's use of her intimate nickname, Lila had winced. More than the military contraction of Hightower, Lila; it was a sideways reference to the High Life they'd savored in liberated Paris, in the heady days when it was clear to the Supreme Command that victory was imminent; when, bivouacked at Versailles, they'd managed overnight leaves in small, outer arrondissement hotels, late nights in the steamy, smoke-filled jazz clubs the French called *caves.* Liberated Paris had been heaven. Which, in comparison, made the bureaucratic pencil-pushing of Eisenhower's Washington hell.

"Excuse me, *sir.*" She'd pictured him seated at his desk, three-star khakis, all starch and polish and self-justification. "I thought you wanted *out* of Washington?"

"Goddamn Dulles, all this talk about the military's New Look. 'We've got The Bomb,' he says, 'so who needs a standing Army?' Can you believe that crap? And Ike—*Ike, for*

Chrissake—appears to be buying his massive-retaliation bull-shit! Max says Ike's talking about cutting the budget, gutting the ranks. No way can I walk away now, no way in hell."

Lila felt stung. The Army had always been The General's first and favorite mistress. "With all due respect, sir, I thought we had a deal." Her tone had come out sharper than she had intended.

She'd heard his quick intake of breath, pictured him stiffening his spine. There was a pause. "Look, Lila," he'd said raggedly. "Can't you think of this as added acreage to our little dream farm in Virginia?"

"You do that, sir. All I see is the added months—*years,* no doubt—of pretending to be something I'm not."

"What's wrong with Special Assistant to the Assistant Chief of Staff?" he'd groused.

"Titles don't do for me what they do for you, J.P."

"Goddamnit, Lila! I thought you'd be thrilled for me. For *us!*"

"Negative, sir," she'd replied, deliberately adding fuel to his fire.

"Christ Almighty, woman!"

She'd cut him off. "My regards to the lovely Kitsy, sir. Gotta go now, sir. Good-bye, *sir,*" she'd said, then slowly, deliberately, hung up the phone.

Of course, Jazz had sent flowers pleading "Patience, Ella. Love, Art." Pink roses, which meant Paris to both of them. So far, she'd not replied, would not reply until the full force of her anger and disappointment subsided. Maybe, she wouldn't reply at all.

Lila squints at the door's polished brass fittings, gleaming in a slant of midmorning sun. *What if I don't go back? What would the Assistant Chief of Staff do then?*

Lila reaches for her coffee. *Bleh!* She sticks out her tongue at the gone-cold taste. *A hot cup would be nice, but*—she sighs— *there'll be no more coffee out of Sissy this morning.*

Aimless, in search of distraction, she returns to the stack of files in front of her, fingers the tabs whose typed titles list legal cases and rulings. *Nothing here,* she thinks, and pulls another stack toward her.

On these folders, the tabs are handwritten in her father's slashing scrawl. Some files are more interesting than others— particularly those with the names of local and state politicos. It would be easy, she thinks, to chart the Judge's rise to political power, his increased fortunes in citrus and cattle, through the number of chits, favors, and payoffs, given and received, and carefully noted, in the margins of his chronological files. Through the years, she sees, his sidebar comments show a keen astuteness, an instinctive sense of timing, advantage, and opportunity. *Sly old bastard,* she thinks, begrudging him her respect.

In another stack, there's a file hand-tabbed simply and mysteriously "Ben." Inside: a Certified Pedigree and Receipt of Sale for one "purebred gray Brahma herd sire, calved June 30, 1950, at 87 lbs., purchased April 3, 1953, at a certified weight of 1,029 lbs. Registration transferred from Breeder B. T. Hallwelle, Houston, Texas, to Owner Howard T. Hightower, Lake Esther, Florida, on April 3, 1953, for the sum of $750.00 plus shipping."

Hooah! Lila thinks, wondering if this is the very same blue-ribbon bull promised to Big Jim Yates, the soon-to-be-ex-Governor, at his panhandle ranch next spring.

In other files are other Receipts of Sale for other bulls and cows, *a whole herd,* which Lila sets aside for forwarding to her father's estate attorney, Paine Marsh. There was no specific mention of cattle in the Judge's will, she recalls. Kyle claimed, and everyone assumed, the Judge had "transferred the herd to him months back." Maybe he did, or maybe he didn't. She'd have Paine inquire.

In the meantime, what *was* she looking for, really? Would this be the place to find it?

Here was another file tabbed simply "Missy" in her father's own hand. She'd been surprised at how many "Missy" files there were, seeded throughout his cabinets, containing odd pieces of artwork, or school assignments, her Red Cross swimming certificate, a handmade Christmas card "To Daddy, From Missy-toe." She and Louis must've been in first grade at the time, maybe second, about the same age as Franklin Dare's little 'Becca.

It was impossible to imagine the old man saving such things, tucking them away in tidy file folders with her nickname on it. Why were they still here? Had he forgotten them? Or, deliberately left them for her to find? Proof that, no matter what had passed between them, he was a good and loving father after all? *Sonofabitch, manipulative to the end, weren't you?*

Lila checks her watch—*quarter to twelve*—and wonders what her chances are of getting lunch. Sissy's a tough old bird and, when riled, likely to pout till supper. *I'll give her another half hour,* Lila decides, *then make a sandwich myself.*

She turns back to the stack. Midway down is another folder tabbed "Louis." *Bastard,* Lila rails at her dead father. Her twin brother's files, scattered as randomly as her own, tugged at her in ways nothing else could. Flipping this one open, expecting some yellowing certificate from Pop Warner football, she's surprised by the two small pieces of paper: On top, an address and phone number, written hastily, almost illegibly, in her mother's hand. In "Jaxvile," which was, no doubt, Jacksonville, Florida. The second, a personal check, also in her mother's looping script, made payable to—she feels her heart fist inside her chest—"Bill Roy Thompson" for fifteen hundred dollars. With the Jacksonville phone number written on the memo line, bottom left.

Lila knew the date without looking: January 9, 1943, the day before she and Louis turned twenty-one, when, legal at last, Louis had planned to announce his engagement to Lynette Thompson, Bill Roy's only daughter.

The day of the party, Lynette went missing. Louis spent hours looking for her, and, that night, accused the Judge of buying Lynette's father off.

"Where is she, you sonofabitch?" he'd roared, oblivious to all the others in attendance. "Tell me, or I'll shoot your god-damned head off!" he'd threatened, brandishing the Judge's own revolver in his face.

The Judge had sworn "before God and these witnesses" that he knew nothing about Lynette's disappearance.

"Besides, Louis-honey," Violet, already deep in her cups, had crooned, "everybody knows that girl's nothing but trash. Even Kyle's had her," she'd said, slick as a snake. "Haven't you, Kyle?"

And, right then, in front of everybody, Kyle DeLuth had bald-faced lied, "Sure. Matter of fact, we had a kinda slipup. She's in Jacksonville right now gettin' it taken care of."

Everyone was stunned. Louis was shattered. And, the betrayal—not by Lynette, Louis knew her heart—but by his own parents and his supposed best friend propelled him into a spitting, flailing, pistol-whipping rage that took half a dozen grown men to subdue.

In the end, it was Hamp, talking calmly, who took the gun, gently, out of Louis's hand. And walked him out of the house, a companionable arm flung around his shoulder, to "get some air." Lila could have, should have, joined them. But she'd felt frozen, statue-like, in place, wondering if what she'd seen had actually happened. Was it possible she'd imagined the whole thing?

Afterward, Louis left. Without one single word to her. On the joint birthday that was supposed to get them both out from under the Judge's thumb forever. It wasn't a deliberate cruelty—her brother wasn't capable of the kind of calculated abuse that was so clearly their parents' stock in trade. The pain Louis caused was haphazard, accidental, on account of his lifelong inability to see the big picture.

They found his car outside the Army recruiter's office, who confirmed he'd presented himself "for immediate enlistment" and been transported to basic infantry training at Fort Benning, Georgia.

No doubt he would've contacted her eventually. But, before that happened, Louis Hightower, her heart's twin, was dead in Tunisia—in the bloody hand-to-hand fighting beneath the date palms of El Guettar—and, in a manner of speaking, so was she.

After the funeral, the dismal folding of the flag, the bleak descent of the coffin, she'd meant to drive home, meet Hamp. But the road east, to the coast, came first. And she found herself turning, following the narrow black ribbon through miles of brooding hammock and pine woods to the broad blank sands of Daytona Beach. She'd stood for hours, staring at the gray ocean of tears whose far side wept on the shores of North Africa.

Her own eyes were dry. Numb with grief, dumb with despair, she must have drawn the attention of the women, dressed in olive drab, strolling the boardwalk. Someone took her hand, drove her car, parked it near the pier in front of the

W.A.C. recruitment office, escorted her onto the bus, and into the nearby basic-training camp. Weeks later, way too long to ever make it right, she realized, with a jolt, that she'd done to Hamp exactly what Louis had done to her.

STILL ON THE FLOOR, Lila rocks back, shaking off the same sense of dizzy paralysis that kept her away from high places, the tops of tall buildings. What some people called fear of heights was, for her, the terrifying urge to jump.

She looks down at the check, surprised to find it still in her hand. The truth, the shocking proof, of—*Wait a minute.* Questions and answers fly up, hard and fast, out of the looping holes of Violet's signature: The check was drawn off a joint account. But when, in Paine Marsh's office, Lila had wondered why all of the Judge's accounts were in his name only, Marsh had replied, "Oh, your daddy took your mamma off things years ago." *How many years, exactly?*

Lila pulls in her feet, cradles both knees between her arms. *Was it possible that Daddy's oath that night was true? That he had no more knowledge of Mamma's scheme, or Kyle's connivance, than I did? That, all these years, I've hated him for something he didn't do?* The check, released, seesaws to the floor.

Of course. Why hadn't she seen it before? Louis's public betrayal was too clumsy, too obvious, too out-of-control to have had the Judge's hand. It violated one of the old bastard's cardinal rules: "If you set out to trap an alligator, you better damn well be prepared to catch one!"

When did he find out? Why didn't he tell me? But, of course, after Louis left, she'd shut both of them out, then left herself. And when she returned, he was on his deathbed, unable to speak. *Except—EXCEPT—through this file, planted innocuously, a deceit to Mamma's prying eyes, yet here nonetheless, directly in my path.* "The truth will out," he always said.

Oh, Daddy. Lila's eyes stray back to the floor, the awful affront of the check's amount. Fifteen hundred dollars. *How could so much loss and suffering be purchased so damn cheaply?*

With a cold hand, one careful thumb and forefinger, she reaches out, turns it over, sees the endorsement.

"Bill Roy Thompson," it says, with a valiant flourish at the end. Underneath his name, Lynette's father had added and underlined, in bold, block letters, the chilling pronouncement:

"BURN IN HELL!!!"

We did. Anguished eyes rise to the ceiling, toward her mother's velvet-draped, bottle-shaped cell. *We do.*

32

Early afternoon, Daniel calls to Aunt Lu, who sits at the kitchen table reading library books—a whole stack of 'em brought out by the newspaper lady, Miz Barrows—to the girls.

Lu comes outside to check his work. "You done a fine job on them bean rows, boy," she says, and releases him to the woods. "Supper's at sunset. Don't keep us waitin', hear?"

Feeling like a noose unloosed, Daniel races out of the clearing, across the field, past the circle of Sampson's beehives. *One of 'em,* he notes, *looks woppy-jawed.* He stops briefly to investigate, spots the series of small tracks, five-toed, some with the inner toe splayed open like a thumb. *Dad gum possum,* he thinks, and sees with a shock the striped husks, piled ankle-high, in front. *Sucked the life plum out of 'em!*

Daniel scans the field for signs of the possum's path, a den or a burrow. *Mebbe Pap'll come out on a possum hunt tonight,* he thinks. And he feels his taste buds swell and sweat in hopes of possum slow-cooked with carrots, onions, and sweet taters.

He slips a dozen or so of the husks into his pocket—*to show the Ol' Seminole, if I see 'im, or Pap, later on*—and, after straightening the hive top, runs on to the waiting woods.

The sandy trail, now hardened by the rain, is where he remembers it, narrow and hugged by pines. He slows to a lope. Shafts of sunlight sift through the high branches, speckling the ground with bright flecks of light, like powdered sugar on a griddle cake. Dozens of birds caw and chitter.

"Woods is woods," Sampson had said. But these are mightily different from the ones up home. Missing are the hardwoods, so colorful this time of year, the hickory and sassafras, dogwood and maple. Here are oaks of a different kind, and scrawnier pines, and the tall brooding sentinels he knows to be cypress. But there's the familiar flicker of redwing; the ratchet of woodpecker; the thrum and drone of a million insects, and, everywhere, the spring of ferns, the thrust of seedlings, the determined clutch of vines. The lushness of life never fails to set his heart leaping like a grasshopper from stem to stalk.

Daniel finds it easy to retrace his steps, to find the big tree root that, just two days ago, sent him sprawling through the bushes to the river where Sampson caught the catfish. Aunt Lu had soaked that fish overnight, as Sampson had said, and fried it crispy with cornmeal, the meat flaky and sweet. Beyond the root, the path parallels the whisper and scent of the river, then hooks right, over a rise, into denser growth.

At a fork in the trail, Daniel hesitates. *The left,* he thinks, *crooks back toward the water; the right ambles deeper inter the woods.* In the midst of his decision making, he hears, off to the distant right, the whistle of an almost whippoorwill. "It's him!" he yelps and sets off like a dog to the hunt.

Up ahead, in the heart of a clearing, surrounded by pines as high as a church house, Sampson stands grinning welcome.

"How'd you know I was in the woods?" Daniel asks, breathless.

"Got my ways, heh?" Sampson tells him, pointing to a saw-grass basket suspended by a string off a tree limb.

"What's that?" Daniel peers up at it. Then adds, with a sharp intake of breath, "A beehive in a basket?"

"Small one, guards camp."

Daniel feels his face scrunch up in disbelief.

"Hive has guards all over th' woods," Sampson patiently explains. "Fly faster than a man can walk. Sets off a warnin' dance for the others, shakes the bones for me."

Daniel studies the quivering basket, and the jangle of dried fish bones dangling beneath it. "It's a signal," he marvels. "And you knowed it was me?"

Sampson shrugs. " 'S why I whistled."

Behind the old man, Daniel sees something else that fills him with wonder. "That your house?"

"Chee-kee," Sampson says, giving a name to the three open-air structures of cypress poles, supporting peaked roofs of palmetto thatch. "Sleep, eat, work, heh?" Sampson points, each one containing objects that bear witness to its use. "Thirsty?" He turns to the fire in the clearing's center, ladles a liquid out of an iron pot into a tin cup.

Daniel follows him, takes the warm cup and asks, "What's this?"

"Sofkee, Seminole, drink," he says, with an encouraging wave of his hand.

Looks like tea, Daniel thinks. "Tastes like corn," he tells him.

"Yes." Sampson pours himself some, sits on one of the two log stools beside the fire. Daniel joins him, openly staring 'round the clearing where Sampson lives, taking in the jumble of deer hides and hammock where he sleeps, the pinewood bench and table where he eats, and the cast-iron pots, the racks of honey jars, the odd tools and frames and stacks of wood for constructing hives. Off to the side of the work structure— *chee-kee, he called it*—is the three-wheeled cart he used to transport his hives into their field.

"You live here alone?" Daniel asks.

"Yes." The Ol' Seminole nods, sipping his drink. " 'Cep' for Mose."

"Mose?" Daniel scans the camp again, as if he missed someone.

"Mose, heh?" Sampson laughs and pats the hump beside his stool that Daniel had thought to be a rock.

"A turtle?" Daniel exclaims. "Biggest ol' turtle I ever seed!" he says and gets up to examine the thing.

Mose's head, halfway out of its shell, casts an angry eye at Daniel, then retracts back into rocklike stillness.

"Look at him!" Daniel rubs a hand across the ancient hump, traces the shape of a brown six-sided section.

"Hex," Sampson says, softly.

"What?" Daniel looks up.

Sampson points to the shell section beneath the boy's finger. "Hex," he says. Then, in explanation, "God's Eye."

"God's what?"

"Eye, eye, heh?" the old man points to one of his own dark eyes, then back to the turtle. "God's Eye."

"You talkin' Indian stuff?"

Patient, Sampson spreads his wide smile. "God," he explains gently, "loves ever'thin'. Some more'n others. Fav'rites have the hex, called God's Eye. Turtle shell . . ." he traces a six-sided section of Mose's shell lightly. "Honeycomb, snow-flake . . ."

"Feldspar?" Daniel asks quickly, remembering the familiar six-sided shape in the mineral's creamy crystals.

"Yes. And you." Sampson holds up a hand, palm forward, separates his thumb from his fingers, and his fingers in the middle, two from two. Daniel, curious, does the same. The old man bends forward, and, softly, traces the six-sided shape that outlines the boy's palm: little finger to center, one; center to pointer, two; pointer to thumb, three; thumb to wrist, four; across wrist, five; wrist to little finger, six. "God's Eye, on *you,* heh?"

Daniel studies his palm, wondering what it means, to have a hex on your own hand? It was, indeed, the identical shape, almost the same size, as the six-sided hex on the old turtle's back. The same shape that defines a honeycomb, and a hornet's nest, and so many of the rock crystals he'd collected up home. What does it have to do with God? And with this ancient Indian who seems to know more than any man he's ever met?

"God's Eye means special," Sampson says, in answer to Daniel's thoughts. "Special to God, heh? Means honor the Most High. Means protect the Least Low. In children, means grow. And live!"

"Live?" Daniel says, baffled. "Ever'one does that."

"No. Some families fall apart. Hives fail. Children die young."

"Oh, hives." Daniel suddenly remembers and reaches in his pocket to retrieve the bee husks. "Possum got inter one of yourn. Left a pile of these outside." He shows Sampson the empty, weightless remains.

"Ohhh." The old man says it sad, mournful. He takes the husks, cradles them in both hands, lifts them up. "Honor the

Most High," he says, his voice like smoke rising skyward. "Protect the Least Low," he whispers, lowering his palms reverent as a prayer. Then, with a look that Daniel recognizes as genuine sorrow, he bows his head, lets each husk slip slowly, silently into the fire.

33

A few years ago, when Ed Cantrell, Principal of Lake Esther Elementary, volunteered to take on the Tuesday Night Youth Group at Lake Esther Methodist, his wife, Alice, had railed, "Are you *nuts?* You spend all week with kids. You've got three of your own. Why take on the teenagers, too?"

He'd found it hard to tell her the truth: that these same teenagers had been among his first students. That he relished the opportunity to see what kind of people they'd become. That their honesty, and earnestness, and painful striving, was a powerful antidote to the increasingly mind-numbing bureaucracy of his day job. That their youthful idealism reminded him of his own, before he'd got snookered out of the classroom, into administration. And, that, on an almost weekly basis, they needed him to remind them who they were, before puberty, and their parents' private battles, and the whole country's postwar posturing, pushed them into The Box he now called his life.

Instead of trying to explain any of these things to Alice—whose entire life's goal was a new split-level outside of town—he'd merely shrugged and said, "I've known these kids most of their lives. I know it sounds odd, but it's like we grew up together."

He rarely prepares a text. They inevitably present one of

their own. And, the anticipation and surprise of it, what things they choose to discuss, from serious to absurd, is the highlight of his week.

As is his custom, Cantrell arrives early, unlocks the Youth Room door, turns on the lights, and arranges twelve folding chairs in a circle. The kids arrive in spurts.

"Hey, Mr. C.," Bobby Reid, the burly high-school fullback, calls from the door. "This here's Lois Ann." He proudly introduces the tiny, ponytailed blonde who wears, and appears lost in, his big scarlet-and-white varsity jacket. "She's a Lutheran, but I told her you wouldn't mind."

"Promise not to bite," Cantrell assures her, as the two take their seats opposite him.

"Hey, Brainiac," Bobby turns to greet skinny, pasty-faced David Getz, arriving just behind them. "Meet Lois Ann."

David Getz nods, flushing red, and moves awkwardly to the seat on Cantrell's left as three more girls—Gwen Moore, Janet Giles, Connie Wells—all brunettes, billow in together, pastel skirts swinging wide above their black-and-white saddle shoes. "Hey, everybody!" they call, wave, make their way gracefully to side-by-side chairs on Cantrell's right.

Behind them, the Gardener cousins, Jim and Jerry, shuffle in, in clashing plaid shirts, holding the door for pretty, raven-haired Mary Lou Meyers, in a slim blue shirtwaist, soft Capezios, and a waft of Shalimar.

Cantrell notes, and relishes, the palpable rise in energy, the rush of noise as the group—rounded out by gangly, spectacled Charles Patterson, who places his Bible and a magazine on the only empty chair—settles into the circle.

At seven o'clock, they bow their heads for Cantrell's brief opening prayer. Afterwards, he looks up and, smiling 'round, asks, "What'll it be tonight, folks?"

Across from him, Bobby Reid, one arm draped around the back of Lois Ann's chair, shrugs, and looks to the others to name the game. On Cantrell's right, the three girlfriends— Gwen, Janet, and Connie—smile prettily and cast their eyes sideways to direct attention elsewhere.

Next to David, Charles, intensely earnest, clears his throat and reaches for the magazine on the chair beside him. "Well, um, Mr. C.? David and I were talking outside, about this week's *Time* magazine? Y'all seen it?"

Charles flips open to the Viewpoint page, shows the column headlined "In Lake Esther, Florida, Nobody Cares."

Cantrell, who'd secretly hoped this might come up, asks the others, "Everybody seen it?" Two of the three girls, both Gardener cousins, Mary Lou—nod their heads. Others— including Bobby Reid and his girlfriend—shake theirs. "It's fairly short. Why don't you read it to us, Charles?"

Charles jabs a finger at the bridge of his horn-rimmed glasses and, again, clears his throat. "Well, it's about those Indian kids, the Dares," he says, by way of introduction, then goes on to read the four paragraphs, which Cantrell, since yesterday, has virtually memorized. At its end, Charles looks up. "I don't know about you, Mr. C., but seems to me, these kids got a raw deal."

"I have to agree with you," Cantrell says quietly. And finds he's relieved to admit it.

Solemn David Getz tells the group, "My little sister had one of their cousins—SaraFaye—in her class. Sheriff barred her and her sister, too."

"Their daddy works for mine down at the lumberyard." Mary Lou Meyers leans forward. "Like Miz Barrows at the *Towncrier* says, they're not Nigra, they're Croatan Indian."

Bobby Reid squints. "So why'd the Sheriff yank 'em out of school?"

"You know Sheriff DeLuth." David frowns and shakes his head.

"But, they ain't Nigra, right?" Bobby is persistent, determined to understand. "Why don't he let 'em stay? 'Steada makin' us the laughin'stock of the whole durn country!"

Ruefully, Charles closes the magazine, stares down at the glossy cover.

"This stinks." Bobby looks hurt by the whole thing.

Gwen and Janet nod in agreement. Beside them, Connie rearranges her dress pleats.

The two pimply-faced cousins eye each other uncomfortably. Jerry, the one on the right, wiggles a blue-sneakered foot on his chair rung.

"What can we do?" Bobby asks no one in particular.

Cantrell, not wanting to assume the leadership role, looks expectantly around the circle of young faces. David, the one nicknamed Brainiac, doesn't let him down.

"We have free speech, right?" David asks. "Couldn't we write *Time* magazine and tell 'em we disagree?"

Yes! Cantrell thinks, but keeps his face impassive.

"But, there's not very many of us," Mary Lou Meyers protests. "What if we drafted a petition and got the whole high school to sign it? Wouldn't that be something?"

Good girl! Cantrell thinks but, keeping his tone neutral, asks, "What's everybody else think?"

"Well, nobody would *have* to sign it, if they didn't want to, right?" Connie sounds nervous.

"Of course not," Gwen says impatiently.

Charles—who initiated the discussion—swallows hard.

Beside Gwen, Janet shifts into organizing. "We could set up a table outside the auditorium."

"Or the lunchroom?" Gwen suggests.

"Nah, nah, the gym!" Bobby says. "Everybody takes P.E. I'll square it with Coach myself."

"But what would this petition say?" Charles wants to know.

"Good question," Cantrell answers.

Connie, pouting, examines her nail polish.

"Lois Ann, you got any paper in your purse?" Bobby Reid asks.

FORTY MINUTES, and a heated discussion later, David, who'd reluctantly, but at Bobby's insistence, served as the group's "team leader," asks Lois Ann, who wrote everything down, to read the finished draft.

" 'Dear *Time* magazine,' " she begins.

" 'In your October twenty-seventh issue, under the 'Viewpoint' section, reporting the Dare family story, you say that Lake Esther is: ". . . a town, where nobody, not one person, cares." We would like to correct that statement. WE CARE.

" 'We have not been asked our opinion, but we would like to state it anyway.

" 'Our country was founded on principles set forth in the Ten Commandments, the Golden Rule, and the Sermon on the Mount. We are proud of our country.

" 'The Constitution says all persons are innocent until they are proven guilty, and that a man is to be considered truthful until he is proved to be a liar.

" 'We feel Daniel, 'Becca, Minna, and SaraFaye Dare got a

raw deal. Their right to an education has been taken away because of the opinion and prejudices of one man.

" 'To be expelled for violation of Florida segregation laws is one thing; to be expelled because of unfounded suspicion is another.

" 'Therefore, we believe the Dare children should be permitted to remain in school until the Sheriff can prove they don't belong there.

" 'That is our position and we want the world to know it.' "

At this, Lois Ann looks up, around the circle. Her smile is tremulous. The others—except for Connie and the plaid-shirted cousins, who have remained silent throughout the discussion—burst into spontaneous applause.

Ed Cantrell, watching, feels his chest ache with pride. He keeps his eyes, which have unexpectedly turned watery, on the speckled linoleum floor as a resolute Charles suggests, and leads them in, the closing prayer.

34

This is probably a mistake, Lila reckons, as she wheels past the overblown stone entrance of the new subdivision—"Welcome home to Fon du Lac"—onto a street so freshly asphalted the stink of tar still taints the air.

"Fon du what?" she'd asked.

"Fon du Lac, Lila!" Ginger had chuckled. "Charlie says it's French for Passion Point, where we all used to go 'to watch the submarine races'? 'A whole lotta fondlin' went on at this *Lac,'* Charlie says."

Why the hell did I say I'd come? Lila searches for the street name and number among the modern, low-slung houses, too wide and too white for their narrow lots, bright green lawns still showing the tight grid of fresh sod, not yet grown in. She remembered Charlie Jackson, the class clown who'd apparently followed his father into real-estate development, and Ginger's eager phone call:

"C'mon, Lila, you've been a hermit ever since you got home! It's Wednesday night, just a few of the old gang. I'm mixin' cocktails; Charlie's burnin' meat. Get yourself out of Lady Violet's lair. Come have some laughs with us!"

Laughs. All things considered—Lila had just received General J. P. Atkinson's formal assent to her formal request for extended leave—it seemed like a good idea at the time. But now? *Hooah!* She parks at the bare curb, two houses past the Jacksons' place. *If I don't like it, I'll just leave,* she decides, stepping around the neighbors' small mountain of moving boxes, a forgotten tricycle, a spindly soon-to-be-planted chestnut tree.

The double black doors reek of fresh paint. Ginger—flaming red hair, red lips, billowing red polka dots—engulfs her in a big-bosomed hug. "*There* you are, lookin' gorgeous as usual! Your perfume is divine. Helen, come smell Lila's perfume, it's simply *divine!*"

Helen Morton, the same pudgy pink face amid blond pin curls that had secretaried their senior class, wrinkles her pug nose and sniffs the air just left of Lila's neck. "Delicious, Lila! French? I *knew* it!" She takes Lila's hand and tugs her off the landing into the living room. "Everyone, come smell Lila's delicious French perfume!"

Lila cringes. There appear to be four, no, five couples here, plus her and—*Oh, God*—at the bar across the room, offering up a quickly poured glass of Jack Daniel's, Hamp Berry.

This is going to be awful. One quick drink and I'll excuse myself, she resolves as Hamp hands her a glass, and interrupts the cicada chorus of cooing women with, "You must see their boat dock,"—he cups her elbow, ushers her toward the big sliding-glass door facing the lake—"it's Charlie's pride and joy." And thus they escape, past Charlie Jackson and Brady Morton poking the smoking barbecue pit, across the Bermuda-grass lawn to the wooden dock and its brand-new Chris-Craft runabout, hoisted up above the water, like a prize or a pig on a spit. The acrid smell of fresh sealant and Charlie's recent overuse of lighter fluid assaults the more fecund scents of wet weeds, dark mud, and stagnant lake water.

"For the record . . ."—Hamp eyes her intently—"I didn't know *you* were invited, either."

Lila swigs her drink, thanks him for the rescue. "I don't know why I agreed to come."

"Well, Ginger's a force of nature, to be sure. But, when she promised entertainment, it never occurred to me that you and I were the floor show."

"What if we just left, Hamp? Jumped in the boat and got the hell outta here?" *Jesus,* Lila thinks, *the Jack's gone straight to my head.*

Hamp, suddenly dead serious, says, "And go where, Lila? And do what?"

Lila instantly regrets the awkward pause, the discomfort that's dropped like a stone between them. "Oh, Hamp, I'm sorry. I feel like a raving lunatic . . ."

He laughs nervously. "And you sound like one, too." He's let her off the hook, again, switched to concern. "Too much time with Our Lady of the Purple Shadows?"

Lila shudders. "Mamma's even worse than I remember. And, as you well know, my memories aren't pleasant." Solid, unflappable Hamp had been the only friend she'd ever brought home, exposed to Violet in all her screeching, slurring, stumbling-down-the-stairs glory.

Hamp shakes his head, calls up memories of his own. "After you left, there was only Sissy, and Kyle, and occasionally me, to run interference between the two of them. Of course, your daddy blamed her for the fact that both of you were gone."

"Turns out he was right."

He lets her comment pass. "At a certain point, two, three years ago, he didn't bother to hide the fact that there were other women. Though, he did have the phone lines in the bedrooms and the kitchen removed, everywhere except his office, so she couldn't eavesdrop or interrupt his calls."

"So Mamma became the spitting recluse she is today?"

"Word was her 'breakdowns' became longer and more frequent, if that's what you're asking. In the beginning, the Judge carted her off to several different high-powered doctors, hoping for help. Each one came up with something different—passive-aggressive, manic-depressive, paranoid-schizophrenic. But all of them recommended he commit her to some high-priced sanitarium."

"Why didn't he?"

"He couldn't. Or wouldn't, I suppose. The last diagnosis was acute alcoholism and an enlarged liver. She came home, as usual, swearing she was off the sauce forever."

"God, what a mess."

"Yes, but—well, Lila, aren't you leaving soon? 'End of the month,' you said."

"Well, no, not exactly—" she begins.

"Hey, you two!" Ginger hollers from the sliding door. "The calf is cooked, and the carnivores are getting restless!"

At the long table, the men have congregated at one end around the fragrant, steaming slabs of barbecued beef. The women at the other end busy themselves with the passing of roasted potatoes, baked beans, cole slaw, and dinner rolls. Lila and Hamp take the empty seats in the middle, opposite each other.

Talk at the women's end spins and tilts like a top toward their unseen children, stashed with sitters for the evening: Halloween costumes, this weekend's school carnival, kids' preferences for candied apples versus caramel popcorn, concerns about tooth decay, and pin-curled Helen who's announced she's expecting their fourth—"Brady just looks at me and another rabbit bites the dust!" Seated beside Hamp, she flushes pink, from apparent happiness, but, Lila notes, Helen's eyes are lined and shadowed, and her shoulders slump with an older woman's weariness.

Between Helen and Ginger at the end, Mary Kaye Wilson, as puny and timid as ever, nods readily, drinks steadily— "Another touch of sherry, anyone?" While on Lila's left, pert, ponytailed Trudy Stokes and greatly pregnant Nancy Roberts discuss the merits of Tidee-Rite Diaper Service versus a brand-new Maytag. Each of the wives, Lila sees, keeps a sly eye on her husband, with the same wary watchfulness as a G.I. on his General.

At the men's end, the topic is commerce: price of land, price of housing, price of citrus, fertilizer, pesticides, and the new frozen-fruit-concentrate plant going up outside of town. It seems odd to Lila that politics—which dominates talk in Washington—isn't mentioned until she brings it up.

"So, which way's the election goin' next Tuesday?" she asks, in a tone brazen enough to gain the attention of both ends.

Helen, listening in on the Tidee-Rite discussion, turns a shining pink face toward Lila, looks blank. Beside her, Mary Kaye tosses a wavering grin toward the man on Lila's right. "Jimbo's the political one in our family."

"Why, Mary Kaye, shame on you," Ginger, their hostess, chides her with a playful tap of red nails. "A woman's got to have a mind of her own!"

"Yeah, Mary Kaye, you should do what Ginger does," Charlie, their host, calls from his end.

"What's that?" Mary Kaye, wide-eyed, asks.

"Well, it's simple, really," Ginger, now the center of the table's attention, preens. "I was a dyed-in-the-wool Democrat until Truman—all his talk about integrating the Armed

Forces—turned me Republican. Now, anything with an 'R' by it gets my vote!"

Next to Ginger, Nancy Roberts cups her belly like a beach ball, nods in eager agreement. There's low laughter from the men's end.

"Including Kyle DeLuth?" Lila's trying to keep the edge off her voice.

"Now, Lila." Charlie's tone exudes patient reason. His pale blue Banlon shirt emphasizes the hot red of today's sunburn. His aqua eyes glitter in a perpetual joker's squint. "We all know there's no love lost between you and Kyle. He's more brawn than brain. Always was. But, you weren't here when the Nigger war veterans came home, struttin' up and down Main Street like they owned the damn place."

"Lounging 'round the bus stops bold as could be," Ginger says, "whistling at white girls, winking at grown women."

"Ol' Kyle got 'em off the streets, though," Ken Roberts, Nancy's gangly, hawk-eyed husband, drawls, "with his vagrancy law."

"They stopped whistling once they found themselves on the chain-gang," Ginger says. Up and down the table, except for Hamp, heads bob.

"And, you missed out on that New Jersey union organizer, too," Charlie continues. "Eatin' pigs' feet with the Nigger pickers, filling their sorry heads with the promise of *union* wages. Can you imagine what union wages would do to the citrus business?"

"Kyle ran that boy's Yankee butt straight outta town," Jimbo adds. Mary Kaye sends a blurry beam in his direction. The other men murmur agreement. "Kick Ass kicked his ass." "You bet!"

Lila leans in, turns toward Charlie. "But, surely, you see he's completely outta bounds with these Dare children."

"Awww, Lila, probably." Charlie smiles amiably. "Everybody makes mistakes. Look at those fool Senators up your way tryin' to censure Joe McCarthy. But, hell—an occasional fumble ain't reason enough to yank your best player outta the game, especially if he's a bona fide All-American!"

Good God! Lila feels fit to explode. Angry arguments assemble on her tongue. But a sudden heavy foot covers hers under the table. Hamp's expression urges control, reminds her that she's a guest at the Jacksons' table. Beside him, Helen's flushed face pleads patience. Beside her, Mary Kaye tenses, sensing a fight.

Lila takes a long drink from her glass, regroups. "Well, Charlie," she says, trying to match his amiable tone, "I couldn't agree with you less. And, from a purely business perspective, Fred Sykes has the better game plan."

Trudy Stokes brightens, chuckles. "Well, Sykes's is a sight better looking than Kyle, that's for sure."

Buddy Stokes glares at his wife. "Looks got nothing to do with sheriffin'. It's all about upholdin' the law, ain't it, Hamp?"

Like everyone else, Lila turns her eyes on Hamp, who shifts thoughtfully in his seat. "Well, strictly speakin'," he drawls, "there's upholdin' and there's holdin' up. Seems to me, over the years, Sheriff DeLuth may have lost track of the difference."

"And I've lost track of Helen's scrumptious potatoes," Ginger says smoothly, surveying the tabletop. "You guys hoardin' 'em down there, Charlie?"

"Well done, Counselor," Lila says softly.

"Why, thank you, Judge," Hamp replies, with a slow smile.

*　　*　　*

PALE SUNLIGHT through strange striped curtains, the sound of a garbage truck clanking tin, breaking glass close by, a heavy arm flung across hers in hairy familiarity—Lila knows with a sudden, startling certainty: *I'm awake. This is not a dream.*

This strange room, round walls converging in a high point above the bed, is real. This strange young man, smelling of Scotch, cigarettes, sweat, is—She turns her head, slightly. *Don't panic. For God's sake, don't wake him.* She shifts her shoulder, adjusts her hip, rolls slowly out from under his embrace. And holds her breath as he folds in, turning, groaning, toward the wall.

She stands, takes stock—*Nothing like this has ever*—stoops to pick up twisted panties—*never before*—strewn bra—*and never*—draped blouse—*ever*—folded slacks—*again!* She steps into the tiny bathroom with its own small, slanted window, avoids the mirror, forgoes the light, and dresses hastily. She washes her face, rinses her mouth at the sink, spits carefully to avoid his shaving kit balanced on its rim, and wonders, sticking to specifics, *Comb, keys, shoes?*

In the half-light of the room with the sleeping stranger, she locates her purse and shoes beneath the room's only chair, steps across the trail of men's clothes that leads to his side of the disheveled bed, and glances back at the burrowed chin, its small, handsome cleft the only clear memory she has of the night before. Her head aches. Her hand on the door shakes. Like a swimmer straining toward the surface after a too-deep dive, she emerges, gasping for air.

Outside, sunlight, memory, explanations rush cruelly in. Her brain, addled from who-knows-how-much alcohol last night, reels and, at the same time, records the facts: The room's strange slanting walls, its high convergent ceiling are common to the units at the WigWam Motel. The garbage must have been collected from the adjacent ThunderCloud Cocktail Lounge, where a green truck—"Hightower Groves, Lake Esther, Florida"—sits alone in the side parking lot.

Inside the truck, fumbling key into ignition, she remembers, *His name began with a "T," something short. Ted? Todd? Tom? Yes, that's it.* "TomTom in a WigWam," she'd joked. *Oh, God!*

She heads north in the early-morning traffic, recognizes the road (*South Trail,* South Hylandia's Orange Blossom Trail, forty minutes from Lake Esther), recalls the moment when, after the Jacksons' disastrous dinner, after Charlie suggested "we all take a walk around the lake, to the Point, where we used to park. Relight the old fires, huh?" (he'd added a wicked wink at Hamp), she'd fled.

Her intention, if she had one, was to head south, as far as she could go. Miami maybe, or, if she felt like it, Key West. But the WigWams caught her eye, and the ThunderCloud Lounge next door held it. She'd stopped, feeling clouded all right, by the thunderclap insight that marriage—in the five forms she'd seen it that night, in the many guises she'd observed at Officers' Clubs on three continents, in the way it might have been with Hamp, or she'd hoped it would be with Jazz—was not for her.

The Lounge was noisier, more crowded than she'd expected. She made her way to the bar, bought her own drink over the protests of an older, expensively dressed regular who sat in the corner, sharing sarcastic asides with the bartender. A man more her age, a cocky smiling salesman, made a run with "What's a doll like you doin' in a dump like this?" and the bartender shooed him away.

It's so obvious: The problem with marriage, she'd thought, *is that even under the best of circumstances, with a guy as fine and fair as Hamp, for example, it's all compromise and capitulation. And with Jazz? Jazz, who in the company of his cronies could be every bit as insufferable as Charlie Jackson? Marriage with Jazz wouldn't be a deliverance* (as she'd always thought); *it would be, more than likely, a demotion, a relegation to the wives' end of the table!* What *had* she been thinking? She was a round peg and marriage was a square hole. She, who suffered no fools lightly, had, for the past nine years, been fooling *herself*! The realization mushroomed in her mind like an atomic cloud, and she felt herself, without warning, reduced to dust, vulnerable to the slightest breeze, the least waft of wind.

Then Tom—she'd let young Tom slip in beside her because he'd asked, in a polite Midwestern farm-boy twang, "May I buy you a drink, ma'am?" She'd liked his solid, wholesome looks, and the fact that he was Army, "temporarily assigned to recruitment, ma'am." (She'd resisted telling him that, according to the new Assistant Chief of Staff, his job was in jeopardy. Or that, under other circumstances, her rank, several grades higher than his, would dictate a salute.) He wore his loneliness openly, unarmored. An eager young buck who'd not yet lost all the soft, green felt off his antlers. He'd seemed, she remembered vaguely, a safe place to fall.

How much time, how many drinks passed, before he suggested she take a look inside his wigwam? ("Though folks around here appear ignorant about real Indians, ma'am. Technically, it's a tepee.") She'd never know.

The only thing she did know, with a certainty as sharp and clear as this morning, is that an entire life of running away— from Louis's death, the perception of her parents' betrayal, her engagement to Hamp, and, last night, the very idea of marriage itself with Jazz or anyone—was getting her nowhere.

Wherever she went, the pain followed, made heavier by the shame and guilt that attended her leave-taking. Not to mention the sordid shock of waking up next to a stranger! *Oh, God.* The memory makes her cringe. *NEVER again!*

What was it that compelled her to leave, usually without thought or explanation? How was it that other people stayed—*like Daddy, for instance, sticking with Mamma all those years, enduring far worse than I can imagine?*

Wheeling north, through the tree-lined streets, past the stately Victorians, the tidy storefronts that define Lake Esther, Lila wonders, *What am I doing here, really?*

And finds herself wishing, *Once, just once, I'd like to feel like I was running toward what I want, instead of away from what I don't. Or, better still, that I had what it takes, in advance, to know the difference.*

35

This is it, Ruth thinks. The dreaded day of reckoning, her self-imposed deadline when, with the additions from this afternoon's mail, her bottom-left desk drawer will no longer close. And she can no longer hide from Hugh the number of subscription and ad cancellations that have been streaming in for days.

We'll have to talk. Ruth lights a cigarette, stubs it out without tasting it. *He'll be furious. Worse yet, hurt,* that she'd deliberately withheld evidence of what was becoming painfully clear—that their editorial outrage and detailed coverage of the Dare family's dilemma, their aggressive stance against K. A. DeLuth, and support for Fred Sykes, was costing them business on every level.

He'd warned her she was pushing too hard, too fast. This weekend's full-page photo essay, titled **Separate but Equal?**, had dared to compare the local white school's brick and mortar respectability, its spanking new gymnasium, gleaming floors, and glistening locker room showers to the ramshackle 58-year-old converted horse barn that housed the colored school, its battered hand-me-down desks and textbooks, its rickety row of outhouses lining the playground, and its appalling "science lab" equipped with one Bunsen burner and a bowl of goldfish.

Shedding light on the broader injustice of segregation (toward which the community had, for decades, turned a deliberately blind eye) had been a calculated risk. Ruth looks at the overfull drawer with disgust. But after last week's horrors— the school board's insanity, Gordon's poisoning, the Sheriff's maniacal rant—*what did you expect?* That, over the weekend— having viewed the paint and the posters out front, the pictures in the weekend edition—the Mayor, the Town Council, someone, *anybody* would rise up? Decry DeLuth? Demand resignations from each and every school-board member? Thank the *Towncrier* for its outstanding journalistic vigilance?

Fat chance. Instead of collective outrage, her desk drawer was full to overflowing with cancellations from all over the county. Instead of voices raised in support, her office was enveloped in a sickening silence.

Ruth watches the snake of smoke still rising from the cigarette in her ashtray. It writhes up, curls over, fans out briefly like the head of a cobra, then disappears into the air. She sighs. *Later today, we'll have to talk.*

"IS MIZ BARROWS IN, please? I'm Miz Carolyn Ellis. We have an appointment."

Ruth swivels her chair from the typewriter at her side to the front of her desk, to take a look at her two o'clock.

Carolyn Ellis is slim, thirtyish, a beautiful blonde, hair done up in a perfect French twist. Flawless skin, ivory pearls, trim red suit, discreet black bag and pumps. *Probable waste of time,* Ruth thinks. She tended to be impatient with beautiful, well-groomed, stylishly dressed women. Not because she envied them. But, too often, she found them more effort than they were worth. Ruth's own mother had been beautiful once—before age, disappointment (not the least of which was her mousy, myopic daughter), and an overabundance of bathtub gin robbed her of the very thing she valued most. Women who wore their beauty like armor, flaunted it like a prize, expecting to be courted and admired, were the worst. Occasionally, however, one of them would surprise you. Like Lila Hightower, who bore her looks lightly, as an addendum or afterthought to her surprisingly keen intelligence. *Prize or surprise? Which, Mrs. Carolyn Ellis, are you?*

Carolyn's entrance into Ruth's office is smiling, graceful, Ruth's welcome polite but perfunctory. The younger woman sits, declines Ruth's proffered cigarette, and launches into her reason for coming.

"Miz Barrows, my husband and I have a relatively new business on the Trail, about ten miles north of town. House of Linens, it's called. We sell sheets, towels, window coverings to new families moving into all the new subdivisions going up out there . . ."

Well-spoken. No doubt good with the ladies in trauma over pink versus blue kitchen curtains, Ruth thinks.

"We also have a line of table linens and party wear, so if anyone's having a party or any kind of bash, we generally know about it firsthand."

Good for you! But why are you bothering me?

"About a month ago, our son, Richie, signed on with your man, Donny, to run a paper route in our neighborhood. Richie was so excited, went 'round signing up everyone on our street and a lot more in our subdivision, ShangriLa Shores. But last week, he started hearing that a number of his customers were canceling their subscriptions."

Ruth sets her cigarette on the lip of her ashtray, crisscrosses her arms. *Let's all cry a river for poor little Richie.*

His mother continues. "Poor thing worked so hard to get the papers out on time, even in all this rain we've been having, toss them on the doorstep, things like that. Richie was devastated, convinced that he'd done something wrong. But my husband and I told him that sometimes things aren't what you think, and the only way to know for sure what's wrong is to go around and ask. Long story short, Miz Barrows, Richie's customers told him, 'Hey! If it's *our* newspaper, how come *we're* not in it? Except for Fred Sykes,' they complained, 'the *Towncrier* is all about the folks in town. What about *our* end of things? Where are *our* Boy Scouts, *our* birthday parties, *our* ladies' luncheons?' So, Miz Barrows,"—Carolyn stops to smile prettily—"here's where my proposal comes in. I worked on my high-school newspaper, took a few writing courses in college. Got to wondering . . . What if, on the page opposite your 'Tidbits from Around Town,' I provided you with 'Blurbs from the Burbs'—a weekly column about what's happening in the subdivisions?" Carolyn extracts two sheets of paper, typewritten, double-spaced, from her bag. "Here's an example of what I have in mind."

Ruth gives the copy a distracted scan. Carolyn's proposed column is packed with the kind of information—names, dates, details of events—that will play well in the new house farms taking root north of town. But her overly alliterative style—"Bright-eyed and bushy-pigtailed Becky Palmer has bagged Brownie Scout Troop 220's top title for Best Door-to-Door Girl Scout Cookies Sales Scout"—will require some heavy editing. *Until she gets the hang of it,* Ruth thinks.

"Our store's right in the middle of things," Carolyn persists, "so it would be an easy thing for me to do. And maybe you and I—well, we could work a trade—my weekly column in exchange for a regular display ad for House of Linens?"

"Why, Mrs. Ellis—may I call you Carolyn?" *And may I take back every petty thing I thought about you?* "What a delightful idea."

Minutes later, as Ruth escorts Carolyn to the lobby and bids her good-bye, she sees the jalopy, an older model with a rumble seat, pull up out front, and six, no seven, teenagers pile out onto the sidewalk. One of them, a burly football-type, opens the front door, then, seeing Carolyn, steps hastily aside to hold it open for her and, behind her back, gives the other two boys an appreciative eye roll.

Beauty doth of itself persuade the eyes of men. And teenage boys, Ruth thinks. She pauses to watch the rest of the group burst through the door into the lobby, crowing "Hey, Peggy!" to the receptionist, barely out of high school herself, and crowd 'round her desk. "We're here to see Miz Barrows." "She in?" "Nice desk," they chatter.

Peggy turns wide eyes toward Ruth who, leaning against her office doorjamb, says, "I'm Mrs. Barrows."

As the teenagers move toward her, obviously intent on invading her office, Ruth steps aside, hears herself suggest to the boys that perhaps they should bring in a few more chairs from the lobby.

As the three boys grab chairs, and the four girls direct the placement of seats, Ruth returns to her side of the desk to survey each one individually.

"Miz Barrows, hi!" the pretty black-haired girl up front in pink angora says, "I'm Mary Lou Meyers and I—well, *we* read your article in *Time* magazine, the one about nobody cares?"

"Yes," Ruth says. *Meyers? Meyers Lumber and Construction?* She checks her mental list of prominent local family names and businesses.

"And we, well, respectfully disagree," Mary Lou says. "And,

have brought you a petition, signed by sixty kids at our school, that says so. We'd like your help sending it to *Time* magazine, please." As Mary Lou thrusts the two sheets of paper onto Ruth's desk, the two girls on either side of her, both brunettes, one in voluminous blue polka dots, the other in pleated red-and-white plaid, nod and murmur and smile their agreement.

Ruth turns the petition around, so the title—"We Care!"—is at the top, quickly reads the text, then glances over the list of signatures below and on the following page. More familiar local surnames, *though none from the county's big-money citrus or cattle families,* she notes. And she can't help but ask, "Do your parents know about this?"

"Well, yes, most of them do," Mary Lou answers, without smiling.

The crewcut football-type behind her chimes in, "We'd prob'ly had more sign it, but a lot of kids said they'd get in trouble if they did."

"And, these are all students? Any teachers? Adults?"

"Nope, just kids from the high school," the fourth girl, a curly redhead with bright blue, protruding eyes, says.

"Who came up with this idea?" Ruth asks. *Charlie at* Time *is going to love this.*

"Well, ma'am," Mary Lou says, seriously, "a bunch of us just felt it was the Christian thing to do." The polka-dot brunette beside her nods in sober agreement. "We were just sick over what happened to those children, felt so helpless about helping them. So we decided we had to do something. Maybe it will wake up the adults."

Ruth sits back, wanting a cigarette badly. "You kids have done a fine thing here, a very fine thing. I'm sure your parents are proud of you. I would be." She reaches for the fat, two-inch-thick file on her desk. "And I want you to know you're not alone. These are telegrams, wires, phone messages from people all over the country who agree with you." She flips open the file cover. "This one, from a lady in Nashville says, 'Please know that there are many, many people who do care what happens to the Dare children and others in similar cases.' Wired the family five dollars, too."

There's a sort of sigh, a settling, on the other side of the desk. Looking at their young faces, Ruth senses something that prompts her to ask, "Taking the high road isn't always easy. Was there any trouble?"

Eyes shift away from her toward the floor. The tall, skinny boy in the back, gaze earnest and intense behind thick glasses, says, "We set up the petition table inside the gym. Outside, somebody put up signs saying 'Nigger Lovers Enter Here'."

Ruth winces. "I wish somebody had called me." *Damn, another lost news photo!*

The burly one beside him frowns. "We tore 'em down once we got wind they were there."

"But, somebody put 'em back up this morning," the earnest boy says.

"And, a few people," the plaid and pleated brunette adds urgently, "got stones pitched at them for signing."

Ruth grabs her pen. "Who? And who did the pitching?"

"Well, uh . . ." The spectacled boy in the back flushes.

"Actually, Brainiac here was one of 'em, but the guys who did it have been set straight, ma'am."

"We did have sixty-two signatures." Mary Lou resumes leadership. "But two kids came back, said we had to take their names off, on account of it might hurt their daddies' businesses."

Their faces, so bright and shining upon their arrival, flicker with disappointment. *So young,* Ruth thinks with a pang. "I want to thank you for bringing this in. You've done a brave and bold thing and I'm sure *Time* magazine will want to cover it." *We certainly will,* she thinks.

"And, will you tell the Dares, too?" Mary Lou presses. "Let them know not everybody in this town is against them?"

"Of course. This should make their day," Ruth says. "It's certainly made mine." *Unbelievable.* "Can I get a quick group shot of you kids holding the petition, please?"

FOR RUTH, the rest of the afternoon blurs in Friday's hustle for Saturday's edition. Gene in the darkroom grumbles over the last-minute inclusion of the teenagers' photo. Walt the typesetter growls over the tight turnaround on a logo for Carolyn's column and the ad for House of Linens. And at six o'clock, on her way out the door, Peggy, the receptionist, announces she's not feeling well and will probably stay home tomorrow.

Ruth stands, key in hand, locking the front door behind Peggy, as the modern sedan purrs into the parking space out front. An older gentleman, distinguished, conservative suit, gets out, makes his stiff-jointed way toward her. *Now what?* she wonders, releasing the deadbolt.

"Mrs. Barrows? We've not met in person, but we've spoken on the phone. Dr. John Leighton, Clark Christian Academy." He offers a bony, freckled hand.

"Of course. You referred me to the article by the Reverend Billy Graham. Thank you again. Please come in."

Dr. Leighton places his hat, a brown, center-dent fedora, on the chair beside him and sits formally, hands clasped in his lap. "I enjoyed your story on the two Billys," he tells her. "Men like Billy Hathaway are despicable—exploiting other people's fears for their own profit. And I applaud your efforts to expose him."

"Why, thank you . . ." *Wish I could say the crowd of cancellations in my desk drawer agreed with you.*

"Mrs. Barrows"—Dr. Leighton leans forward—"yesterday, I called Sheriff DeLuth to inform him that my school, which is a privately funded Christian institution, would welcome the Dare children into our midst."

"Wonderful!" Ruth says in a rush.

"But, unfortunately . . ." Dr. Leighton holds up his hand to stop her. "the Sheriff informs me that, were I to do so, I could be subjecting the school to *criminal* charges."

"What?!"

"For violating state laws on segregation. Which, of course, the Sheriff says, he would be duty-bound to prosecute."

"Oh, Lord!" *Kick Ass strikes again.*

Dr. Leighton purses his lips, as if trying to rid his mouth of a bad taste. "Of course, I cannot, in good conscience, break the law. But . . ." Eyes solemn, he presses the fingertips of both hands together in a prayerful tent, "neither can I sit by while the minds of these children go unattended. I have discussed this matter with the leadership of my faculty. And I am here to offer the Dare family, through you, the voluntary services of two highly qualified tutors."

"Tutors?" *Brilliant!*

"There are four children, I understand, in grades one, two, three, and five? The tutors, who teach at Clark Christian during the day, will come at night, twice a week, and instruct the children at home. In addition, we will provide all required books and materials."

Ruth sits back. *What a brilliant, goddamn beautiful idea!*

"Mrs. Barrows, I'd like you to reassure the parents that I will personally supervise the quality of instruction."

"Your offer is wonderful. I'm sure they'll be delighted. And much more receptive than our demented Sheriff."

"We are a *Christian* institution, Mrs. Barrows. As I told Sheriff DeLuth: he, as a lawman, knows his duty; just as we, as Christians, know ours."

After Dr. Leighton's formal farewell, Ruth hears the mechanical grind rising to the rolling roar of the giant flatbed press in the back. Saturday's edition was out of Hugh's hands and into the capable grip of sweating, swearing pressman Joe Stephens.

Ruth sits, listening to the rhythm, like a heartbeat, of the press pumping ink onto newsprint. She smokes, sending gray rings spinning toward the ceiling. She surveys her desk: on her left, the still unclosable bottom drawer; on her right, Carolyn Ellis's first "Blurbs from the Burbs"; and, in front of her, on top of the kids' "We Care!" petition, Dr. Leighton's card, which she'll drive out to the Dares' place first thing in the morning.

Jesus. Days of wondering if anybody's listening, days of wishing someone would do something. And then this one. Ruth leans forward, presses the cream-colored button. "Hugh?" she calls into the interoffice speaker.

"Yep?" she hears his raspy, distracted voice yell over the rumble of the press.

"Can you come up front? We need to talk."

36

Finally, after supper Saturday night, Pap agrees to walk out with Daniel and "take a look-see at them possum prints."

"I hope they're still there," Daniel tells Pap as they make their way across the field, Pap holding the piney wood torch high above his head.

They are. But, once Pap gets a look at them, he squashes the idea of a hunt straightaway.

"This 'un here"—he points to the clearest print, with the toe like a hooked thumb on the side—"is her back foot. Ain't a possum alive make a print that deep less'n she's carryin' five or six, mebbe more, younguns on her back. Cain't hunt that possum till the younguns are grown and gone."

Daniel is doubly disappointed. Not only is the hunt off, the pile of bee husks he'd told Pap about is gone.

"Them empty bee husks was right here, Pap. I swear it. A whole heap of 'em, sucked plum dry," Daniel tells him, pointing to the spot where the husks used to be.

Pap grins in the torchlight. "I'm sure they was. But bees can be as persnickety 'bout their hive as any woman. Probably carried 'em off out inter the field somewheres."

"What?"

"Ants the same way. Don't bury their dead, jus' carry 'em off someplace away from the livin'."

"That true, Pap?"

Pap eyes Daniel and nods. "They's gone, ain't they?"

"But what's to keep that possum from comin' back, gettin' into ever' one of these hives?" the boy worries.

"Well, I'll tell ye." Pap drops a hand on Daniel's shoulder, heads him back toward the clearing. "The first thing is plum laziness. That possum had to work all night to make a meal outta a bunch o' bees. With all them mouths to feed, ye gotta b'lieve she's lookin' fer somethin' easier—field mouse mebbe, or, since the rain softened things up, some big ol' earthworms. The second thing is: tomorr', ye gonna find yoreself a camphor tree, pull off some branches, bring 'em out here and step on the leaves, crush 'em up a little, see? Then, sweep ye a wide circle round them hives. Possums don't take to camphenated oil anymore'n people do."

Daniel laughs, catching Pap's joke. Mam thought camphenated oil cured everything. She was forever pestering them to "rub a li'l oirl" on Pap's sore shoulder, Daniel's cut foot, 'Becca's runny nose. Pap, especially, hated the smell of it. "Get away from me! That stuff stinks to high heaven," he used to tell her.

At the cabin, Daniel places the piney torch in an iron bucket by the steps, and the two of them sit in rockers, watching sparks sail up off the torch and into the dark clearing.

"Spent most of the day in the woods again, did ye?" Pap asks quietly.

"Yes. Sampson's teachin' me how to fish Indian style. I ain't got the hang of it jus' yet, but I will."

"A boy b'longs in the woods. I b'lieve that." Daniel hears the slow creak of Pap's rocker, then a sudden stillness. "But, for the next couple weeks, I need you home with Lu and the girls."

"Why?"

"There's things goin' on, boy, in town. Got nothin' to do with us. And ever'thin' to do with us. Could spell trouble."

In the trembling light of the fading piney torch, Daniel sees Pap's hawk nose, his scowling brow, in profile. "What things, Pap?"

"Accordin' to Miz Barrows, there's people in town want y'all back in their school. And, there's people who don't. Bunch of high-school kids signed a paper sayin' they's on our side. Bunch of Klanners painted up the newspaper office, killed their dog, sayin' they ain't. Accordin' to Miss Lila, there's a lawyer down at the Courthouse wants to take the school board to court. In the meantime, Miz Barrows is bringin' out some teachers from a private school Monday night, catch ye and the girls up on yore lessons. The worst of it is, there's an election come Tuesday to see if that Sheriff DeLuth gets to stay Sheriff or not."

"Mebbe they'll vote 'im out, Pap."

"Well . . ."—Daniel sees the match, hears the suck and flare of Pap's pipe. Pap takes a long pull. Beneath his nose, the tamped-down tobac glows crackly red—"ef they vote 'im out, Sheriff's likely to rare up ugly, like a bear throwed out of his den. And, ef they vote 'im in, he could jus' as easy bloat wild, like a b'ar hog gone crazy on gooseberries. Either way, could be bad."

"But, me and Sampson are—"

"Not now, Daniel." Pap sucks hard again. There's no mistaking his father's steely resolve. Daniel's heart sinks.

"What d'you want me to do, Pap?" he asks.

"I want ye here for Lu and the girls when Will and I ain't,"

Pap replies, eyeing Daniel through the rising, meandering vine of pipe smoke. "I want ye to unwrap yore twenty-two and my shotgun, and clean 'em up good. I bought some new shells today, we'll keep 'em at the ready. I don't aim for ye to do any shootin', boy. But I do want ye keepin' an eye out."

Daniel feels the weight of his father's request fall, like a whole cupboardful of coverlets, across his own bony shoulders. He hangs his head. "All right, Pap," he says, his voice and his hopes gone hollow.

She Who Decides is unspeakably relieved.

Just days after the disaster of the clawed intruder, the Young One, the favored of He Who Provides, arrives to cleanse the colony's grounds of the intruder's lingering scent.

The Young One's action, She knows, destroys the markings that might otherwise invite additional trespass. In their stead, he creates a powerful, repellent moat; its scent a soothing balm to Her fearful, grieving kin.

The children are safe, She assures the Old Ones. We are all now safe, She tells the rest, many of whom counseled flight against the fear of another ruinous fight.

We stay, She Who Decides pronounces. We weather the Winter and trust Spring's promise. And we watch, She decrees, that the Young One who comes daily to offer his protection, is protected as well, within the free range of our shared ground.

37

As the Reverend Tommy Childs begins to read the names from the pulpit of the First Baptist Church, K. A. DeLuth bows his head and tries to look pious. But, inside he's grinning from ear to ear. *As far as this election game goes, it's a helluva fourth quarter.*

"Bobby Reid, Lois Ann Allen . . ."

This week alone, there'd been that crazy old coot runs the Christian reform school outside of town. We'll welcome them Niggers in our midst, the old coot says. Over my lily white dead ass! Set him straight, didn't I?

". . . Getz, Mary Lou Meyers, Janet . . ."

That fat bastard Cantrell instigating these kids in Youth Group— Youth Group!—to get up their "We Care!" petition. Spreadin' that bleedin'-heart bullshit all over the high school. Could've arrested the whole lot of 'em for pollution of county property, if I'd known about it.

". . . Charles Patterson, Gwen Moore . . ."

Need to have Miss Emily down at the post office give Cantrell's mail the once-over. I'll lay five to a dime he's a member of what?—the Progressive Party, the Civil Rights Congress? Probably subscribes to The Daily Worker, *or some such shit. His ass is grass.*

". . . Charlotte Stone, Dottie . . ."

Course, that little twat Ruth Barrows had to air it all out in

Time *magazine. Their covers are always red, ain't they? The idea of seeing my name inside a Red wrapper makes me wanna puke. But, like the Judge always said, good or bad, publicity's still publicity.*

". . . Lee, Joan Marie Cuozzo . . ."

Have to hand it to Fred Sykes. He and his wife, three kids, bunch of Realtors, Jaycees, handing out free trick-or-treat bags to the station wagons downtown. "Your Future Sheriff Wishes You a Safe and Happy Halloween!" Probably had 'em printed up at the Towncrier's *print shop. Lila wastin' the Judge's money like that. Bet the ol' man's turnin' over in his grave.*

". . . Louise Hewitson, Angela Stout . . ."

Back of the treat bags, Sykes and his wife and kids make a pretty picture. But, it don't beat mine on Ol' Blue. Clive Cunningham says it reminds him of Roy fuckin' Rogers on Trigger, and you can't get more American than that!

". . . Elizabeth Finneran, Joanne . . ."

Halloween on a Friday night! Goddamn Niggers went crazy with their numbers. Biggest haul I can remember. Have to call Hallwelle in Houston on Monday, tell 'im I'm ready for another bull. Gray one, this time. Spice things up a little.

". . . Anne Knickerbocker, Marty . . ."

Barbecue at the Cattlemen's Club went great yesterday. Like Clive said, "Sykes'll take a few of the new subdivisions up north, but the rest of the county knows what's what. You can eyewash it all you want, but the Sheriff's job is to keep the Niggers in their place. And Kick Ass knows how."

". . . Blye Phillips, Karen O'Rourke . . ."

The topper was Clive's wife. Standin' up there sayin' somethin' should be done about these poor misguided kids, the sixty who signed the petition, listed on the front page of the Barrows' Saturday rag. It was Sarah Cunningham's idea to call all the Baptist preachers in the county, create a public prayer list, announce their names from the pulpit, ask the Good Lord to show them and their parents the error of their ways. That it wasn't Christian to question God's divine plan, or the established state laws on racial segregation.

". . . Don Hardy, Vicky Newell . . ."

In the pew beside him, Birdilee reaches over and squeezes his hand, hard, and gives him a dirty look. Had he chuckled out loud? *Sorry, darlin',* his eyes tell her, then return to the high-gloss shine on his Sunday boots. *Course Birdilee didn't much like Sarah Cunningham's plan. "Aren't these kids entitled to free speech?" she said, or some such nonsense. We all had a good laugh over that one!*

DeLuth shifts position in his seat, rearranges his pants' seam to the center of his knee. *After this election, think I'll take ol' Clive's advice, hire a deputy, maybe two. Yeah. One white, one Nigger. So nobody can accuse Sheriff K. A. DeLuth of being less than fair-minded. Hope I run into Fred Sykes downtown today. Have to tell 'im, "You are three and out, buddy. This game was a blowout 'fore you even suited up."*

38

Tuesday morning, Lila's in the kitchen, sharing a second cup of coffee with Sissy, when sounds from the second floor suggest that the Lady Violet is on the move.

"What's she up to?" Lila asks Sissy.

"Lawd knows. Reckon she decided to get outta bed?"

"I sure hope not." *As if there's not enough going on today already.* Lila locks her jaw.

" 'S election day, ain't it? Mebbe she g'wan to do her patriotic duty."

"If I find out she's votin' for Kyle DeLuth, I'll wring her neck!"

"Awww, c'mon now, Missy," Sissy cackles. "She don't like the Sheriff any more than she did the Judge."

"Then why the hell did she stick with 'em both all these years?"

Sissy eyes Lila sideways. "Your mamma ain't like you, girl. She need somebody to stick to."

"Right. Like a black widow needs her web."

"It's true, girl. The Lawd give her two feet, but she ain't never learned how to stand on 'em."

"Stand on what?" Violet asks, pushing her way through the

kitchen's swinging door. She's dressed in a lavender suit that appears a tad tight across her belly; plus heavy powder, bright lipstick, and an overdose of Violettes de Nice perfume.

"Two feet? One's own ground? Principle?" Lila taunts.

"Who we talkin' 'bout?" Violet wants to know. At the counter, she picks up a leftover piece of bacon from its serving plate, holds it between two fingers, pinky elevated, as delicately as a canapé.

"You, Mamma."

Violet takes a bite. Eyeing Lila, she retorts, "Spiders eat their young."

"So far," her daughter says softly, "you're one for two."

"You cats g'wan t' fight," Sissy grumbles, "you best take it outta mah kitchen."

Violet laughs. "We're not fightin'. Lila never fights. She hits and runs. Don't you, girl o' mine?"

Lila feels herself at once rising to and resisting her mother's bait. *Don't do this, do NOT do this with her,* she tells herself and puts on a saccharine smile. "Does this mean you're over your nervous breakdown, Mamma?"

"Well, of course, it does." Violet grabs a dishtowel to wipe the bacon grease off her fingers, checks her seventeen-jewel Lady Hamilton watch. "The polls are open. You headin' out anytime soon?"

"Not till ten," Lila tells her.

"Ready when you are, Missy," Violet says, her tone awash in sweetness. Then she asks Sissy, "Any more biscuits?"

AT TEN, Lila emerges from her father's office, hoping her mother's changed her mind. But Violet sits primly at the kitchen table, purse and white gloves in hand, smiling like a birthday child awaiting her presents.

"Mamma, I've got one question before we go. You votin' for Kyle or not?"

Violet looks hurt. "Not," she says, pouting pansy-colored lips.

"Let's go then," Lila sighs, grabbing the keys to the grove truck off the rack by the back door.

"Oh, can't we take the Cadillac? I'll never get into the truck in this skirt."

Lila loathes the royal blue Hightower Cadillac. Even now, it reeks of her father's cigar smoke and her mother's pretensions. "You could drive yourself, you know."

"Oh, I'm hardly strong enough for that," Violet shoots back and hands her the Cadillac's keys.

Once they're on their way into town, Lila tells her, "I have a few errands to run. Why don't I drop you off at the polls? When you're done voting, you can walk across the street to the Women's Club. I'll pick you up there, at eleven."

Violet clasps her purse, feigns shock. "Drop me off? *By myself?* I think not! Run your errands. I'll just wait in the car till you're done."

The sunny streets of downtown Lake Esther are thronged with cars and people. Violet's eyes dart left and right. She rests her arm on the open window, waves a white-gloved hand weakly and smiles wanly at those she knows.

As if they've all come out to welcome her back, Lila fumes silently. *From what? A month of breakfast, crossword puzzles, and bourbon in bed!*

*   *   *

WHEN LILA PULLS IN FRONT of the law offices of estate attorney T. Paine Marsh, Violet sits up, eyes brightening at the prospect of being fawned over by the old gentleman. "Paine's office?" she exclaims. "Can I come?"

"Just dropping off a few files, Mamma. Won't be a minute," Lila tells her. "Wouldn't want you to exhaust yourself on the stairs," she adds, moving away from the car as quickly as she can.

Although Paine Marsh was never a part of the Judge's tight circle of Courthouse cronies, her father trusted him. "Only lawyer in town worth his shingle," Judge How-High used to declare. Marsh's family was among the county's original settlers. He's a solid, old-school gentleman, tall with an attentive stoop, white-haired, impeccably dressed in a charcoal gray suit. Today, he greets her warmly, with the affection of a special uncle for his favorite niece, and ushers her into the high-ceilinged, mahogany-paneled office that smells pleasantly of pipe smoke, leather books, and Olde English furniture polish.

When she presents him with the stack of Receipts of Sale for the Judge's Brahma herd, he shakes his head, lets out a long, slow whistle. "So, top of everything else, our Kyle could be a cattle thief?"

"You got any title transfers in your file?" Lila asks him. " 'Cause Daddy didn't have any in his."

"Not a one. Shall I present our query before or after the final vote count?" he asks, blue eyes twinkling beneath silver brows.

"Sooner's better than later, don't you think?"

HER NEXT STOP, two blocks away, is the campaign headquarters for "I LIKE SYKES, Future Sheriff."

In the seat beside her, Violet cranes forward to scan the hubbub of anxious and expectant faces milling about—*new people,* Lila notes, *nobody who'd know who she is*—then sits back dejected. "I'll wait here." She sighs, closing her eyes.

Fred Sykes, handsome in a pale blue dress shirt with a loosened red tie, stands behind the row of hunchbacked volunteers who are working the phones to get out the vote. Despite a noisy industrial-size fan in one corner, the room is hot, ripe with the smells of sweat, strong coffee, and stale pastries.

"How's it goin' today?" Lila asks him. They've spent the past four days campaigning together.

Sykes's smile is confident, but his eyes are deeply tired. "DeLuth's high jinks with the Baptists, turning the kids' petition into a public prayer list, seems to have backfired with the Methodists and Presbyterians," he says.

"Yeah, but what are the numbers? Don't the Baptists outnumber the others two to one?"

"Three to one, actually." Sykes says it ruefully.

"How about the Jaycees? The Junior League?"

"We got 'em. We got just about everybody who's not hardshell Baptist, racist, or somehow in business with our present Sheriff. The question is, will they be enough?"

"When do you think we'll know?" Lila demands.

"Polls close at seven, should know something for sure by nine. Win or lose, my wife's putting on a party at the New Haven Community Center tonight. Will you come?"

"I'm not much for parties." Lila masks a small shudder at the memory of Ginger and Charlie's barbecue. "But will you call just as soon as you hear?"

"Of course. And, Miss Hightower . . ."

She sees in his face the start of some kind of emotional

thank-you. "You're welcome, Fred Sykes, Future Sheriff," she interrupts, releasing them both. "Just beat the bastard, would you please?"

Sykes presses his lips, a determined half-frown, turns tired eyes back to the phone banks. *He's done his best,* she thinks, *but, hooah, it's still a crapshoot.*

VIOLET'S RECEPTION at the precinct is as predictable as leaf curl in late summer. At the door, Lila stands back, watches the ladies manning the polls embrace her mother as the invalid restored, with gentle, outstretched arms, soft shoulder pats, and the quiet clucking of hens.

On her part, Violet plays it to the hilt, smiling heroically, thanking all graciously for their concern, dabbing a lavender linen handkerchief delicately to dry eyes. The prodigal penitent returned.

How many times over how many years has she played exactly this part? Lila wonders. *And how often have these same women sanctioned her charade with their ritual acceptance?* Was this a white-gloved triumph of good manners over Violet's social chicanery? Or, was it a sincere act of Christian charity on their part? *Probably,* Lila realizes, *a bit of both.*

Predictably, the ladies invite Violet to join those who are breaking for lunch at the Women's Club across the street. Violet turns a preening face toward Lila, who stands at the exit, Cadillac keys in hand.

"Well, if Lila doesn't mind picking me up in an hour or two . . ."

Lila, who's had quite enough, smiles slyly. "Of course not, Mamma. Shall we say two? Or, if the juleps are as good as you remember, four?"

Violet, her back to her friends, slits her eyes, and says, in full sugar, "Maybe I'll just call you when I'm ready?"

"No, no, no!" Pearl Lee Bagwell steps forward—Pearl Lee, who was their neighbor on Beech Street before the Judge and Violet built the big house outside of town, who shared many an afternoon sherry with Violet in those early days, who is no longer allowed to drive and has a Negro chauffeur—"you go on, Lila. Jack Henry and I will see your mamma home."

Lila nods, waves, and is off, wondering how Pearl Lee's liver is holding up after all these years.

On a whim that surprises her, Lila turns the Cadillac toward Beech Street to drive past her childhood home. It's still there, the simple two-story clapboard beneath the solitary live oak, then and now, the biggest tree on the block. When they were children, Louis told her that the oak, with its tremendous trunk split just outside his window into five massive limbs, reminded him of a huge hand flung up, outstretched, toward heaven. *We believed in heaven then. When was it I stopped?*

At the end of Beech Street, Lila finds herself turning east onto Old Road, toward Pine Forest Cemetery. It's election day, and if things go as she hopes, she'll be leaving soon. She feels a gut-level urge to say a proper good-bye to Louis (she'd avoided his grave during the Judge's funeral) and to deliver an overdue apology to her father.

Just beyond the heavy wrought-iron gates at the cemetery's entrance, rusted open her entire life, she slows to make the sharp turn through the trees toward the family plot in the sunny southwest corner. Still in the shade, she sees ahead— *What the hell?*—and stomps on the brakes, hoping the thick layer of pine needles masks the sound of her sudden stop.

In the clearing, beside the Judge's grave, a tall man in

uniform holds on, leans upon a small slip of a woman. His shoulders shake; he appears to sob. With one slim hand, she braces herself stiff-armed against his squad car. With the other, she rubs his back gently, in small consoling circles. Kyle DeLuth and his wife. *Here? Now?* Then it hits her: *Election day. His first without Daddy. Of course. Is it grief alone you're feeling, Kyle? Is there a bit of fear there, too? Are you wondering, as I am, who you are without him? What are you, Kyle, without the Judge to call the shots, set the limits, define the boundaries of your existence?*

Lila shakes her head at the scene—*pure pitiful*. Slowly, she slides the Cadillac into reverse, and backs it out of sight.

On Old Dixie, heading toward her parents' house, she rolls up the Cadillac's windows, flips on the air conditioner against the afternoon's gathering heat—hot for November. The cool air reminds her how much she misses her air-conditioned apartment in Georgetown, its smell of sandalwood, its pen-and-ink prints purchased from the stalls along the Quai de Montebello, its thick-walled sense of privacy and inviolable space.

In Washington, not necessarily at the Pentagon but inside the Beltway, there was the definite air of possibility, the distinct quickening sense that it was possible, with the flourish of a pen or the strike of a gavel, to alter the course of human destiny, allay the suffering, improve the lot of millions across the country, if not the world.

So unlike the air of transparent, patent inevitability in Lake Esther where, like the Judge always said, "everyone's chickens come home to roost."

THAT NIGHT, with Violet (who'd been helped, stumbling, up the stairs by Pearl Lee's patient Jack Henry) tucked into bed, Lila sits at the desk willing the phone to ring.

Just before nine, it does. It's Sykes, sounding genuinely hopeful. "Miss Hightower, I told you we'd have the results by nine. But they're telling me it's still too close to call!"

"How much longer?"

"An hour, they're saying. Maybe less."

"Call me the second you hear," she tells him.

"Of course."

AT TEN-FOURTEEN, the ticking of the clock has become unbearable. Lila, on her second pot of hot tea, jumps at the phone's insistent ring. "Well, did we kick his ass or not?"

"Why, Missy, of course we did."

Lila feels her blood freeze. "What the hell you doin', Kyle?" she demands icily.

"Makin' the same call I've made every election night of my life," DeLuth says smoothly. "Old habits are hard to break, I guess."

"You won?" Lila's voice falters on the word, on the very idea.

"Why, yes. B'lieve it was the Nigger precincts put me over the top. Little slow addin' up their final figures."

On her end—*Goddamnit to hell!*—Lila's speechless.

"It's customary for the loser to congratulate the winner, Lila." Kyle's tone comes at her, awful as an ice pick.

"You . . . insufferable . . . bastard, rot in *hell!*" she hears herself roar and slams the receiver against the rumble of his laughter.

Damnit, Lila fumes. *Damn him, and every ignorant, goddamn, moronic, backwoods fool who voted for him! How in the hell . . .* She wrenches open the county phone book, flips the pages, scans the columns for the number.

Ruth Barrows's tobacco-raw voice answers abruptly at the first ring, *"Towncrier."*

"This whole damn town *oughtta* be cryin' if what I just heard is true!"

"Just confirmed it with the County Registrar. Who told you?"

"The horse's hind end himself. How the hell did this happen?"

"My best guess is a bunch of ballot stuffing in the Negro precincts," Ruth tells her. "The very ones you'd think would vote him out kept him in. Any idea why?"

"Classic Fascism . . . fear beats out enlightened self-interest every time." Lila says it bitterly.

"You think DeLuth fancies himself the local Il Duce?"

Lila hears the quick click of Ruth's Zippo, the hungry pull on her cigarette. "No need to study the newsreels," Lila says wearily. "Kyle's nothing but a junkyard dog gone rabid on power. In someplace reasonable, they'd get a gun and shoot him, put us all out of his misery."

39

Wednesday, the morning after the election, Principal Ed Cantrell's in a piss-poor mood.

"May!" Cantrell groans, dropping the front section of the morning's *Towncrier* on her desk. "What the hell's wrong with the people of this county? Reelecting Kyle DeLuth Sheriff, plus Jim Gibbons and Sam Higginbotham to the school board?"

"Well, at least it was close," May consoles him. "That's progress."

"They *won,* goddamnit," Cantrell rages. "Four more years of idiocy!" he grouses, spilling coffee. He grabs a towel, does a lousy job of sopping up his mess, and barrels into his office. "No calls," he snarls.

Minutes later, he hears the lobby door open, hears May call out from her desk, in welcome and in warning, "Why, Superintendent, Chairman Roberts! And *Sheriff,* good morning!"

Good Christ, now what? Cantrell groans.

"Ed in, Miss May?" he hears Superintendent Larry Bateman ask.

"Well, sure," May replies. "C'mon in. Get y'all some coffee?"

"No, thanks." It's Zeke Roberts, Chairman of the school board. "We won't be staying."

"Gentlemen," Cantrell says, rising. Seeing the fourth man in his doorway, he adds, "May, another chair in here, please."

But DeLuth, closing the door in May's face, holds up his hand. " 'S all right, Ed. My new deputy, Carl Paige." He jerks his chin toward the new man. "We'll stand." Carl Paige's look is rawboned, lanky, and vacant. But his clothes, Cantrell notes, are, like DeLuth's, military pressed.

Cantrell sits. Across from him, Superintendent Bateman clears his scrawny throat, says, "Well, Ed—", then stops. Instead, he reaches inside the breast pocket of his coat, pulls out a white Clark County School District envelope, slides it across the desk.

"What's this?"

"Letter of resignation, Ed. We'd like you to sign it, please."

"Me? You want *me* to sign it? Why? What for?"

Bateman's Adam's apple bobs like a float on a fishing line. A career bureaucrat, he eyes Zeke Roberts, then passes the buck. "The school board has directed me to ask you to leave."

Big Zeke Roberts, Chairman, nods his jowled chin. "It was unanimous, Ed."

"But, you haven't told me why. What's this all about?" *Should've seen this coming,* he thinks.

Behind Bateman and Roberts, DeLuth unfolds his arms, hitches up his uniform pants. "Oh, cut the crap, Ed. If you'd done your job in the first place, told them Nigger kids to take a hike the day they got here, the school board wouldn't have its tit in the ringer over all this. If you'd kept your mouth shut in your Youth Group, 'stead of fomenting that petition, the whole damn country wouldn't be readin' about your foolishness in the Pinko Press. To my mind, you've either gone stupid or Red. Which is it?"

The man's a goddamn lunatic, Cantrell realizes, and drops his eyes back to Zeke Roberts. "What if I refuse to resign?"

"Then we'll have to fire you, Ed. Blackball your record. You don't want that." Zeke's big bulldog head sways as he threatens Cantrell with the end of his career.

Pencil-necked Bateman, at Roberts's side, dips his head. "Ed, the board's bein' more than fair."

Cantrell sits back, his swivel chair complains. *Think, THINK, goddamnit!* "I'd like to think about this," he says. *Should I call an attorney? Who?*

"Thinking time's past, Eddie-boy." DeLuth steps forward. "Sign it or not. We're here to escort you off the premises."

"Now?" *What the hell's their hurry?*

"Ed." Pencil Neck hunches forward, apologetic. "No need to make this unpleasant. Principals and school boards part ways all the time. In your case, the board's giving you the option to resign and go. Don't make us fire you. Just go."

Beside him, bulldog Roberts purses his lips. Behind him, the lunatic DeLuth fondles the ivory handle of his gun.

Cantrell has the dizzying sensation of watching the room but not being in it, watching himself open the Superintendent's envelope and read its brief paragraph. They'd have him resign for "personal reasons." *Personal? The race of the Dare kids, a small part Indian, is* personal? *The teenagers in his Youth Group, seeing right from wrong clearer than most adults, are* personal? *Bullshit! What will be personal is May's face when she hears about this. And, Alice. Goddamnit. Alice's face when she learns the split-level's off. The question is how's he to go? Resign or be fired? Flight or fight? Scapegoat or martyr?*

Cantrell sees himself shake his own head to clear it, finds himself wondering what the squat, balding guy on his side of the desk will do.

"Well, boys," he hears his voice, miraculously steady, say, "looks like you all need a fall guy, and I'm it. I'll go,"—he sees himself lean forward, smiling—"but not without telling you you're a bunch of goddamn dinosaurs. You're trampling the law here, the very moral wall between right and wrong, to suit your own pathetic prejudices." Cantrell sees himself sign the letter with a flourish, flick the signed letter across the desk toward DeLuth, the biggest dinosaur of them all. "Today, you're getting away with it. Four more years, maybe a few after that. But not forever. Someday, your kind will be extinct. Schoolkids will study your bones, wonder how in the hell you were allowed to live."

40

Wednesday midmorning, Lila, dressed in workshirt, pants, and heavy grove boots, steps off the porch and strides toward the far-off sounds of the picking crew at work in the southwest-corner grove.

This being early November, she's bound for the acres of big, arching navel trees, where the crew has been working to strip the heavy limbs of their first-ripe fruit. This being the day after the election, the steel-gray clouds, threatening an afternoon thunderstorm, match her mood perfectly.

In passing, she studies the fragrant oval fruit on the long rows of tangerine trees; the larger, rounder Temples; the pouty-lipped tangeloes; and the freckled Parson Browns. All appear to be ripening nicely toward their January-through-March picking dates. *Though, God knows, I'll be long gone by then,* she remembers. "Won't I?" she wonders aloud, casting suspicious eyes toward the darkening sky.

She charts a diagonal course through the orderly tree rows, across the thick sandy soil that grasps and battles each step, toward the throaty calls and sporadic laughter of the pickers, each on his own high ladder. Finally, she spots the big green grove truck and, standing beside it issuing pick tickets (one for each box picked), foreman Franklin Dare.

"Miss Lila." He drops his chin in greeting, raises watchful eyes to meet hers.

"Well, he won the election. I guess you know that."

"Yes, ma'am."

"But, he's lost his support in Tallahassee. I just spoke with the new Governor and he's definitely on our side."

Dare says nothing. But a nearly imperceptible shake of his head reminds her they are not alone. All around them, the grove's gone quiet as a graveyard.

Of course. "Let's take a walk, shall we?" she suggests and turns toward the secondary grove road behind them.

"Nate," Dare calls. A dark figure descends a nearby ladder. Dare hands him the ticket book and the pen, says, "Thank ye, Nate," and falls into step beside her. He has the smell of lye soap, leather work gloves, and something else—*cornbread?*—upon him.

"Sorry," she tells him softly.

"Most of 'em don't cotton to the Sheriff any more'n ye do, ma'am. But, this bizness 'bout my younguns . . . well, t'ain't that mine are any better than their'n."

"You're right." *What was I thinking?*

"My younguns jus' are what they are, that's all. And cain't nobody say diff'rent."

Dare's demeanor—as politely considerate of the Negroes on his crew as he is of her—reminds her of something his son, Daniel, said at the newspaper office. "Got hisself a Silver Star, a Purple Heart, and everythin'," the boy said. And Lila knows, from a multitude of attended ceremonies, that the Army's Silver Star is awarded "for gallantry in action against the enemy." *What did he do?* she wonders. *Who did he save, and at what cost?* Dare radiates the decency of a man who'd refuse to leave a buddy behind. *It's an admirable quality, but not advantageous,* she thinks, *against a viper like Kyle DeLuth.* Kyle requires powerful reinforcement.

"Fortunately, the Governor-elect agrees with you."

Dare stops at the road. They both do. He stands for a moment, hands motionless at his sides, eyes studying the approaching thunderclouds. "What's that mean, ma'am, exactly?"

"It means, one way or another, you and your children are goin' to get your day in court. But, I'm afraid you're goin' to need more evidence than you have. It might mean a quick trip back to North Carolina to collect some specific documents."

"But the crop—"

"Will get picked, whether you're here or not." Her tone deliberately issues the order. She watches his resistance flicker briefly then retreat.

"Yes, ma'am," he says, flatly, with all due respect.

LATER, WHEN THE STORM BREAKS, Lila finds herself alone—Sissy's gone out grocery shopping, and Violet's retired to her bed "to nap." No doubt, Dare's got the crew in the shelter of the storage shed until the worst of the torrent passes.

Standing at the window of her father's office, Lila watches the downpour, streaked silver by the frequent flash of lightning, struck mute by the heavy drum of thunder.

Dimly, as if across a great divide, she hears the Westminster chimes and thinks of London, the great green expanse of Bushey Park, the burst of buzz bombs, the confusion of fires and ambulances afterward. Again, the chimes, this time too near, too thin to be the real Westminster. *Good Lord, someone's at the front door! Who the hell's out in weather like this?*

She opens her door on the apologetic young officer—rainwater streaming off his cap, drenching his olive drab jacket—and

236 Susan Carol McCarthy

recoils from the memory of that other young officer standing just there, just so, with the yellow telegram announcing
Louis's death. She notes the sharp planes of his cheeks and chin,
the wariness of his eyes, the chevron on his shoulder sleeve.
He's not as young as she thought.

"Sergeant. Please come in."

He steps inside bringing the scents of damp wool and military starch with him.

"What in the world brings you out in a storm like this?"

"Hand delivery, ma'am. Major L. Randall Hightower."

"Really?" It was Jazz's joke to address important mail with
her middle name, sealed with Top Secret security tape.

"Is he here, ma'am?"

"He who?"

"The Major. No offense, ma'am, but this one's marked Eyes
Only."

"*I'm* Major Lila Randall Hightower, Sergeant, Special Assistant to Lieutenant General J. P. Atkinson who, no doubt,
sent me that case you're carrying."

The Sergeant's eyes flatten. "Ma'am," he says, striking a
salute.

"At ease, Sergeant," she tells him. "Do you have a pen?"

ALONE, Lila carries the flat, black attaché case back to the office, sets it in the center of the Judge's desk, and stares at the
label. Her name, in Jazz's careful hand.

What are you up to? she wonders. Knowing Jazz, it could be
anything: an official memo or a *Stars and Stripes* cartoon, a Top
Secret report, or the review of some new New York jazz club.
Always, always there would be one message within another,
one meaning overlaying the next. Like Art Tatum, his favorite

piano player, Jazz could mentally riff, scat, jam on the surface, while underneath there was always an intense strategic intelligence at work, in tight, tactical command. Like Tatum, what others could only imagine, Jazz could envision and ruthlessly execute.

Ike had spotted him early—they'd been together in North Africa—and reeled him into Supreme Headquarters in London. At Bushey Park, Jazz had spotted Lila, not in person but by name on a series of Air Reconnaissance maps and their attendant analyses. He'd strolled into the W.A.C. map room demanding, "Where's this genius named Hightower?" Then, he'd taken her to task for a number of small misinterpretations. Finally, he'd quietly had her transferred to G-2, Army Intelligence, authoring their daily reports to the Supreme Command.

He picked her, he claimed, because she had "the brains of a General, and the good sense not to blush, or back down from an asinine superior officer, like I was, the day we met."

Their relationship was all business, until Paris, and the devastating massacre of America POWs at Malmedy—"Eighty-one of our boys with bullets in their heads; their bodies left to rot in the snow. Damnit, Lila, we knew those butchers in the Waffen SS were on the move! With better intelligence, we might have rerouted that battalion, instead of sending them in, like pigs to slaughter." In the emotional maelstrom that was Paris, January '45, they sought solace in the smoky jazz caves off Rue de la Huchette, and found it, finally, at the Hotel Bonchasse.

He'd made promises then: "Soon as this war's over, I'm out of this Army *and* my marriage." Promises that Ike rendered impossible with their transfer, after V-E Day, to EUCOM. And her temporary assignment to W.A.C. Command for the Berlin

Airlift, the most harrowing 328 days of her life. After Berlin, he'd promised her Virginia: "Just you, me, and half a dozen horses, kid." Then General Ridgeway summoned them to Korea for Operations Thunderbolt, Killer, Ripper, and Piledriver, and the frustrating "armistice without peace." Then Ike offered up the prestigious War College, the chance to set straight the Army's next generation. The excuses were endless until, just six weeks ago, she'd dared to believe Jazz again: "This time I really mean it, HiLi. We are history!" And now he was Assistant Chief of Staff.

I can't do this anymore, Jazz. She eyes the package, her name in his hand. *It's been too much, too long. I just can't do it anymore.*

But it won't hurt to look, will it? a part of her argues. *To hear what he says, to see what he's sent? Of course not.* She reaches for scissors and slits the Top Secret sealing tape. Inside, with no greeting or explanation, is a vinyl disk, a 45 record, with its label removed.

Curious, she switches on her father's hi-fi, removes the record from its anonymous sleeve, and sets the turntable spinning.

"Perdu," the voice croons, an older, mellowed version of the young male chansonnier they discovered in Paris. "Lost," he despairs, with a melancholy swell of strings. Beyond help, beyond hope, he feels like a king toppled from his throne, a priest bereft of his faith, a tenor robbed of his voice. *"Chérie combien je suis perdu sans toi"*—Darling, I am lost without you.

Oh, Jazz, how many dark, down-the-alley record shops did you have to comb to find this? She resists the memory of young Charles Aznavour on stage in the Rue de la Huchette, light sculpting his impudent, ironic face, shadows cloaking the effect of his songs on the couples in the corner booths. *Oh, Jazz . . .* She wills her fingers to lift the needle, turn over the record.

The reverse is worse. *Did he know it would be?* Accompanied by a single, plaintive piano, Aznavour pleads, *"Reviens, mon amour, ma vie"*—Come back, my love, my life. A miserable repentant, he admits his mistake, begs her forgiveness, entreats her to return, to lay her head once more *"au creux de mon épaule"*—in the hollow of my shoulder.

This time, the pictures hold: The rain-soaked walks to the Hotel Bonchasse, the entwined rides up the ancient iron elevator, the shameless, shared shedding, begun in the dark hallway, of coats, clothes, zippers, clasps. Inside the shuttered room, on the small, swaybacked bed, Lila recalls, the knowing slide of his hand on her hip, the greedy glide of arms, legs, tongues—*oh, Jazz*—turning, twisting, teasing—*oh, you, oh*—until the swelling tide, bidden, the surging waves, ridden, broke—OH!—over them, on them, in them—*YES!*—heaving them apart, breathless, rolling them, softly, back together—*yes*—and afterward, always afterward, in the sighing ebb, the warm, safe settling into—*where else?*—the hollow of his shoulder.

The song ends. In silence, Lila drifts toward the window, stares out at the now whispering streams of rain. She has the sense that someone—Sissy, Franklin, and the picking crew—will be returning soon. And she struggles to regain herself.

Oh, Jazz . . . What was it about him that had always pushed her past thought, past reason, into the abyss of all-forgetting passion? And kept her there, in the private heaven and hell of their nine-year affair?

In the early days, he'd seemed like some powerful planet pulling her into orbit around him. Like the moon to his Earth, or Earth to his sun, she'd surrendered, hungrily, to his greater gravity. But through the years, the endless circling had left her dizzy, the broken promises tilted her off course. She'd begun to wobble, and to wonder: *Was it his irresistible pull, or my own aching need that kept us spiraling through time and space together?*

Oh, Jazz . . . Lila looks out at the rain, abating. *You and I both know that you've never, in your entire life, been the least bit lost. And I . . . well, I'm not exactly sure—not yet—but I am most certainly past* perdu.

LATE THAT AFTERNOON, Lila's outside settling up the day's wages with Dare and the crew. Sissy opens the back door and calls, "Phone's for you!"

" 'Scuse me, Franklin," Lila says and calls back, "Can you take a message, please?"

"Somebody from Washin'ton! Sounds important!"

"Franklin, sorry, will you finish up?" she asks, moving toward the house without waiting for his answer. *Jazz?* she gasps inwardly, putting on a mask of mild interest to get past Sissy and into the office, behind the closed door. At the desk, she sits, takes a breath, picks up the waiting receiver. "Hello?"

"Lila, is that you? It's Myrt! Myrt O'Reilly. You are one tough cookie to get hold of. Sorry to hear about your father."

Lila pictures Myrt's broad, smiling face, her stocky frame, her ultra-efficient manner with the men loading and unloading the planes at Wiesbaden during their shared stint in the Airlift.

"Myrt, it's been years! Five? Six? How in the world are you? *Where* in the world are you?"

Myrt treats Lila to the hearty chuckle she remembers. "I'm in D.C.—where you should be, dear girl—on Secretary Hobby's staff."

"*Secretary* Hobby! Bet *that* took some gettin' used to."

For Lila, and W.A.C.'s everywhere, Colonel Oveta Culp Hobby was their patron saint, organizer and first commander of the Women's Army Auxiliary Corps. They revered Hobby for getting the Army's all-male Top Brass to accord female volunteers the full military rights they deserved as soldiers in the Women's Army Corps. After the war, Hobby retired and went home to Texas. But early last year, Ike tapped her to become the first Secretary of Health, Education and Welfare, the nation's only female cabinet member.

"Well, we don't have to salute her, if that's what you mean," Myrt says. "And, as you can imagine, I do *not* miss the uniforms!" Poor Myrt. She'd spent months complaining that neither olive drab nor khaki did a thing for her florid, freckled looks. "But, what about *you*, kiddo? Had enough sunshine? Ready to get back to work?"

"Well," Lila stalls, wondering how much Myrt knows, and from whom. "Rumor is, as the Assistant's Assistant, I get a whole new cubbyhole."

"So I heard. But, hell, the only war going on now is over budgets between the Joint Chiefs. All the big action's in our area."

"What do you mean?"

"Don't they have newspapers down there? In Health, we've got a whole country full of children to vaccinate against polio. Hospitals, nursing homes, and treatment centers to build. In Education, 'cause our vets are populating like rabbits, we've got seven billion dollars' worth of schools to build—in the next *three* years! And Welfare—the latest report is we'll have ten million more Americans on Social Security before the end of next year!"

"Somebody's gonna be busy," Lila teases, impressed.

"Well, hopefully, one of those somebodies is you."

"What?"

"Listen, Lila. On the Q.T., we've got half a dozen high-level posts to fill but quick! Like I told Secretary Hobby, you'd be a dream-come-true liaison for us with the boys on the Hill. Or, if you wanted something more specific, this school program's a tiger in need of somebody to grab its tail."

"But General Atkinson—"

Myrt interrupts, "Has kept your wagon hitched to his stars long enough, don't you think?"

"Well, I—uh—"

"Will think about it, at least?"

"Well, yes, Myrt, of course. Once my head stops spinning."

"General Atkinson—who was not happy to hear from me, by the way—says you're due back to him on Tuesday, December first. Any chance you could come back a day earlier, meet with the Secretary and me?"

41

"District Attorney's office." A young woman, a girl's voice really, attempts no-nonsense efficiency.

"Yes, hello. This is Ruth Cooper Barrows, *Lake Esther Towncrier*. Hamp in?"

"Please hold while I see if the District Attorney is available."

Okay, girlie, you do that, Ruth thinks, dragging on the last of her Pall Mall, considering if there's time to light another. She pictures the District Attorney's small Courthouse office with its tiny reception area out front. *Swivel 'round your chair, honey, and ask him if he'll take my call.*

"Miz Barrows, I'll put you through, now," the voice decrees.

Good, Ruth thinks, grinding out her stub, grabbing a pen.

"Hamp Berry."

Ruth pictures the frat-boy handsome face, bores in. "*Mr.* Berry, I'm investigating a rumor that the Governor-elect has asked you to sue the local school board for denying the Dare family due process."

"Off the record, *Miz* Barrows, the Governor-elect has called me twice."

"And?"

"Off the record, we've discussed the political ramifications involved in the Great State of Florida suing the Board of Public Instruction of one of its counties at this time."

"And?" Ruth shakes another cigarette out of its pack.

"And, off the record, the Governor-elect has suggested an alternate, less inflammatory tack."

"AND?" Ruth asks, scanning her blotter. *Where the hell is my lighter?*

"Off the record, the Governor-elect suggests a civil suit, a Bill of Complaint by the Dares filed against the Board and Superintendent Larry Bateman."

"Who's going to do that?" She gives up on the lighter, tugs open her desk drawer in search of a matchbox.

"Off the record . . ."

"Oh, hell, Hamp, I heard you the first time. I won't quote you."

"Not even as a 'Courthouse source'?"

"All right!" Ruth strikes a match, inhaling quickly. "But who's going to take the case?"

"I b'lieve, at this very moment, the lovely Miss Hightower is twisting the arm of the highly esteemed Mr. Thomas Paine Marsh."

"Paine Marsh? Really? Think he'll take it?"

"Paine's a good man. Fair. And the Dares' complaint is cut-and-dried. Either they're one-eighth or they're not. The bigger question is whether the Fifth Circuit will hear it."

"Judge Woods?" *Could be trouble.*

"Winston K., the Third. High side is he and Marsh are life-long huntin' buddies. Low side's that he's got Congressional ambitions, might be disinclined to risk an unpopular ruling."

"Jesus. What's the timing?"

"Well—and, of course, I never said this—the Governor-elect wants it wrapped up before Christmas, so there's no overflow onto his inauguration. That's seven, eight weeks, Ruth. Requires a judge who'll keep the defense attorney's feet to the fire."

"Who's the school board got?"

"Nobody yet. Ticklish assignment. But lots of potential publicity."

"What're the Dares' chances?"

"With Lila *and* the Governor-elect in their corner, Judge Woods on the bench? Fair to middlin', I'd say."

Jesus. Ruth grounds out her smoke in the ash-filled tray. "Thanks, Hamp."

"Welcome, Ruth. Call anytime."

She hangs up the phone, stands, slips her pack of Pall Malls, pen, and a small notepad into her jacket. Inside the pocket, her fingers find her missing lighter. *That's where the damn thing is,* she thinks, and steps outside, blinking in the late-morning glare. At the curb, she squints up Oak Street toward the two-story brick offices of Thomas Paine Marsh, Esq. Parked out front, the big green Hightower Groves pickup is easy to spot.

Eyeing the sky's thin clouds, relishing the fresh air, Ruth strolls a pleasant block up Oak and leans casually against the green truck's curbside wheel well.

Minutes later, Lila Hightower emerges from Marsh's office, dressed, as usual, in dark tailored slacks and a crisp, open-necked shirt. *Does the woman even own a skirt?* Ruth wonders, as she waves and calls, "Mission accomplished?"

Lila's smile appears triumphant. "Had lunch yet?" she calls back.

Ruth reads the promise of details in Lila's eyes and shakes her head.

"Hop in then." The younger woman swings easily into the truck's driver's seat and leans over to wrench and push open the rider's door.

Ruth, regretting her own short legs and narrow skirt, grabs the door handle and jamb and launches herself—*All the grace of an old cow!*—into the truck. "Mind if we stop by my office?" She's suddenly remembered: "I've come off without my purse."

"Oh, please." Lila laughs. "I'm only talking Uncle Willie's. My treat."

"Uncle Willie—the peanut man?"

Lila glances at her sideways. "How long you lived here?"

"Three years last month."

"And you've not eaten out back of Uncle Willie's?"

At the end of Oak Street, Lila wheels the truck onto the highway then whips it abruptly off the shoulder at the massive live oak where crude, hand-painted signs announce "Hot Boilt P-Nuts" and "BBQ Pork." A temporary-looking, tin-roofed structure slumps against the tree trunk. To one side, an ancient, wiry Negro stirs a big, steaming pot suspended over a smoking wood fire. At the sound of the truck, he turns and, beneath the wide brim of his palmetto hat, welcomes them with a crooked, toothless smile.

"Hey, li'l Mith," he lisps warmly.

"Hey, yourself, Uncle Willie! This here's Ruth. Come for a couple of PBJs. Okay?"

Ruth negotiates a clumsy, jerking slide onto the hard-packed, nutshell-crusted ground and nods her acknowledgment to Lila's introduction.

"Comin' rithe up," Uncle Willie says.

Ruth trails Lila behind the big oak, past a second shed fragrant with roasting pork, to a shady picnic table next to the small stream—a large culvert, actually—that parallels the highway. At the half dozen tables, covered with red-and-white oilcloth, Ruth notes that she and Lila are the only white people present.

"Locals only," Lila tells Ruth as a few dark faces, mostly men, nod respectful recognition in their direction.

"What's a PBJ?" Ruth sits, facing Lila.

"Well, it ain't peanut butter and jelly." Lila chuckles, then looks up and smiles at the tiny, brown gnome of a woman (*Mrs. Willie?* Ruth wonders) with the loaded tin tray.

"Plate uh pork, bag uh bolt nuts, jar uh 'shine." Mrs. Willie announces each item she places in front of them.

"What flavor today, Annie?" Lila holds up the Mason jar half full of liquid the color of white wine.

The old woman squints at the glass, sucks on a side tooth, with a quick little kissing sound, and replies, "Right good pear, Missy." Her nod encourages them to give it a try.

Ruth lifts her jar and sniffs. A sharp, familiar fume sears through her sinuses. Bracing herself, she sips. The taste is a surprise . . . clean, mildly fruity, with a quick afterburn not unlike a good brandy.

Lila smacks her lips. "Lovely," she tells Mrs. Willie, who sucks her tooth again in gratified approbation, picks up her tray, and sidles off.

Lila plunges a plastic fork into her shredded pork and Ruth follows suit. The meat is juicy tender, glistening with a vinegary-pepper sauce, and delicious. There's a small side of slaw.

"Best barbecue I've had in years," Ruth says, enjoying the moment. But, at the same time, wanting to broach the subject of Paine Marsh and the Dares' civil suit. *Eat first,* she decides.

Lila, swigging 'shine, levels her eyes over the rim of her jar. "He's agreed to take it," she says quietly.

"Marsh? The suit?" *Terrific!* "How'd you get him to say yes?"

Lila shrugs. "Asked a good man to do the right thing. Piece of cake."

Lila's nonchalance, her air of utter confidence, prompts a question that Ruth is surprised she hasn't asked before. "What do you do in the W.A.C.'s, Lila?"

"Currently?" The younger woman squares her shoulders, snaps a wry salute. "Special Assistant to General J. P. Atkinson, Assistant Chief of Staff, ma'am."

Jesus. "Top Brass!"

"Originally, G-2, Army Intelligence, for S.H.A.E.F.— Supreme Headquarters, Allied Expeditionary Forces."

"No wonder you thought Paine Marsh a piece of cake," Ruth says, impressed. "Though, of course, some people I know might say 'Army Intelligence' is a conflict of terms."

Lila chuckles. "Some people *I* know would prove your people right."

"So, after the war, you . . . ?"

"After V-E Day, we moved to Berlin, part of EUCOM, the Airlift." She shudders. "After that, we spent an eternity in Korea, then back to the War College."

"What the hell are you doing *here?*"

Lila frowns, takes another swig, tightens her lips around the taste. "Officially, I'm on extended leave to inter my father, comfort and settle the affairs of my grieving mother."

"Unofficially?"

"I'd say I'm conducting a little personal archaeology."

On whom? For what? "Digging up dirt? Can I help? I'm pretty good at it."

"Dirt!" Lila spits out the four-letter word as if it were the pinnacle of profanity. "There's enough dirt in my father's files to reroute the St. Johns River. No, Ruth, I'm not digging for dirt."

"What then?"

"Oh, hell, I don't know . . . It's . . . well . . ." Lila drops her gaze, bows her head, thinking. After a moment, her eyes flick back to Ruth. "Do you get ever worn out? You know, with the way things are? I mean, the way the world—or the people who seem to run it just don't give a damn about what happens beyond their own puny selves—just wears me right *out*."

"Some days—this past week, for example—you bet."

"What I don't understand is—what *are* they thinking? How does my father, for example, who loved this county, nurtured it like a child, helped it grow—how does he leave it, like an orphan, in the hands of a straw dog like Kyle DeLuth? What goes on in the minds of the men who run for the school board—do the community an important service—then *arbitrarily* deny innocent children their education? Or the men in the Senate letting Joe McCarthy run roughshod over the Bill of Rights as if it never even existed? How can they argue about whether or not he should be censured?"

Ruth grimaces. "Your guess is as good as mine."

"These men don't stand *for* anything but themselves," Lila says, staring down into her drink. "They stand *against* whatever fears will help get them reelected. And they're the only ones who are truly free—free to trample the rights, the individual liberties, the justice due anyone who gets in their way."

Mrs. Willie arrives with a jug, to refill their Mason jars. Lila thanks her with an upheld hand. "I'm switching to sweet tea, please."

Ruth nods—"Me, too."—and turns back to Lila. "Plato."

"Pardon me?"

"Or maybe it was Plato quoting Socrates: 'A society is only as just, and as safe, as the justice and protection provided the least of its members.' "

Lila pauses to consider this. "My father used to say there were two types of politicians. Those who rise on the scaffolds of the people's hopes and dreams—Lincoln, for example, Churchill. And those who ride in on the back of the people's fears—Hitler, Mussolini, even Truman, with his Smith Act, his Loyalty Oaths, his Internal Security Acts. Why, Truman set the stage for Joe McCarthy, just as surely as my father did for Kyle DeLuth!"

Ruth cups her empty jar in both hands. "And where does Eisenhower fit in?"

"Eisenhower's pure Army, Ruth. A West Point warrior. Which means securing of positions, procurement of provisions, and preparation for the next war. Not to mention payback to the big contractors that put him there in the first place."

"Spread the money among your friends, and consolidate the enemy?"

"Absolutely. My father called it 'The Terrifying It.' 'Doesn't matter what It is,' he'd say, 'so long as people are scared silly of It, and a candidate can convince them that he's the one who's gonna save 'em from It!' "

"The Red Menace, the Yellow Horde—"

"The Colored anything, around here."

Mrs. Willie returns, removes their empty Mason jars. Both women murmur "Thank you" as she replaces them with sweating tumblers of iced tea.

Ruth eyes Lila. "So how do you go back?"

"I'm not sure I will. It's been ten years, Ruth. After ten years, the questions have changed from 'Can I?' or 'Can't I?' to 'Will I?' or 'Won't I?' From what I'd call 'competence' to—well— 'conscience.' After ten years and two wars, it seems to me that in some ways the world has changed completely. But in other ways—ways that count—nothing's changed at all. Or, maybe— given that we have The Bomb, and men who are willing, if not itching, to use it—we're worse off now than we were before."

"Then, perhaps you'll stay?"

"Impossible." Lila juts her jaw. But abruptly, she adds, "Oh, hell!" and gives a deliberate shudder, a hollow laugh. "Who knows where I'll wind up?!"

In the lined rim of Lila's eyes, the small break in her voice, the quiver in her right hand reaching for her glass, Ruth senses, again, the whole-lot-more behind what-meets-the-eye. "None of us knows, really, what lies ahead, but,"—Ruth shrugs—"*Illegitimus non carborundum!*"

"Illie-what?"

Ruth pulls out pen and notepad from her pocket, writes the words, rips out the sheet and hands it to Lila. "One of my husband's favorite sayings—*Illegitimus non carborundum:* 'Don't let the bastards wear you down.' "

Lila smiles. "Plato again?"

"No," Ruth says. "General 'Vinegar Joe' Stilwell. A born Floridian, by the way. In Burma, he also picked up one of *my* favorite quotes—'Keep smiling,' he'd say, 'the higher the monkey climbs, the more you can see of his backside.' "

"But, who gives the monkey the right to the better view?" Lila asks sharply.

"Why, he does, of course. Until somebody climbs up behind him and knocks him out of the way."

"Another monkey just like him?"

"Not necessarily. I've been known to climb a few trees. And how about you, Lila? Afraid of heights?"

"Well, no." Lila folds Ruth's note into a small white square, slips it into the side pocket of her slacks. "Not exactly."

42

Late afternoon Friday, Daniel peers across the field to that place in the distance where the dirt road to their property intersects the blacktop into town. *Any time now,* he thinks. And then, he sees it, the hump and flash of dark metal, the moving mound of dust rising off the road. "They're home!" he hollers to Aunt Lu who, with the girls, is shooing the chickens back into the coop.

Daniel, man of the house, rises out of his porch rocker, solemnly sets his .22 aside, safety on, muzzle up, and leaps off the porch yelling "Wahoo!"

Coming up the drive, Pap and Uncle Will wave hello from each side of the truck. Daniel bolts across the clearing to Pap's side and greets him with, "Kin I go, Pap? Kin I? Now?"

"Yes, boy," Pap tells him through the window, "ye kin go. Be home 'fore full dark."

"I will," Daniel calls over his shoulder as he races across the field, past the hives, toward the sandy path through the woods. He's been waiting all week for this moment, endured the long days of work and boredom with the girls, the nights of schooling with Miz Jenkins, the short, blocky teacher from the Christian school, and the photographs for Miz Barrows and her newspaper story on their "School at Home." It had been a hard week to put by. The girls had pestered him something awful. But, this moment, the hours just ahead of him will make all of it worthwhile. This is the day he's going to catch his first catfish, Seminole style.

In the woods, Daniel races past the now familiar landmarks, the long-needle pines, the big, tripping tree root, the magnolia by the banks of the river, the hook right, away from the water, the sudden fork that takes him deeper into the woods, and, at last, the clearing surrounded by tall pines.

Sampson stands, grinning welcome, by the fire.

"Did I beat them bee guards?" Daniel peers up at the buzzing basket, the tangle of bones tinkling below.

"Cain't. Wings faster than feet, heh?"

Watching the basket, Daniel's mood suddenly darkens. "Need t'get me one of these," he says.

"Guard bees?"

"Pap, town stuff." Daniel wags his head to shake off his thoughts. "Ready to fish?" he asks eagerly, avoiding the ancient eyes that probe him.

"Grab your goblin today, heh?" Sampson nods, and points the way, down a different path, out of the clearing. Behind him, Daniel marvels at, and tries to mimic, the way Ol' Sampson's big feet take such light, silent steps.

They speak quietly along the way. Sampson reminds him that a catfish doesn't see real well, but it's got the hearing of a hunt dog, so there'll be no talking once they reach the water. He's scouted the spot, a murky hole between the knees of a cypress in a slowed-down crook of the river.

In his haste to leave home, Daniel's forgotten his kerchief. Sampson takes off his and carefully wraps the red cloth around Daniel's right arm, from above the boy's elbow to his wrist, leaving the tail of it extended between his finger and his thumb. "Shake it at 'im, like you stickin' out your tongue," he instructs. "Big fish gonna come at you, gonna swallow your arm whole. Don't be 'fraid. Remember you bigger. Jus' grabble onto whatever you can, inside. Then, lock your other hand on his lower lip. Don't worry 'bout his teeth, ain't nothin' but nubs, heh?"

AT THE RIVERBANK, Sampson points and winks. He pantomimes wiggling the red tongue, shoving his right arm forward, grabbing his elbow with his left, raising both high above his head, and throwing something heavy onto the bank. Daniel nods solemnly and wades in.

The water is about the same temperature as the air, so the boy feels at first only the sensation of wet, sweeping from his ankles up to his waist. He steps toward and around the big folded knob, like a bent knee, of cypress root. In front of the dark narrow hole, between two knees, the water is the color of brown ink with a faint rainbow of oil slick on top.

Daniel takes a deep breath then dives under, extending both hands gently in front of him. *Cain't see a thing, but somethin's there, slick and smooth.* Moving his hands slowly upward, he feels the shape of a fin, on top, angling sharply up to the left. "Higher on the left puts his head on the right," Sampson had said. Daniel backs off and rises for air.

At the surface, he looks at Sampson, points to the right, and drops down again. Underwater, he wiggles the cloth tongue and thrusts his right fist in the spot where he guesses the head to be. There's a sensation of—nothing! *Where'd he go?* Suddenly there's a vicious clamping, a painful turning on his upper arm. *I'm in him!* Daniel realizes, and, in shock, opens his fingers onto the fish's soft, squishy innards. *His lower lip!*

Where is it? Daniel slides his left hand up, above his elbow, finds the hard ridge of fish lip, grabs it, and hoists his arm overhead.

Lungs about to burst, he kicks up, yells when he hits the surface, "I got him! I got him!" And, suddenly, Sampson's there, too, grabbing gills, yanking the monster, the ancient goblin face, off his arm and onto the sandy bank.

"You shore did!" Sampson laughs. "Wheweee! Look at 'im! Twenty pounds, for sure." Then scowling at the catfish, he crows, "The boy got you, Ol' Ugly. His name's Dan'l. And he got you, all by hisself!"

Daniel is awash with water, pride, and the remains of his fear. His upper arm is rubbed raw and sore. But, the sight of his fish, now strung up by its huge lower lip on a nearby tree branch, thrills him.

This time, it's Daniel who, under the Ol' Seminole's patient direction, digs the hole in the sand beneath his fish, and guts and cuts the meat off its carcass. Later, refilling the hole, he offers the Indian the catfish head for stew. But Sampson refuses, saying, "First head, all yours."

It's getting on dusk when the two of them return to Sampson's clearing, Daniel carrying the monstrous fish head by the piece of wire strung through its lip, Sampson carting the leather pouches filled with water and fillets.

The boy insists that the old man keep one of the pouches. Sampson accepts, on condition that he walk the boy home.

There's a hiss and a crackle as Sampson lights a gas lantern with a stick from his still-smoldering fire. Daniel watches him carry the lantern to the third chee-kee, the one where he works, and rummage around for what looks like a small, woven bowl.

"What's that for?" he asks.

"See soon, heh?" Sampson tells him. The old Indian crosses the clearing to the tree where the bee basket hangs quietly on guard. Only when he holds the bowl in front of the basket does Daniel realize *it's not a bowl atall,* but the basket's lid. With quick but gentle hands, Sampson seals the basket, and removes it from its perch, the web of fish bones tinkling below.

"Why'd you do that?" Daniel wants to know.

"Make you a present of it," the old man says, then, holding the now-buzzing basket in one hand, the lantern in the other, nods, "Go now, heh?"

Daniel scoops up the catfish head and the dripping leather pouch. Together, they retrace his steps through the woods and the field to the cabins in the clearing.

43

K. A. DeLuth parks his freshly washed and waxed Sheriff's car in front of his Main Street office downtown. *Do folks good to see their reelected Sheriff workin' hard on a Saturday afternoon,* he thinks, chuckling, as he grabs file folders and the fat paper sack from Big Nick out of the backseat.

Unlocking and relocking the door, flipping on the light, he notes that his new deputy has swept the floor, polished the wooden reception counter, and stacked the mail neatly on his desk.

He'd hired Carl Paige on Clive Cunningham's recommendation. Paige was Sarah Cunningham's younger brother, a Korean War vet, and, like Clive said, "Carl ain't the sharpest knife in the drawer, but he can shoot straight and knows how to take orders." Though it had only been a few days, DeLuth was enjoying having Deputy Paige around. On top of everything else, *he's a tidy sonofabitch. Should've thought of this myself years ago.*

Seated at his desk, DeLuth removes the gunmetal gray cash box from its spot, beneath the false bottom of his lower desk drawer.

Tossing the paper sack into the trash, he recounts the stacked bills of his Bolita share into the box, enters the amount and new total in the small journal, and replaces the box in his bottom drawer. *Not as big a take as last weekend, Halloween night, but better than the week before. Next week should be better still,* he thinks, grinning at the memory that, a few hours earlier, *that Greek Nigger didn't like my demand for a bigger piece of the pie, but he's too smart to say no.*

Turning to the top file folder, he reads again the letter from Paine Marsh, requesting "copies of any and all documents proving transfer of title of the following animals purchased by Howard T. Hightower from breeder B. T. Hallwelle of Houston, Texas." The list contained references to practically his entire herd!

Damn the ol' man! Toward the end, the Judge had promised DeLuth again and again that he'd sign the papers. Kyle had even gone so far as to secure the forms from Hallwelle in Texas, type them up himself, and present them, at the Judge's bedside, at least half a dozen times. But, there'd always been something that got in the way—a coughing attack, the spitting up of blood, too tired, needed some sleep, and, finally, Lila, come home to bar him from the bedside.

Setting the unsigned stack of forms aside, DeLuth pulls out a blank sheet of paper and another document, an old writ signed by the Judge last year.

In the sharp sunlight pooling on his desk, DeLuth begins, slowly at first, then with increasing confidence, to practice the hacking verticals, the slashing crossbars of the Judge's distinctive initials H.T.H., mastering later, the slicing horizontals, looping, like a snake, in between and after.

AROUND SIX, on his way out to drop the big envelope into Marsh's mail slot, DeLuth phones Birdilee at the hospital to suggest a steak supper at the Cattlemen's Club. She agrees "so long as you don't mind my Pink Lady uniform. And it's just us, right? I don't have what it takes to make nice with the Cunninghams tonight."

But, of course, Clive and Sarah were there—he'd known they would be—with the Matthewses, the MacGregors, and the Fraziers. And they'd all wound up, the county's biggest beef men and their wives, at the banquet table in the back. Too bad Birdilee was so tuckered out. She was quiet all evening and, on the way home, closed her eyes claiming she was "too tired to talk." But, not him! No way! He was all keyed up over the evening's triumph—the first night, "the first *time,* Birdilee!" he'd actually "sat with the big boys and felt like I *belonged*! All those years—ten *years,* Birdilee!—of being the Judge's chief boot-licker are behind us! Thanks to Ol' Ben and Big Nick, we are *in* like Flynn!"

Around ten, having squired Birdilee home, he heads out again, in his truck, to meet the boys. He'd guaranteed Zeke Roberts that this whole mess with the Nigger Dares and their suit against the school board would go away. *And he, by God, was a man of his word!*

44

After supper Saturday night, Daniel sits on the porch in Pap's rocker, cradling his father's shotgun in his lap, staring up at the slice of melon moon. *Wish he was here,* the boy thinks. *Or better yet, that there'd been a way for Pap and Uncle Will to take me with them.*

It was all that lawyer man Mr. Marsh's fault. He was the one give Pap the list of things—marriage certificates, death notices, wills, and the like—to collect from up home.

Up home. If they drove straight through, taking turns like they planned, Pap and Uncle Will are there by now. He can picture them, sitting on Uncle Dolph's porch, with his cousins Jack and Frank. If word got 'round in time, there'd be others there, too. Maybe Uncle Dolph has busted out his banjo, Cousin Jack his box, and Aunt Angie her fiddle. They're all up there now, picking to beat the band, something old and lively like "Cacklin' Hen," or sweet and sorrowful like "Wildwood Flower."

Daniel swats a mosquito off his arm and rocks, hearing the strains of "Wildwood Flower" in his head, wishing he had a box to pick out the notes. He'd been promised one once, but that was before Mam and the move off the mountain and all.

Before Floridy and the Sheriff at the school and all. Before Sampson taught him how to catch a catfish.

In the dark, Daniel smiles, remembering his catfish. Aunt Lu had done a fine job on his fish for supper. And he'd had fun scaring the girls with the head. Even now, drying and hardening on the porch post, that head was monstrous ugly and plumb beautiful at the same time.

Across the clearing, Aunt Lu appears in the doorway. "Daniel, sure you don't want to come in with us?"

"Got a better view of things from here," he calls back.

"All right, then, but don't sit out all night. Them skeeters'll eat you alive."

"All right," he calls and goes back to rocking.

Sometime later, not meaning to, he dozes off, hearing in his head the sound of up home singing "I Am Weary, Let Me Rest."

THAT'S A QUARE NOISE, the boy thinks. Stirring stiff in his chair, Daniel doesn't recognize it at first. But, swimming up into awake, he remembers. The tinkling sound of the bones strung off Sampson's bee basket. He'd hung it off the live oak beside the house. *Them bees are hard at it,* he thinks. Wondering why sits him straight up now, clutching the cold, heavy metal of Pap's shotgun.

The clearing and the wide field are deeply dark, except for the pale light from the slice of moon. Everything's hushed, but for the bees buzzing angry and rattling the tangle of dry bones.

Way off in the distance, a pair of headlights turns off the hardtop onto their road. And another pair. And another after that. Five of 'em in all, the dust kicked up from the car in front smearing the headlamps of those behind.

Daniel's up and running. "Aunt Lu!" he yells as he slams into the kitchen. "Git up! Git the girls somewheres safe, under the bed, back o' the cupboard. Now!"

Once he sees his aunt, with Uncle Will's rifle in her hand, he races back into the clearing between the two cabins and watches and waits.

The line of headlamps makes its way around the field and up the drive. When the light of the first car, *or mebbe it's a truck,* hits the cabins, it stops. The two behind it pull up alongside, the other two stop behind. Three pairs of bright white eyes stare into the clearing where Daniel stands frozen, staring back.

He hears the sharp mechanical wrench of doors jerked open, slammed shut. He sees the shapes of men dressed like ghosts, the flash of gunmetal against their chests. "It's the boy," he hears one man call to another.

"Where's your daddy, boy?" a hard voice yells from behind the lights. "Get 'im out here!" "And your uncle, too!"

Daniel's shaking. He wonders desperately what to yell back. His mind skitters through his options. But before he can say a word, a single word, all hell breaks loose among the ghostly men behind the headlights.

The outermost guards saw it first. The waiting at roadside, the passing of jugs, the gas and gunning of angry engines. They turned and, imperceptibly to the intruders, sent the alarm. "Some come!"

The message was passed from guard to guard, from outer rim to inner wall, from watchful eyes to anxious hearts. "Some come!"

Those assigned to the Young One's defense took flight immediately. Others followed from neighboring commands. Only a few, and the Old Ones, stayed behind to guard their communal treasure. Sensing the alarm ("The Young One and his sisters, are they safe?"), She Who Decides emerges from Her chambers.

The forwardmost flank attacks first; their enemy, though large, a thousand times outnumbered. In waves, the defenders assault their intruders, each strike a single soldier's sacrifice. Word of the battle flies to and through the woods. He Who Provides rises, alert, to their report.

45

Sunday morning, as part of a new weekly series spotlighting local clergy, Ruth stands outside the arched double doors of the First Methodist Church, having a final cigarette before the service begins.

Among those milling around the base of the church steps, one man mentions his disappointment over the past week's election. A woman chimes in her upset over the school board's firing of Principal Ed Cantrell. "They say Ed resigned, but that's a bunch of hogwash," she declares, hardening red lips.

Plump, henna-haired Patsy Denby, Doc Denby's wife, nods. "Seems to me Sheriff DeLuth's on the warpath. Had the Klan out to those Indians, the Dares' house last night," she confides, eyes bright beneath pencil-thin brows.

"*What?*" Ruth gasps, nearly swallowing the stub of her half-smoked cigarette.

"Why, Patsy, how *on earth* could you know that?" Patsy's sister, Sandra Moore, married to the local pharmacist, demands.

"Because," Patsy says, "five of 'em came to our house afterward, rousted Charles outta bed for help with bee stings! Said they were attacked by a whole cloud of bees. Must have had forty, fifty stings apiece! One of 'em, Leroy Russell, bit so bad he couldn't walk or talk!"

"But why in the world did they bother Charles?" MaryEllen Ranson scrunches her face at the veterinarian's wife.

Patsy grins. "They were ranch hands mostly, from the Cunningham place. Told him he was the only doctor they knew!"

"But, Patsy," Deacon Red Phillips interjects, "how'd Charles know they were Klanners? Where they'd been?"

"Well,"—Patsy eyes the circle that had now grown to a dozen or so—"they were still in their robes and all, covered with bees. Most of the bites were on their hands and faces. And Charles made them tell where it happened."

"Was anybody home? Did they say what they did?" Ruth asks it urgently, knowing full well that Franklin Dare and his brother are away collecting documents for their suit against the school board.

"Said they saw the boy, but then those bees came and they had to get outta there," Patsy tells her.

George Meyers, owner of the local lumberyard and Will Dare's employer, scowls mightily. "But both the Dare men are in North Carolina till late Monday."

"So that poor woman and the children are out there all alone?" His wife lays a pale hand on his brawny forearm.

"It didn't take long, three minutes flat," Ruth tells Hugh on the phone, "for those Methodists to organize a forty-eight-hour prayer vigil out at the Dare property, to protect Lu Dare and the children till the men come home. The congregation's still smarting, you know, from the Baptists turning their kids' petition into a public prayer list. I'm on my way out there now, to photograph the tire marks, and let Lu and the kids know that the Methodist Cavalry is on its way!"

*   *   *

LATE THAT NIGHT, as Ruth, exhausted, slips into bed, Hugh rolls over and turns on the light.

"Well?" he asks quietly.

"Damnedest thing you ever saw," she replies. "The women showed up first carting casseroles, carrying coffeepots, pitchers of iced tea. Set up camp in the clearing between the two cabins. George Meyers and the men came afterwards with a couple truckloads of scrap wood from his lumberyard. They parked their cars in a barricade across the drive, then built a huge bonfire, flames initially as high as a house.

"Every hour, on the hour, they pass out pieces of wood— 'prayer logs,' they call them—and gather 'round the fire. The minister or one of the deacons begins. Then, round robin, each one adds something—a special thought or appeal—and tosses their prayer log onto the fire. I imagine that sounds corny, or strange. But, I'll tell you, Hugh, it was something else entirely. In between prayer circles, the women sing—turns out Lu has a lovely voice—and I actually heard them invite her to join the Methodist choir! And the men tell stories to entertain the children. One of them, Red Phillips, has a guitar and is teaching Daniel how to play. Hell, even Lila Hightower showed up. Somehow she knew that 'Becca, the one with the nose, who never talks, has a favorite kind of cookie—thumbprint, they're called, round with a dab of strawberry jam in the middle—and Lila shows up with a whole platterful. Had that little girl grinning from ear to ear.

"The whole day and into the night—the men are taking shifts tonight, the women will be back tomorrow—standing 'round that fire felt—I don't know, Hugh—instead of corny, it felt . . . communal, a community of good people gathered to do the right thing. And, instead of strange, it was somehow . . ." Ruth stops, searches for the exact word, which, when she finds

it, comes out surprised, in a whisper. ". . . true." She shakes
her head, reaches over him, turns out the light. "Damnedest
thing you ever saw," she says softly, settling next to him in the
dark.

TUESDAY MORNING, Ruth drives eagerly to the courthouse.
Rumor has it that Judge Winston K. Woods, a Methodist, is
fit to be tied. According to Paine Marsh, the Judge has cleared
his docket and summoned all parties involved in the *Dares* v.
the Clark County School Board suit to his courtroom for an immediate preliminary hearing.

In the hallway, Ruth greets an amused Lila Hightower.
"Isn't this a *bee*-yootiful day?" Lila demands. And together
they find seats in the back.

Up front, Ruth spots the row of defendants in their suits:
Superintendent Bateman, Chairman Zeke Roberts, and the
rest of the all-male school board. Their attorneys, one old, one
young, stand and face them, answering softly spoken queries,
nodding reassurance.

Opposite them, the Dares seem dwarfed by the Victorian
furniture, the high ceilings, the calculated grandeur of the courtroom: Pigtailed Minna and snaggle-toothed SaraFaye stare
goggle-eyed up at Will; rail-thin Lu cuddles baby June in her
lap, whispers to a somber 'Becca by her side; and the two stoics,
Daniel and Franklin, sit ramrod straight on the aisle. In front
of them is the quiet, dignified, silver-haired figure of attorney
Paine Marsh, studying a thick, open book. Behind them is a
rather large contingent of people from the prayer vigil.

Although identical in design, the Fifth Circuit courtroom,
where Judge Woods presides, lacks the highly polished luster
of Judge How-High's Number Two next door.

Judge How-High was a stickler for appearances, Ruth recalls. While Judge Woods, also called The Whittlin' Judge, is known to arrive at his bench with a handful of sticks. At preliminary hearings, he announces to attorneys on both sides that he has deemed the case a two-stick, four-stick, anywhere up to a six-stick case. Which means he will listen patiently for the time it takes him to whittle down the designated number of sticks—curled shavings piling up in front of him, occasionally brushed off onto the floor—and at the very end of the last stick, he will rule.

Veteran attorneys know to match the length of their arguments to the length of the sticks. And that Judge Woods looks harshly on those who attempt to eat up more than their fair share of shavings. Ruth wonders if the school board's attorneys understand this and privately hopes for their ignorance.

Two minutes before ten, there's a brief, sharp exchange at the back of the courtroom. Sheriff K. A. DeLuth has arrived, and the Bailiff is requesting he surrender his firearm.

"No guns in the courtroom," the Bailiff, a thin man with thick glasses, says.

"C'mon, Henry, I'm not about to shoot somebody in front of all these witnesses," DeLuth jokes.

"Please, Sheriff. Judge's orders."

"No deal," DeLuth says, abruptly serious, and brushes past the Bailiff, his ivory-handled pistol still in place. Ruth watches the big man sweep down the aisle, solicitously tipping his hat to the school-board wives seated behind their husbands, seizing the empty seat next to Zeke Roberts. Beside her, Ruth feels Lila bristle with contempt.

At precisely ten, the Honorable Winston K. Woods enters his courtroom, carrying one stick. He has the look of his name: tan, rough-hewn features, a shock of unruly hair falling over his forehead, and a rawboned build that moves with the unexpected grace of a born hunter.

As the Bailiff announces the case, Judge Woods scans the courtroom and catches sight of DeLuth's pistol. "Bailiff," he says sharply, obviously rankled, "did you or did you not request that the Sheriff surrender his firearm?"

"I did, sir."

Woods turns an angry eye onto DeLuth. "Sheriff, you will surrender said firearm this instant or be found in contempt of court. And I will personally see that you serve time in your own jail!"

DeLuth stands, bowing his head, pouting his lips like a penitent schoolboy. Then, with a flourish, he unholsters his gun and presents it to the Bailiff.

Judge Woods, not pleased with the Sheriff's showboating, turns a vicious glare onto the school board's attorneys.

"Gentlemen, I have summoned your clients, as well as the plaintiffs, to inform you that this is hardly even a one-stick case, let alone two. The law is exceedingly clear. If the children in question are one-eighth or more Negro, your clients may refuse them entry to the white school system. If they are not, your clients are, by law, bound to provide them free, unfettered access to their education.

"Now, as I understand it, the plaintiffs claim to have legal proof that these four children are white. And the defendants claim proof they are not. One week from today, both sides will present said proof and I will rule. And, for the record, if you intend to clutter up my desk with any sort of Motion or Stay or any other such nonsense that might delay a swift and final decree on this case, I will find you in contempt. Further, if you are considering a Writ of Certiorari and Motion to Vacate, I can save you the trouble by informing you that the head of the Supreme Court of Florida has, this very morning, advised me it will be denied.

"Finally, Sheriff DeLuth,"—Judge Woods sets his cross-hairs on the big man whose grin hasn't faltered—"I charge you with the responsibility of providing round-the-clock protection, against all unruly elements, to the plaintiffs in this case. In days past, I understand, residents of the community have been forced to do what is clearly your elected duty. You are to mount a twenty-four-hour roadblock at the entrance to the Dare property, denying access to all persons not appearing on a list provided you by their attorney. And, make no mistake, Sheriff,"—the Judge grates, stabbing a bony finger at DeLuth—"if, between this moment and next Tuesday, anyone harms so much as a single hair on one of the heads of these four children, *or* their parents' property, this court will hold *you* personally accountable. And, I assure you, Sheriff, I will *not* be kind."

Judge Woods pauses to survey his courtroom and, Ruth suspects, catch his breath. After a moment, he returns his gaze to the three attorneys up front.

"Gentlemen," he nods, picking up his gavel in one hand, his stick in the other. With one smooth stroke, he strikes the sound block, stands, and, in five long strides, returns to his chambers.

46

Paine Marsh's secretary, Bea Marquette, greets Lila with a sly grin. "Heard tell Judge Woods gave 'em both barrels at the Courthouse this mornin'."

"Oh, he was in full bore all right," Lila tells her. "And rightly so, I'd say."

"Paine said the same thing. But, Lila? One thing bothers me." Bea knits her penciled brows. "After Paine wins their claim, do you think those children are going to *want* to return to Lake Esther Elementary?"

"One thing at time, Bea," Lila says, shaking her head. "One thing at a time. He ready for me?"

"Oh, sure, honey, go right on in."

THOMAS PAINE MARSH rises from his big leather chair and warmly clasps her hand. After both are seated, on opposite sides of his desk, he observes, "Saw you in the back this morning."

"Wouldn't've missed it for the world. Any chance we'll lose?"

"Not hardly."

"Good," she says, buoyed with relief and gratitude. And something else, something rare—*trust*. "Thanks again for taking this on, Paine," she tells him impulsively.

"Simple thing, really," he replies. "Now." He lays his hand on the thick envelope on the desktop. "Want to see what showed up over the weekend?"

"Yes, sir, I do."

Marsh turns the envelope over, undoes the little string wrapped in a figure-eight closure on the flap, and slips out the stack of official-looking forms. Turning them 'round, top to bottom, he slides them across the desk to her.

Lila takes a minute to look them over. All are similar, in format, to the Receipt of Sale forms she'd found in her father's files. But these are titled Livestock Transfer. They bear similar information as to each bull's or cow's description, original breeder, pedigree, and so forth. But at the bottom of each form is one glaring difference.

"They're forged," Lila says.

"What do you mean?"

"This is not my father's signature."

"Lila, I've seen the Judge's signature hundreds of times. Looks like it to me."

"Looks like it, yes. But, tell me, Paine: In any of those hundreds of times, did he ever once sign anything with a ballpoint pen?"

"Can't say as I ever noticed."

"When we were kids," Lila tells him, "he read somewhere that J. P. Morgan always used a fountain pen. He ordered his special-made in ebony with fourteen-carat gold trim. From the day it arrived, he never used anything else."

"Well, now that you mention it . . ."

"Don't you remember, he almost always had a black ink stain on his writing finger, from that damn fountain pen?"

"Yes, I do remember that."

"I challenge you to go through every document of his that

you have, and anything filed down at the Courthouse, or anywhere else, and find one thing not signed with that fountain pen. You won't. He was a fanatic about it."

Marsh picks up his own pen, and makes a note.

"Another thing," Lila says. "These are in blue ink. Daddy hated blue ink. Refused to use it. One time, he found an essay Louis had written in blue ink. Made him copy the whole thing over in black."

Marsh shakes his head sympathetically. "He was tough on you two."

Lila pushes away the memory of Louis, tears streaming down his face, writing and rewriting his eight-page essay, for no good reason other than their father's whim.

"The last thing, Paine, is the date on these things. By this date, Daddy was bedridden downstairs, in the office. Had his phone, his typewriter, his stationery, everything, including his precious ebony fountain pen, by his side. There is no way in hell that on this date, he would have signed anything with something else. Most particularly, a blue ballpoint pen!"

"If we can *prove* all this," Marsh says, level-eyed, "we're talking forgery, material alteration, legal efficacy, and out-and-out fraud—felonies all."

Lila, arms criss-crossed on top of the stack, meets his gaze. "Daddy didn't sign these, Paine. No way, no how."

He frowns in thought. "I won't file anything till next week, after the Dares' hearing. In the meantime, I'll request a document search from the Clerk of the Court. And, at some point, I'll need to depose Sissy, and probably your mamma."

Lila makes a face. "Well, make sure you talk to Mamma in the mornin'. She's not what you'd call reliable after noon."

Marsh stares at her, troubled. "How you holdin' up?" he asks gently.

"Oh, Paine, you know . . ."

"What I know is—your daddy left you with a terrible burden, but not without the resources to see it through."

"What do you mean?"

"I mean—many's the time he sat right there where you are, bragging about you being Top Brass, setting the Allies straight, giving the Russians, the Koreans what for. To hear him tell it, you practically ran the Berlin Airlift single-handed!"

"But, Paine—" Lila sits straight up, openmouthed. "Daddy and I parted on the worst of terms. I didn't call, never wrote—except occasionally to Sissy and she was sworn to secrecy. How could he . . ."

"Your daddy"—Marsh shoots her a knowing look—"had ways of finding things out. A Congressman here, a Senator there, someone in Defense, the Armed Services Committee. He got regular reports. 'That Lila,' he'd sit right there and crow, 'she has got what it takes!' "

"To do what?" She's surprised to hear the words in her head come out of her mouth.

"I always took it to mean: Anything you want to, girl. Anything you want."

Lila sits back, shaken. For weeks now, she'd endured one disaster after another—Jazz's betrayal, the Jacksons' barbecue, young Tom in the WigWam, Kyle's reelection. *And, of course, Mamma's check in Daddy's files.* The cumulative effect had become a paralysis of guilt, shame, and uncertainty—*I've been walking around for days waiting for the next awful thing, the other shoe to drop.*

But not once had she expected this: *He knew!* Her father, whom she'd ignored, rejected, come home to bury without reconciliation, *knew* that one day she'd uncover the truth. The Judge, whom she'd bitterly blamed for Louis's death and sentenced to ten years of silence, had refused to judge or reject her. *He even contrived, through his files, to show me the proof of his innocence. And, through kind old Paine Marsh here, to send me his blessing.* The extent of his faith in her, his uninterrupted pride in his only, unloving daughter, overwhelms her. *In spite of everything, he forgave me my shortcomings, and continued to believe I've "got what it takes."*

Something inside her turns, clicks, sharpens; a memory from her tenth summer. The Judge had bought a new boat, and decided it was high time that she and Louis learned how to water ski behind it in a glassy cove off Lake Marjorie. Louis, the athlete, got up on his first try. But Lila struggled. Time after time, she faltered, fell, came up sputtering, feeling like a waterlogged failure. For nearly an hour, she tried, the Judge and Louis patiently circling back, calling encouragement over the side. Finally, she'd had enough.

"I can't do it," she'd cried.

"Sure you can," her brother insisted.

"No, I can't! These skis are too long, and the rope's too short. I'm wearing the wrong bathing suit. I need to go home and change it."

The Judge had removed his sunglasses and given her the same eagle eye he gave repeat offenders or ill-prepared attorneys in his courtroom. "Only thing you need to change, Miss Priss," he'd said quietly, "is your mind."

Angry, determined, intent, she'd gotten up on her next try. *He knew.*

An hour later, Lila steps briskly out of Marsh's office. The sky overhead is a clear, see-forever blue, rimmed by a range of white clouds that high winds have whipped into snowy bright peaks.

Wheeling her pickup into the noontime traffic, bound for the Pine Forest Cemetery, she decides to stop by the Courthouse near the center of town. She'll be leaving soon. And this time Hamp, most especially Hamp, deserves to know when. And why.

His secretary's desk is empty. *Out to lunch,* she thinks, and raps softly on his door.

"Come in," he calls, and looks up expectantly from the stacks of books and files blanketing his desk. "Lila!?" He shoots to his feet, comes around the desk, makes a show of settling her in one of his chairs. He doesn't return to his desk, but sits down beside her, collapsing the space between them.

They'd spoken only casually, on the phone and in the Courthouse, since the Jacksons' barbecue. He'd called to apologize for Charlie's ridiculous comment about rekindling old flames. She'd disagreed. "You'd didn't do anything. I was the one who bolted like a colt out of the barn."

His expression is pleased, eager, with a shy smile that betrays the guarded hope she wished he didn't have. "Quite a show this morning, huh?" he asks, opening on shared ground.

"Judge Woods's or Kyle's?"

"Pick your player. Either one was a vintage performance."

"I've just come from Paine Marsh who says next week's hearing should be a piece of cake," Lila says.

"Piece of cake and, no doubt, a fine piece of courtroom theater. We could probably sell tickets—make a few bucks on the side."

She eyes him with mock disgust.

He recoils in exaggerated self-righteousness. "For deposit to the Dare kids' college fund, of course!"

Lila feels an inner twinge. This kind of playful repartee had always been the best part of being with Hamp. He had a child's heart really: light, loving, and—*Oh, God*—so easily hurt. There was no getting 'round it. Nervous, she clears her throat. "What I meant was—Paine says next week is it. This business should be over and done with—"

"Ahead of schedule. The Governor-elect will be happy."

"—and with his kids back in school, Franklin will be free to focus on the groves—"

"Just in time for high picking season."

She can see in his eyes what he's doing. "Hamp, this is hard enough without you interrupting. With Franklin in charge—"

"You're leaving," he says flatly.

God, there it went. The child's light was gone. Hurt and disappointment took its place.

"Hamp, I'm sorry. But aside from Paine, you're the first to know."

"Well, there's that, isn't there?" he says, rising, returning to his side of the desk. He opens his drawer, looks up. "A toast to old times?" His face is carefully composed, his smile that of Clark County's tough-as-nails District Attorney. Lila attempts a dry swallow against the rising cotton in her throat. "I—"

"—have not a thing in the world to feel bad about, Lila. A fool and his heart are soon parted," he says, pouring whiskey in both glasses. "Or is it luck, a fool and his luck?" he asks, handing over hers.

"It's money, Hamp. The expression is 'A fool and his *money* are soon parted'—"

"Oh, money. I never gave a rat's ass about that."

"—And you are not a fool, Hamp." *God, this is awful.*

"I beg to differ, Judge. I am most certainly"—he leans over the desk, clinks her glass—"a fool for you."

Worse, worse than I ever imagined. "I won't drink to that, Hamp."

"You don't have to, my dear." He lifts his glass. "This particular fool has learned, two times over, the excruciating pleasure of drinking alone." He tosses back the entire amount in a single gulp. Then, smiling his guarded man's smile, his prosecutor's no-deal-on-copping-a-plea smile, he asks, "Mind if I have another?"

47

Early Wednesday morning, Sheriff K. A. DeLuth gives Birdilee a good-bye peck on the cheek. He'd aimed for her mouth, but, at the last moment, his wife had turned sideways. She'd been quiet, kept to herself ever since their dinner at the Cattlemen's Club, hadn't said a word or even offered to help with the bee stings on the backs of his hands, and out-and-out refused to attend the hearing in Judge Woods's courtroom. *It's about damn time she got over whatever the hell it is she's so upset about. I'll have it out with her when I get back.* "Give you a call from the road, darlin'," he'd told her nicely, choosing to ignore the way she seemed to look right through him, like he wasn't there, or she'd somehow forgot what the man she'd been married to for ten years looked like.

First off, he heads to the office to complete his paperwork, writes out his answers to the list of questions hand-delivered by old Marsh's secretary yesterday afternoon: Yes, he was there when the Judge signed the Livestock Transfer forms. No, there were no other witnesses present. Yes, the date was accurate and the transaction occurred at the Judge's bedside. No, no cash was exchanged. Yes, he would be claiming the fair value of the cattle as a gift on his income tax. *Like hell I will,* he chuckles as he folds and stamps the envelope, and places it in the flip-top mailbox just outside the door.

Next, he makes his follow-up phone calls to the six Police Chiefs in the county who are helping with the court-ordered roadblock of the Dare property.

Finally, he writes himself a check off the county account for "advance on travel expenses" and strolls across the street to cash it at the Lake Esther State Bank.

Paperwork complete, he checks the lock on his office, unlocks his car, and heads south, out of town. At the dirt road turnoff, he sees Deputy Carl Paige standing, sentrylike, in front of the sawhorses that block the entry to the Dare place. With a quick glance at the empty road ahead, DeLuth wheels over, facing south on the northbound shoulder, and kills his engine in the crosswalk.

"Sheriff!" Paige says, and salutes the squad car in crisp, military fashion.

"At ease, Carl."

DeLuth thinks he should probably tell Paige, once again, that a salute's not necessary, but secretly he relishes it. "How's it goin'?"

"Not many visitors 'cept that newspaper woman, the schoolteachers from Clark Christian, and a few Methodists."

"Not exactly popular, are they?" DeLuth says, squinting in the direction of the Dares' two cabins.

"Not exactly, sir."

"Brought you a copy of the schedule for the next few days."

"Yes, sir," Paige says, accepting the sheet.

"Three eight-hour shifts," DeLuth explains, "split between you and the Chiefs from Lake Esther, Opatka, Oscilla, and the others. With occasional fill-in by the Deputy from Tangerine County."

"Yes, sir," Paige nods, without asking the obvious—why isn't his Sheriff in the shift rotation?

"I'm on my way to North Carolina for a few days," DeLuth tells him anyway. "Collect some evidence in this damn case. Find the smoked Irishman in these Indians' woodpile." He grins.

"Yes, sir," Paige says, in a way that makes DeLuth wonder if he even got the joke.

"I'll be checkin' in every night, Carl. Call you at your house, six o'clock, okay?"

"Yes, sir."

Ol' Clive was right, DeLuth thinks, *not much upstairs, but he's a damn fine order taker.*

"Be back on Saturday," the Sheriff says, starting his engine. "Sunday at the latest," he calls, over the car's souped-up rumble.

"Yes, sir. Have a good trip, *sir.*" Paige strikes attention, slicing the air with his picture-perfect salute.

The Deputy's precise execution, his unwaveringly respectful attitude sets DeLuth to thinking, for the next hundred miles or so, of all he could set straight with an army of Carl Paige recruits.

48

Ruth sits staring, hands on the keys of her Underwood, wondering if she has what it takes to truly tell it.

Oh, it would be easy to stick to the bare bones of the attorneys' submissions and Judge Woods's decree, to relate to her readers, simple and straightforward, the now-settled fate of the four Dare children.

It would be easy but it wouldn't be right, she thinks. *No.* Somehow she needs to wrap those bones in the flesh-and-blood drama she witnessed today in the Fifth Circuit courtroom. She has to consider her audience—the raging racists, the quiet liberals, the vast not-really-involved in the middle—new to the community and old, and somehow move them in the way that she was moved by the day's proceedings. She has to . . .

The silence from the back room is deafening. Somewhere, just around the corner, Hugh and Walt and Joe, editor and typesetter and pressman, sit idle, waiting to run Wednesday's edition, already late.

"Saved you the head plus twenty-four column inches, above the fold," Hugh told her when she rushed in from the Courthouse.

"Yeh, in half that many minutes, please," Walt, the clock-watcher, had joked.

Behind him, Hugh shook his head. He, more than anyone, knew how important this was. To the community. *To us.* "We'll wait," was all he'd told her.

Clouding her head was the news—*incredible!*—from Hugh that the Senate had voted—*sixty-seven to twenty-two!*—to condemn Joe McCarthy. That lead would be easy to write: "In 'The Fight for America,' America has won."

But this one. *Where to begin?* With the dramatic face-off between thundering Judge Woods and sneering, leering Sheriff DeLuth? With a cross-reference to McCarthy, and the fact that this hearing, like his, rode in on the backs of what Margaret Chase Smith, America's first female Senator, called "the Four Horsemen of Calumny—Fear, Ignorance, Bigotry, and Smear"?

Too strong? Too philosophical? *Probably.* Better to let the drama reveal itself step-by-step. Engage the reader in the same startling way that every single person in the courtroom was riveted today. *Yes,* she decides, *start at the beginning. And, with any luck, the head and the lead will write themselves afterward.* She grinds out her cigarette, flips open her notepad, and begins:

DRAMA attended the closing of the Dare case that has reverberated across the nation as Americans of all races read of the four children evicted without warning or due process from their school, all-white Lake Esther Elementary, by Sheriff K. A. DeLuth and the Clark County School Board, who, against parental protest, insisted the children were Negro.

The drama was not only in the sudden bolt of its ending but also in the simmering presence of Sheriff DeLuth, who initially, single-handedly evicted the children of Franklin Dare and of William and LuEllen Dare; in the tightly packed rows of spectators, overflowing into the lobby, who sat hushed throughout the morning session, while a determined Fifth Circuit Court Judge Winston K. Woods forced the acceptance of the one and only legal issue at stake: "Are the children Colored within the meaning and intent of the laws of Florida?"

The drama increased when the plaintiff's attorney, Thomas Paine Marsh, produced evidence to show that throughout their lives the Dares have lived as, and been accepted by their previous school, church, neighbors, and community as, white people. It increased again when defense attorneys Charles Sloan and Arnold Cooper, representing the Clark County School Board, at first refused to produce evidence to substantiate their charges that the children were Negroes. When at last forced to produce what they had, by Judge Woods's order to "do so here and now or there will be no other opportunity," Mr. Sloan reluctantly, and somewhat nervously, produced a fifteen-year-old dictionary and a sheaf of photostatic copies of birth certificates from his briefcase.

He then produced a Last Will and Testament, identifying it as that of Franklin Dare's grandfather, John T. Dare, and saying it would be "connected" to the birth certificates.

Except for those of the Dare children, their parents, grandparents, and great-grandparents—which were also introduced by the Dares's counsel to show white and Croatan Indian racial listing—the certificates Sloan submitted to the court were of Negroes by the surname of Dare.

None of the names on the certificates, personally collected by Sheriff K. A. DeLuth, corresponded to the names on the Will as descendants of the children's great-grandfather, who died in 1931. Nor did any of the certificates derive from either Avery or Robeson County, North Carolina, where the family has lived.

Mr. Marsh, given the chance to review the certificates submitted by the defense, argued, "All these Negroes have the name of Dare. I imagine you'll find a thousand Negroes in North Carolina named Dare—hundreds in that state's Dare County alone. We demand to know what witnesses you will produce to connect these Dares to the Franklin and Will Dare family!"

It was then the defense balked for the third time: The first was in their introduction of fourteen declarations as "issues" in the case, a list that Judge Woods whittled down to the single racial issue; the second in their begging for more time in which to "obtain more evidence," which the Judge denied. And in this, the third instance, they asked for an additional month to obtain witnesses—after admitting they had no "expert" witnesses to submit.

After reminding them that they had already had two weeks, since the Complaint was filed, to round up witnesses as did the plaintiffs, Judge Woods gave them "until four o'clock this afternoon."

At the four o'clock session, all parties returned. In response to Judge Woods's query, "Does the defense have any further evidence or expert depositions to present?" school-board attorney Sloan said,

"We are not presenting any names and addresses at this time, because it is not in the best interest of our clients to do so."

Judge Woods, unmoved, demanded a "yes or no answer." Mr. Sloan replied, "We don't intend to introduce anything at this time."

Mr. Marsh spoke for the plaintiffs as he said, "In view of the issue the Judge set forth today, that of race, we feel that the defense has shown no basis or any evidence that this family is not white, whereas we have produced depositions to show—with documents, affidavits, and testimony—they are white, and have always been classed white in every area where they were reared or have lived. The defense was given ample opportunity to prove their charge that the family is Negro. And they have not filed or attempted to file any evidence except the names of Dares who are Negroes. Nor have they undertaken to connect those Negroes surnamed Dare to the Franklin and Will Dare family.

"All of this shows clearly that their charge is a sham—it is patently false and unsupported by evidence or expert testimony of any kind. We move the charge be stricken from the record and that a judgment be granted for this family."

It was here that Mr. Sloan attempted to save the hearing's wreckage as he moved for a trial "so that the defense could question one of the plaintiffs' witnesses."

That witness is Dr. Kendrick McIntosh, a native of Robeson County, North Carolina—the same county of origin as the children's great-grandfather—a professor of anthropology and sociology at Pembroke University who is a graduate of Harvard and the University of Edinburgh, Scotland, and an author, editor, and recognized authority on race.

Dr. McIntosh, said Mr. Marsh, has stated in writing that he has investigated the Indians of Robeson County who are termed "Croatan" and they are not Negro. He knows the community where Mr. Dare's grandfather was born, and he would be willing to testify that the man and his descendants are not Negro "either biologically, politically, or sociologically."

Mr. Marsh also revealed that Dr. McIntosh, in a deposition he was prepared to enter if the case went to trial, was asked this question: "Does the fact that the grandfather's birth certificate lists him as Croatan indicate in any way that he was a Negro?"

Under oath, Dr. McIntosh answered, "It definitely does not."

Again, Mr. Sloan attempted to save his case with a request for trial so that "the defense might examine the physical evidence of the Dare children," and if the word Croatan could, indeed, mean Negro.

Mr. Marsh replied, "The only evidence you've had of that is the Sheriff's dictionary, which we've already shown has been disproved by law."

Mr. Cooper, Mr. Sloan's partner, took little part

in the proceedings. Near the end of the afternoon session, the attorney suggested, somewhat facetiously, that the case be thrown out and "we could start all over again." He laughed when Mr. Marsh commented, "You'd like that, wouldn't you?"

Before ruling, Judge Woods stated that, in his opinion, the question of the children's race hinged "crucially on the racial identity of their great-grandfather, John T. Dare," deemed "Croatan" by his 1847 birth certificate. "That question," Judge Woods told the packed courtroom, "is answered in a letter dated the tenth of this month, and entered into the record, from the Comptroller General of North Carolina. The letter states unequivocally that John T. Dare was a Confederate Army infantryman and that Negroes were not used as anything but camp help during the Civil War. If the Confederate Army did not deem John T. Dare a Negro, then neither, I say, can we!"

At that, Circuit Judge Winston K. Woods granted the motion of the plaintiffs' attorney that the accusation declaring the evicted schoolchildren are Negro could not be upheld.

Tight-lipped Sheriff DeLuth, author of the original now-declared-false accusation, strode out of the courtroom with an angry "No comment."

Judge Woods's ruling allows the declaratory judgment the Dare family sought in its suit against the Clark County School Board—that of the right to attend a white school.

That school is going to be Clark Christian Academy—the choice of the Dare family and a place where, according to Dr. John Leighton, head of the Academy, "Our doors are wide open for them the moment the court rules they may legally attend."

Franklin Dare, father of two of the four falsely accused children, said, "The Lord be praised—I feel like I am living in America again." His sister-in-law LuEllen Dare, with tears in her eyes, added, "It couldn't be any other way. Thank the Lord— we've prayed so hard."

49

From the moment that Judge Woods pounded his gavel, *declarin' for us, 'stead of aginst us,* Daniel noticed, everyone's mood changed. *Like the sun comin' onter the holler after a hard rain,* he thinks.

Except for Miss Lila's clenched jaw at the sight of the Sheriff leaving the Courthouse, and her whispered suggestion to Pap that "You'd best keep an eye out," there was nothing but smiles all around from Miz Ruth, Mister and Miz Meyers from the lumberyard, Mister Red, and the others from the prayer vigil.

After all the shaking of hands, the thumping of backs, and the heartfelt thank-yous to Mr. Marsh, they'd made their way to Pap's truck where Uncle Will suggested a surprise stop at the Dairy Queen drive-in. Afterward, the girls, faces sticky from their cones, knowing they'll be back in school again come Monday, chirped like spring birds all the way home.

This morning, when Aunt Lu discovered that some varmit got into her chicken coop and left a mess of broken eggshells, she laughed. *Laughed!* And, Pap, inspecting the paw prints outside the coop, grinned and said, "Well, Daniel, guess we'll be havin' your possum hunt tonight. Prob'ly taken up in some rabbit hole out-air in our field. Whyn't you walk 'round today, see if you kin spy its den?"

THE GIRLS RUN OUT AHEAD OF HIM, in search of some lucky four-leaf clovers; Minna, as usual, bossing SaraFaye as to which way to go. Even 'Becca, still not much for talking, smiles at him on her way out into the field.

Daniel trails along after them, relishing the feel of his .22, looking forward to the night's hunt with Pap. And, if that weren't enough to make a boy's heart fairly burst with high spirits, *here comes Ol' Sampson trompin' outta the woods with his smoker, come to check the hives on this happy day.*

"Hey, Sampson," "Hey!" the cousins call. 'Becca adds a shy wave.

Sampson grins, tips his hat, then, bearing in on Daniel, adds, "Good day, heh?"

Daniel's given up trying to understand how the Ol' Seminole knows all that he knows. It *is* a good day, for one and all.

"Huntin' somethin'?" the ancient black Indian asks, nodding toward Daniel's rifle.

"Possum, tonight," Daniel answers proudly. "Just sniffin' out his hole today."

Sampson is busy with the smoker and a match. Daniel smells the pine needles light, watches Sampson pump the bellows to release a stream of smoke, and begin to inspect the nearest hive. "Be back soon," Daniel says and sets out himself, eyes to the ground.

On the far side of the field, he hears before he sees the heavy rumble of the Sheriff's car, and, behind it, the Deputy's pickup truck. *Bet they come for their sawhorses,* he thinks, as the Sheriff and his Deputy stop by the stack of two-by-fours on the edge of their road.

Intent on his own hole hunt, Daniel doesn't see, till it's too late, that the Sheriff's walked out to where 'Becca sits alone, poking through the clover.

"Well, looky here," the Sheriff drawls, hands on his hips, "if it ain't the little pickaninny started all this mess."

Daniel sees the Sheriff cock his head, sees 'Becca freeze in the big man's shadow.

"Forgot your name, li'l troublemaker. What is it?"

'Becca looks up, soft brown eyes big as saucers, then quickly drops her chin. Daniel sees her skinny shoulders start to shake, sees her hand, with its small clutch of clover, reach up to wipe away a tear.

"I *said,*"—the Sheriff hauls 'Becca up by a single bony arm—"what's your name, girl?"

"Leave her be," Daniel yells, running toward them, holding his .22 in a two-handed grip.

"Whoa," the Sheriff, thick fingers around 'Becca's elbow, turns on Daniel, "two little Niggers for the price of one. Only asked her name, boy. But 'pears to me, girl's acting uppity. You got any idea what we do with uppity Niggers 'round here?"

"Turn her loose," Daniel says, his breath rasping, eyes boring into the big man's face. Just below his breastbone, his right forefinger releases the .22's safety, levers over into ready.

"Gonna shoot the Sheriff, boy?"—He parts his lips in a slow grin.—"All I want . . ."—He slips his free hand to his hip, unholsters his gun.—". . . is this li'l girl's nigger-nosed name."—He pulls his pistol up and out—"C'mon, now,"— slides the barrel under 'Becca's chin, raising it, forcing her to lift her smudged and terrified face. "I *said,* what's your name, gal?"

Daniel's heart hammers inside his chest. He lifts his rifle to eye level, braces his legs, takes aim. "Turn my sister loose, Sheriff."

The Sheriff's using the tip of his four-inch barrel to trace the outline of 'Becca's nose, now shiny with tears, up one side and down the other. "Nose like this," he says softly, "gotta have a name."

Just below his bead, Daniel sees 'Becca trembling, white-eyed, as the Sheriff's gunmetal caresses her face. He sees the Sheriff, too; smiling mouth beneath cold, cruel eyes. Those same eyes had singled him out in Miss Burch's classroom, not as a boy but as something less—wings outside the duck blind, hooves in the woods, a silvery tail upstream—something to be hunted, trapped, slaughtered for sport. Daniel feels the hot blood of outrage, the searing flush of fear. *"Look after yer sister."* He'd promised Mam. *Now that man had a .38 in 'Becca's face . . . refused to leave her, leave us, BE!*

Bam! The Sheriff's eyes flash surprise. Then, suddenly, his big bear's body pitches forward, off his feet.

"NO!" Sampson, somehow beside him, howls and wrenches the .22 out of Daniel's grip. "No, boy, no!"

"What the hell!" the Deputy shouts, scrambling up out of nowhere. "Sheriff?" He flops the big man over onto his back, recoils from the hole between the Sheriff's eyes. "You crazy Nigger!" he yells. "You *killed* him!" He swoops up the Sheriff's pistol, fires it, point-blank, at Sampson's chest.

'Becca covers her ears, screams and screams.

Daniel cries out, drops to his knees in horror as Sampson crumples to the earth beside him. "Sampson," he cries, flinging his arms around his friend. "Sampson!" he wails as a stain of dark blood blossoms onto the Ol' Seminole's chest. "*He didn't . . .*" Daniel turns to tell the Deputy, but ancient black fingers grasp his shirt, yank him eye to eye.

"Don't say it, Dan'l! Don't! Live, you hear? LIVE!!" Sampson whispers with his final breath.

50

Lila stands, hand on the office door, and yells toward the kitchen. "Sissy!"

"Woo-hoo," Sissy hollers back, her signal that she'll be there in a minute.

Lila waits, eager to be done, until Sissy appears in front of her, wiping soapy hands on her apron. "Come in, would you please?" Lila steps aside to let her pass, then quietly closes the door.

"What is it, girl? Ah got pies 'bout ready to come outta the oven."

"Sit down, please, Sissy," Lila insists gently. She pats the arm of one of the leather chairs in front of the Judge's desk, seats herself in the other.

"Well, jus' for a minute or two," Sissy says.

Lila leans forward. "We got somethin' important to talk about." She reaches to the file folder and flips it open.

Sissy's eyes search Lila's face.

"I'm done here, Sissy. Finished. Leavin' for Washington this afternoon." Got a couple things left to do today, and then I'm gone. For good."

"But it's Thanksgivin' tomorrow. You can't . . ." Lila's look silences her.

"It shouldn't surprise you to hear me say that none of this"—the sweep of Lila's hand takes in the Judge's office, his house, his groves surrounding it—"means anything to me. Truth is, I lost interest in all of it the day we got word Louis was dead. These papers"—she lays her hand on the file—"transfer everything to you."

Sissy sits back like she's seen a snake. "But, your mamma . . ."

"Will be more than taken care of," Lila snaps sharply, then, seeing Sissy's face, softens. "Look, what I'm giving you is a choice. You're a wealthy woman now. You can stay or go, retire in style to East Town, or move to West Atlanta, or, frankly, any damn place you please."

"But your . . ."

"I spoke with Doc Ellis. At the rate Mamma's going, her liver's not long for this world. She ought to be committed. But Daddy didn't have the heart to do that, and neither do I. So Doc Ellis has agreed to arrange round-the-clock nurse care. And Paine Marsh will serve as her legal guardian."

"But . . ."

"Paine's fixed it. You asked me to come back and keep Kyle from gettin' everythin' whole hog. I did. And now, I've given it all to you. And there's nothing, not one damn thing, anybody can do about that."

"But she got a right . . ."

"No, Sissy, she doesn't. Far as I'm concerned, she gave up her right the night she chose to do Louis and Lynette wrong all those years ago."

Sissy's eyes are troubled. "Law, Missy." Her shoulders heave. "That was a terrible thing. You think doin' this to your mamma, or to me, gonna make that right?"

"Nothin' in the world can make what she and Kyle did to Louis right. I know that now," Lila tells her quietly. "But, with Louis and Daddy gone, the only other person in this house I care about, or who truly cares about me, is you."

"Oh, child, you got to lay this all by!"

"I will. I am. Fact is, soon as I let Mamma know what's what, I'm shed of all this forever."

"But, I ain't 'bout to turn your mamma over to some strange nurses. You know that." Sissy's look is fierce.

"Oh, Sissy. In spite of all she's said and done over all these years—Well, like I said, it's entirely your choice." Lila points at the papers. "Paine is expecting you this afternoon to go through all this. Franklin Dare has agreed to stay on, manage the groves. And you may or may not have a cattle herd that you'll probably want to sell. Any other questions, any problems, just ask Paine. He's a good man, Paine is."

"Ah don't care 'bout all that."

"Not now maybe, but you will." Lila digs in the pocket of her slacks, fishes out the truck keys. "I'd appreciate it, after I speak with Mamma, if you'd give me a ride to the airport?"

Sissy takes the keys, cradles them in her apron lap. Lila watches the feelings—*sorrow, concern, love, hope?*—that cross, like clouds, the familiar old face. Finally, her eyes brimming tears, Sissy looks up. "You *mean* this? This be the thing that'll make you happy?"

"It's a start," Lila answers softly. Tenderly, she plants a kiss on Sissy's dark, cinnamon-scented cheek.

Sissy stares at her, sadly. "Oh, girl." She sighs. Her tone is resigned. Then, with a sudden wicked crinkling of crow's feet, she suggests, "How 'bout we take the Cadillac instead?"

51

Mind racing, fingers flying, half-smoked Pall Mall hanging off her lower lip, Ruth is deep into the story of Sheriff DeLuth's funeral, the coroner's swift closing of the double-murder case, and the Governor's dramatic announcement that, at the widow's request, Fred Sykes has been named interim Sheriff until the next election.

Whatever possessed Birdilee DeLuth to ask that her husband's political rival become his replacement? Didn't she claim, "Politics is Kyle's cup of tea, not mine"? What changed her mind? And what prompted the Governor to grant such a thing? Both had refused interviews. But, in the back of her brain, Ruth believes the answer lies in the additional odd elements she's sworn an oath not to tell.

She recalls this morning's phone call to the head of the Clark Christian Academy. Her purpose was to find a home for the nearly four hundred dollars she'd received from donors across the country on the Dare family's behalf. "Franklin won't take it," she'd explained to Dr. Leighton. "I'd like to give it to you, to apply to the expenses of the children's education."

"I'll be happy to deposit it in our school's scholarship fund, but I must admit that tuition for all four of the Dare children has been fully funded."

"By whom?" Ruth asked.

"In part, by a most generous endowment from Miss Lila Hightower," Dr. Leighton had told her cautiously.

"In part? Who else, then?"

"Well, I'm not exactly at liberty to say."

"Oh, please," Ruth had pleaded, "I've worried over this family for weeks; lost almost a third of my business defending them against Sheriff DeLuth and the Klan. You *must* tell me!"

"It's a most surprising source. If I do reveal it, you'll have to promise it will go no further."

"Off the record, you mean?" *Jesus, who could it be?*

"That's exactly what I mean."

Ruth could hear the resolve in the old gentleman's voice. "All right," she'd agreed. "Who?"

"Just yesterday, Mrs. Birdilee DeLuth appeared at my office to inquire after the Dare children."

"Birdilee *DeLuth*, the Sheriff's—" Ruth had been dumbstruck.

"Widow. Yes. I was surprised myself. Mrs. DeLuth said she was concerned that the children had been traumatized by this fall's events and by witnessing her husband's demise. She wanted to make sure their future was secure, with a significant, anonymous contribution on their behalf."

"And she handed you a big, fat check?"

"It was cash, actually, in small, well-used bills."

"But how? Why?"

"All she'd say was, 'Those poor children, this entire community, has suffered enough.' "

In the lobby, the receptionist's voice cuts through Ruth's musing on the mysteries of Birdilee DeLuth. "May I say who's askin', ma'am?"

"Hightower, Lila."

"Oh, Miss Hightower, I didn't . . . Sorry . . . Please, go right in!"

Ruth looks up, curious, as Lila fills the doorway, trim and broad-shouldered, in full W.A.C. uniform—auburn hair tucked primly under flat-topped, small-brimmed hat, khaki shirt, knotted tie, crisply tailored olive drab jacket, matching skirt. *So she owns a skirt after all!*

"Blessed are they who hunger and thirst after righteousness!" Lila sweeps in, sets a good-size cardboard box in the middle of Ruth's desk. "For they shall inherit the dirt!"

"Good God . . ." Ruth bolts up. Her forgotten cigarette teeters on her lip. She grabs it, stabs it dead in the ashtray, and does a broad double take on Lila's gold oak leaves. "You're a—"

Lila grins. "Major, ma'am."

"Jesus! Off to the V.F.W.? Give the local boys a thrill?"

"Airport, actually." Lila's eyes brighten to the point of sparkle. "Back to the Capital."

Ruth's attention is drawn, like a magnet, to the cardboard box between them. "What's all this?"

"As I recall, you said you enjoyed diggin' in the dirt. There's enough here"—Lila opens the box lid—"to keep you in mud pies for a month of Sundays."

The box is crammed with manila file folders. Ruth scans the tabs, some typed, some hand-scrawled with the names of a number of county and state luminaries.

Lila continues. "The Judge had the goods on every bad boy around, here and in Tallahassee. Kept him on top of the heap for years. I figure these'll help you keep Clive Cunningham and the rest of his crew in line. In case they try to stir up another hornet's nest."

Ruth feels her fingers itch, actually tingle, in anticipation of digging through Judge How-High's secret files. (Although, she remembers, she's promised Hugh to "lay off the controversial stuff for a while.") She smiles widely. "So, the prodigal daughter got what she came for?" she asks.

Lila squints out the window. It's a brilliant day, the sky a sharp, clear blue after the early-morning rain. Ruth notices, for the first time, the shiny Cadillac out front, with the tiny brown woman behind the wheel.

"I believe I did, Ruth. I found out the truth." Lila's eyes dart back to Ruth's. "The bare, unvarnished truth about a whole lot of things. And the funny thing is, it's left me feeling . . . *free*, finally free of stuff I've been carryin' 'round for years." *Fire and ice.* Ruth remembers her first impression of the striking Miss Hightower. *But this Lila's lost her polar ice cap, she's practically aglow with warmth and something else—purpose?*

"Congratulations." Ruth reaches out her hand; Lila returns her grip, firm, businesslike. "So you're off to rattle the Joint Chiefs?"

"No." Lila looks down, brushes invisible lint off her sleeve. "Something else, I think," she says quietly, "out of uniform."

What? Why? When? Ruth wants to ask but Lila's face— private, pained—stops her. Lila wavers, closed lips pressed tight against her teeth. *As if she's searching for words, or deciding whether to share a confidence.* A sudden resolve softens her. She looks up. "Oh, hell, Ruth, I've got a shot at something, something pretty big, in H.E.W."

"Secretary Hobby's staff? Terrific!"

"Of course, it's only an interview at this point. But I do have a bit of an in."

"They'll be lucky to have you."

"So,"—Lila favors Ruth with a wry smile—"if this thing works out, I'll take on the monkeys' backsides in Washington— try to knock 'em into building more and better schools instead of bombs—and you'll keep the local *illegitimus* in line?" This time, it's Lila who extends her hand across the desk.

This time, Ruth notes, Lila's clasp is personal, her palm surprisingly warm. In it, Ruth feels the quick, searing sense of impending loss.

"Give the bastards hell," Lila tells her softly.

"Deal," Ruth says, wondering, not for the first time, *Where's the goddamn good in good-bye?*

It is a day of mourning. The Old Ones and She Who Decides such things decreed it. But, long before Her word came 'round, they knew it was to be.

At break of day, the Young One comes respect-fully, bearing smoke. And, for hours on end, he toils alone, refusing the help of all who offer.

At last, when his solitary task is done, the others come, bearing the body to its resting place in the sacred center of the Colony's circle.

There are words and a song and a prayer in his language, then, once again, at the Young One's insistence, the others leave and he toils alone. At last, when He Who Provides is finally at rest, the Young One erects a wooden symbol, crossed bars bearing, at the joint, the Colony's own sacred six-sided shape.

Among them, the Young One stands, weep-ing. Wiping tears, he stops to consider his palms. "God's Eye," he whispers in the language they cannot hear. "Means—" He struggles with memory. "Means—honor the Most High. And—" The Colony falls silent. "And protect the Least Low," He says, in movements they recognize, have prayerfully watched for. At last, the dance begins, the hum of rejoicing. He Who Provides has provided them an Heir.

Acknowledgments

I am grateful to the following individuals who generously allowed their memories, experiences, and expertise to fuel a writer's fires:

Gail Morris of the Lake County Historical Society; Jim Reeves of the American Brahman Breeders Association; Virginia Mitchell of the *Seminole Tribune, Voice of the Unconquered;* Willy Martinez, former "Bolita man"; Madeline McClure, current editor of the *Mount Dora Topic;* and a handful of old-timers who gave me their stories but deferred public acknowledgment.

Thanks are also due to my agent, Lane Zachary, an endless source of sound advice and well-timed "atta-girls"; to my editor, Kate Miciak, who, early on, promised to be my safety net and, with patience and good humor, never fails; and to Bantam's first-rate managing editor Anna Forgione, flanked by copyeditor Robin Foster, and designer Glen Edelstein. It was my pleasure to work with each of you.

To Cris Weatherby, Tricia Rowe, Julie Clark, and Joe Bear, who read the final draft: Your helpful comments both broadened my perspective and narrowed my focus onto overlooked details. To Joanne Martinez, best and most perceptive friend, who soldiered through many different versions of the manuscript:

Your openhanded praise and accurate insights, especially into Lila and Ruth, were invaluable, every time. Finally, to my husband, Paul: You saw what this story could be in the earliest draft. Thanks beyond words for your unwavering faith in it, and in me.

About the Author

SUSAN CAROL MCCARTHY was born and raised in central Florida. Her first novel, *Lay That Trumpet in Our Hands,* received, among others, the Chautauqua South Fiction Award. She lives in California and is at work on her third novel.

Visit the author's website at www.SusanCarolMcCarthy.com.